# The Party and the People Were a Blur . . .

Nothing was real except Luke's arms around her . . .

"Let's get out of here and get some air," Luke said, whirling Rebel off the dance floor and into a darkened passageway. "Don't worry, nobody's paying any attention to us."

"I don't think . . ." Rebel began, but her words were stopped by Luke's.

"Good. Don't. Just feel," he suggested, and drew her into his arms.

His mouth was warm and gentle, and then, as he guided her into an unlighted room, she felt passion stirring within him, a passion matched within herself. His kiss consumed her, depriving her of strength and the will to resist . . .

*Dear Reader,*

*We, the editors of Tapestry Romances, are committed to bringing you two outstanding original romantic historical novels each and every month.*

*From Kentucky in the 1850s to the court of Louis XIII, from the deck of a pirate ship within sight of Gibraltar to a mining camp high in the Sierra Nevadas, our heroines experience life and love, romance and adventure.*

*Our aim is to give you the kind of historical romances that you want to read. We would enjoy hearing your thoughts about this book and all future Tapestry Romances. Please write to us at the address below.*

The Editors
Tapestry Romances
POCKET BOOKS
1230 Avenue of the Americas
Box TAP
New York, N.Y. 10020

# My Rebel, My Love

## Willo Davis Roberts

**A TAPESTRY BOOK**

PUBLISHED BY POCKET BOOKS NEW YORK

An *Original* publication of TAPESTRY BOOKS

A Tapestry Book, published by
POCKET BOOKS, a division of Simon & Schuster, Inc.
1230 Avenue of the Americas, New York, N.Y. 10020

ISBN: 978-1-4516-9852-7

First Tapestry Books printing April, 1986

10 9 8 7 6 5 4 3 2 1

# *My Rebel, My Love*

# Chapter One

THE NOVEMBER WIND WHIPPED REBEL'S COPPERY CURLS free of the scarf which covered them and penetrated her garments with a chill that made her teeth chatter. Already she felt ice in her bones, though she was not half an hour off the train that had brought her down alongside the Hudson River to New York City.

Old Mr. Simpson had been here once, and he'd described the place to the other inhabitants of Lyons Falls, most of whom had never ventured out of upper New York State. Over three million people, he'd said, and Rebel had listened, wide-eyed like the others.

She had not envisioned anything like this, however. She had set out so boldly—that her courage was born of desperation didn't detract from her bravery, did it?—and on the long ride south had kept telling herself that it would be all right once she reached her only living relatives. And now she was so bewildered by the size of the city that it was painful to breathe, and what optimism she'd managed to muster had evaporated.

Rebel tucked her hands beneath her long cloak and held it more tightly to her slender body in an attempt to minimize the effect of the wind. Dear heaven, how was she to find anyone in this place, with all three million of its residents apparently moving about on this very street?

Someone jostled her and moved on without an apology. Half-turned already by the force of the impact, Rebel looked back the way she had come. There were shops everywhere, selling every conceivable product and service, and already she'd forgotten which way she'd walked from the train station.

Not that it mattered. She couldn't return home anyway. There no longer was a home, only friends, and they couldn't be expected to see to her welfare forever.

She looked up at the street signs on the nearest corner, then again at the slip of paper she'd brought with her. The wind nearly snatched it from her, causing her to quickly bring it beneath the cape once more. She knew which street she was looking for, but it wasn't on either of the signs.

An elderly man approached amid the crowd, walking more slowly than the others, leaning on a cane. For an instant their eyes met and Rebel spoke quickly, before he could pass.

"Excuse me, sir. Would you know the location of a shop owned by Arlen Bickford? He's a merchant dealing in diamonds, I believe."

The stranger stared at her as if she were dim-witted, but at least he'd stopped.

"He's my uncle—by marriage, that is—and I need quite urgently to find him—"

The old man shook his head. "Nobody I know buys diamonds. You don't have an address?"

2

She didn't have to pull out the paper again; she knew it by heart. "Fifth Avenue, but the streets all say Forty-something—" She gestured toward the one saying Forty-third Street. "Will I have to walk miles and miles to find Fifth? And which direction is it?"

He was still shaking his head. "Those are streets. Fifth *Avenue* is over that way." He gestured with a withered hand. "The patrolman might be able to tell you more."

Rebel swallowed, both relieved to find out which direction to go and trembling in apprehension over her reception once she arrived at Arlen Bickford's shop. "Thank you, sir," she said to him, and the old man touched the brim of his hat and moved on.

There was no building in Lyons Falls more than two stories high, and not many of those. Here, the streets tunneled between towering office buildings and tenements and churches with soaring spires; it was impossible to see very far in any direction, for the view was blocked by buildings taller and greater in number than Rebel had ever dreamed existed.

The sidewalks teemed with pedestrians, all of them in a hurry, and the streets were clogged with horses and carriages and buggies of every description. Worst of all, no one seemed to pay any attention to anyone else. If she were knocked down, or if she couldn't find Arlen Bickford, would she starve or freeze to death, unnoticed, amid all these strangers?

An old man in rags sat with his back against one of the tall buildings, a bottle held between his knees in hands that had gone slack, for he was either asleep or unconscious. At home Rebel would have investigated and called for help, but here—no, here, she knew instinctively, such people were ignored. As she would be ignored if she grew too tired to walk any farther and sank down onto the curb.

Rebel feared she would be taking her life into her hands if she crossed from one side of the street to the other, yet if Fifth Avenue was *that* way, that way she must go.

She lifted her head in an unconscious attitude of renewed determination and strode as briskly as her long skirts would allow in the direction the old man had indicated.

Luke Kittering hunched his broad shoulders inside his wool coat, his hands jammed into his pockets, and pressed his tall body into the meager shelter of the entrance to a cleaning establishment. He was unaware of the surging crowd and only vaguely conscious of the cold, his hazel eyes fixed on the doorway of a small shop across the street.

A cart piled high with refuse passed, and Luke raised himself above his six-foot height to see beyond it, cursing silently at the slow pace of the worn-out nag that drew the cart.

No one had emerged while his view was blocked, had they? His keen gaze swept the sidewalk in both directions. Reassured by the lack of any familiar figure, he focused once more on the door he'd been watching for the past half hour.

A girl moved into the periphery of his vision, and though he'd ignored literally hundreds of passersby since he'd taken up his post, this one distracted him.

She was young and pretty, with the most startling hair he'd ever seen. It was the color of a newly minted penny, and so curly that her attempts to restrain it were futile. Bright tendrils escaped around an enchanting face with a clear complexion and a tiny sprinkling of freckles across a small, beautifully shaped nose.

She stood uncertainly on the curb, close enough to

Luke so that he could have reached out a hand and touched her. Her eyelashes were coppery, too, over eyes either gray or green; it was impossible to tell for sure from this angle.

She was lost, but he wasn't able to help her. Luke felt a fleeting regret that he couldn't, that this girl was no one he could ever know. Again he scanned the street. Another wagon, this one enclosed and rising higher than the refuse wagon, was coming toward him.

He stepped out of the dubious shelter of the doorway, intending to move quickly behind it to avoid losing sight of his objective for more than a few seconds.

Suddenly, when the horses pulling the wagon were almost upon him, the girl with the flaming hair stepped off the curb right into their path.

The driver yelled a warning. Luke smothered an oath and grabbed the girl around the waist, jerking her backward so violently that her head struck him in the teeth.

She gave a strangled cry. When he released her and set her on her feet, balancing her with a firm grip on one arm, there was moisture swimming in the girl's green eyes. He could see them now that he faced her—the eyes and the delightful freckles, and the rosy lips parted in shock at how close she'd come to being crushed under the horses' hooves or the wagon wheels.

The wagon driver shook his head in disgust and relief. No one else seemed to have noticed anything amiss, for the pedestrians continued to buffet each other as they churned along the sidewalks in their mad pace to get wherever they were going.

"You all right?" Luke asked the girl.

She wasn't. She was upset, her eyes had been blurred by tears, and she hadn't been thinking about the traffic

5

when she started to cross the street. Something inside Luke Kittering twisted; he wondered what was making her unhappy and he was sorry he wouldn't have the opportunity to do anything about it.

Her lips formed an unsteady smile. "Yes, thanks to you. I'm sorry, it was careless of me. Thank you, sir."

"You're welcome," he said, and consciously stored away the sound of her voice—melodic, slightly husky. Was it always that way, or only when she'd just been badly frightened?

He forgot why he was there and what he was supposed to be doing; he was lost in those misted green eyes.

Rebel's heart was pounding. It had been a close call; the horse had actually brushed her skirts. She stared up into the unfamiliar face—the first friendly one she had seen since arriving in this overwhelming place—and felt a sensation sweep through her. It was a sensation she had never known before, but she knew at once that she'd been waiting for it all her life.

She drew in a sharp breath, mesmerized by the countenance she committed at once to memory. Dark hair with a hint of a wave, heavy black brows to match the thick mustache that only partially concealed a wide, sensitive—and sensual—mouth. He had a firm, clean-shaven chin and a strong nose; his eyes were hazel and he had the tanned, fit look of a man who spent much of his time out-of-doors.

His hand—she glanced down to see it still holding her arm, and it, too, appealed to her—was muscular and bronzed. Its warmth came through her coat sleeve, and Rebel felt a sudden, almost desperate, need to keep it there.

Unconsciously, she shifted her weight, for she was

disconcertingly close to this man. And yet she didn't want to move away from him. Common sense had deserted her; she was reacting strictly by instinct, an instinct she hadn't known she possessed.

A small sound escaped her lips, and concern appeared at once in the man's hazel eyes. "Are you hurt?" he asked.

It was a miracle that she was able to respond, for Rebel felt struck dumb. "Ah, my . . . my ankle. I must have twisted it when I started off the curb and then tried to stop when the horse bore down on me. I'm . . . I'm sure it isn't serious."

She wished it *were* serious. She wished she'd broken a leg, or sustained a concussion, or received some other injury that would keep this man at her side.

His voice was deep and assured. "Maybe you'd better sit down for a minute or two, to make sure." He glanced around, then renewed his hold on her, putting his arm around her for support, actually causing her, for a moment, to need it. "There's a cafe right next door, and an empty table by the window. Let's go in for a few minutes for something hot to drink, and make certain you're all right before you try to walk any farther."

Even Rebel, with no experience of the city, knew that accepting such an invitation from a stranger was simply not done. Yet she offered no resistance—indeed, she stepped with obvious care upon the supposedly injured foot—and allowed herself to be guided into the tiny cafe and seated with her back to the steamy window. Her escort reached over and wiped the window clean, then seated himself opposite her, where she had a better look at him.

He was just as attractive from this slight distance, perhaps more so. His clothes were well-cut and of good

7

quality, his dark hair was windblown. He was smiling. "Is it better to be off the foot?"

Rebel sounded breathless, and she hoped he would take this for mild pain rather than for what it was: paralysis of her respiratory apparatus due to his proximity. "Yes, it is good to sit for a moment."

"Would you like a cup of coffee? Or tea?"

"Tea, please," Rebel answered. And then she was struck with such a wave of vertigo that she gripped the edge of the table with one hand and held on, afraid that she would slide off the chair.

His concern deepened, and he covered her hand with his own as if to hold her in place, sending more disconcerting signals through Rebel's body. "You *are* hurt," he said.

"No, no, I only felt a bit . . . faint." One didn't mention to a strange gentleman that a corset was too tightly laced to allow for this peculiarly urgent need for more air than usual. This man was surely old enough— thirty, perhaps?—to be aware of such matters, anyway.

That wasn't how he interpreted her dizziness, however. "How long has it been since you've eaten?"

"Eaten?" She echoed the word, then grappled with his meaning. "Oh, I ate the last of my lunch on the train, an hour or so out of New York. This morning," she clarified.

For a moment she thought he'd demand to know if she had money to buy food, and then he beckoned to the waitress who was bringing their tea. "The young lady would like something to eat," he said. "Soup, maybe? Or a plate of meat and potatoes?"

Rebel was torn between embarrassment and gratitude. She *was* hungry, and she hadn't enough money for a restaurant meal.

"Soup?" he asked, eyebrows raised. When she nodded, he gave the order to the waitress. Rebel was dazzled by the warmth of his smile.

He had lifted his hand from hers and for a moment seemed distracted by something taking place out in the street. She felt his attention leave her, and almost turned to see what he was looking at, but before she could he was smiling once more into her face.

"You're not a native New Yorker, either," he stated.

There was no implied criticism in this observation; indeed, it was as if being from somewhere else bound them together, outsiders against those hurrying, uncaring people.

Rebel nodded. "I'm from Lyons Falls. That's a village upstate."

Something quickened, sharpened focus, in the hazel eyes. "You're only visiting?"

Rebel hesitated, then nodded again. "My aunt and uncle," she said. How could she explain the true state of affairs to a perfect stranger?

"They live here? In this neighborhood?"

Again she hesitated. One could hardly give out such information to a man to whom one had never even been introduced. Yet the alternative was that when they walked out of this cafe, he would vanish forever.

Rebel did not want that to happen. She fell back upon honesty, unsatisfying though it might be. "My uncle has a shop somewhere near here. It's the only address I have; I don't know his home address."

The keen gaze weighed this, finally accepting it as the truth rather than evasion. With acceptance came a slow smile, causing a mysterious fluttering in her midsection and a renewed acceleration of her pulse.

Her mind raced. If she'd known Uncle's address, she'd have given it to him, she thought. Propriety be damned. She'd never met a man like this one before,

9

she didn't want him to walk out of her life as abruptly as he'd walked into it.

He was suddenly solicitous. No doubt he had seen some of the emotion flickering on her face and misinterpreted it. "Is the ankle giving you pain?"

Subterfuge had never been part of Rebel's makeup, but then she'd never needed it before. "Well, a little," she lied.

"Let's take a look at it." To her astonishment, he was out of his chair, kneeling before her, unbuttoning her boot and easing it from her foot. "Can you move your toes?"

Startled, Rebel glanced around the cafe, her cheeks flaming, but no one was paying any attention to this unorthodox behavior. For the first time, she felt glad that New Yorkers minded their own business.

She experimented with wiggling her toes, as if she had actually sustained an injury.

"Good. Means you didn't break anything. It doesn't seem to be swelling, at least not much." He took her stockinged foot in his hands and began to massage it gently. "Does that hurt?"

"N-n-no," Rebel replied. She stared down at the top of his dark head, just above the level of her knees, and was awash in more sensations, even stronger than the initial ones.

She had imagined being kissed and embraced by a handsome gentleman one day, but it had never occurred to her that having a foot caressed could be so intimate, so excruciatingly exciting. It *was* a caress, sending tremors through her entire body; she imagined the hand sliding up her ankle—oh, God! The actuality surpassed the imagination, and she gasped softly.

Her benefactor paused to look into her face. "That hurt, up there?"

She stammered. "Ah . . . ah, yes, a little. But . . . but I'm sure it will be all right, I'll be able to walk on it."

She wished she could truthfully say that it must be broken, that she needed to be carried somewhere—where?—anything to keep him with her a few minutes longer.

He nodded. "Good." He was putting her shoe back on, his large fingers fumbling with the tiny buttons. "I can't get them all, not without a buttonhook, but since the shoe has elastic on the side, I think it won't matter."

He rose and retook his seat, leaving Rebel limp and momentarily unable to speak.

The waitress approached their table, and again the man addressed her. "Bring me another cup of coffee, please, and a piece of that pie. I think the young lady will have pie, also," he added without consulting Rebel. "And could I have something to write on, please."

When she brought the soup, which was thick and hearty with vegetables and tender chunks of beef, the waitress left a bit of paper on the table. Rebel, suddenly starving, had to restrain the impulse to bolt it down, and she was glad her companion had ordered pie for her. It meant they would prolong the time they sat here together, though that would end all too quickly. This man stirred her in a way she'd longed for, without fully realizing the depths to which this was possible; yet within a short time he would walk out of her life as quickly as he'd come into it.

Rebel sought desperately for a way to prevent that, but she couldn't think of a single thing.

Her companion brought out a pencil and scribbled something on the scrap of paper. Then, his pie un-

11

touched, he glanced past her into the street and leaped abruptly to his feet, pushing the paper toward her. "I have to go, I'm sorry—"

To her dismay, he was flinging money onto the table and already moving away, leaving her. He paused, however, to demand, "What's your name?"

"Rebel Moran," she said, and then he was gone. He practically ran from the cafe; he had vanished by the time she turned around to peer after him.

Disappointment washed over her, bringing an absurd prickling of tears. He was only a stranger, a kind man who had saved her from being hurt and taken pity on her; the debt was all on her side, and she had no way to hold him.

The paper lay on the table beside her bowl. Her appetite was gone, now, although she hadn't finished her soup.

She picked up the paper and stared down at what he'd written. *Luke Kittering. Hoffman House.*

Her heart began to pound. Her lips moved silently and then she was able to speak to the waitress, who was collecting the money.

"Please, can you tell me—do you know the name *Hoffman House?*"

"It's a hotel," the waitress said, and was gone before Rebel could form another question.

A hotel. Yes, of course. Hadn't he said, "You're not a native New Yorker, either?" He was a visitor here, and he was staying in a hotel.

And he'd told her which one it was.

Why? Did he think she'd call on him there? No lady would do that; did he take her for a . . . a different kind of woman? But no, Rebel told herself, enveloped in searing heat.

It could only mean that he'd been as attracted to her

as she'd been to him, and though he'd had to leave quickly, he wanted to see her again.

If she chose to do so, she now knew where to contact him.

The waitress, pausing with a tray, stared at her curiously. "Are you all right, miss?"

Rebel swallowed. "Yes. Yes, thank you." She pushed back her chair, needing fresh air, for all at once she felt as if she were suffocating.

"Ain't you going to eat your pie?"

For a moment the words made no sense, and then Rebel looked at the pie Luke Kittering had paid for, the juice running out onto the plates.

"No," Rebel said. "No, thank you."

The woman muttered something about peculiar people, but Rebel scarcely heard her.

What had happened that made Luke Kittering dash out that way? She pushed through the door, welcoming the icy air on her flushed cheeks.

Maybe he'd been waiting for someone, and he'd had to hurry to join them, she thought. But she knew where to find him.

She folded the paper and tucked it into her purse. The idea of contacting a strange man at a hotel was both terrifying and intriguing. For the moment, however, there was something more urgent to attend to.

Rebel was still shaken when she reached the far side of the street, having dodged yet another carriage and two pedestrians who had run into her, one on each side, nearly making her lose her footing.

How did anyone ever learn to walk around in this place? Why would anyone want to live here?

Gaining the relative safety of the far sidewalk, she paused to get her breath.

If it hadn't been for Luke Kittering, she might well

be lying in the gutter now with broken bones, bleeding, at the mercy of strangers.

Rebel inhaled deeply and turned to examine the small discreet sign she had spotted from the other curb. *A. Bickford,* it read. *Diamonds and Fine Jewelry.*

She *was* at the mercy of strangers, she thought. Within a few minutes, perhaps, she would find out whether this unknown uncle-by-marriage would accept her as a family responsibility, or whether she was truly alone in this terrifying city.

Rebel squared her shoulders and opened the door to the shop.

# Chapter Two

A BELL JANGLED OVERHEAD AS REBEL ENTERED THE SHOP. It was a tiny place, so narrow that there was only space for a walkway beside a high glass case along one side of the room. Behind the case stood a portly gentleman of medium height with gray hair and the sharpest gray eyes Rebel had ever encountered.

She felt as if she had come to steal his wares, and that she would never get away with it.

She came to a halt, feeling totally out of place, and knowing she *looked* out of place. Her clothes were not particularly shabby—indeed, she had worn her best black skirt and shirtwaist, though they were hidden by her old-fashioned cloak. The cloak had belonged to her mother but it was of good woolen material, with no moth holes except one that the man couldn't possibly see, though he looked as if he did. No doubt he was also aware of the thin soles of her shoes and the fact that her corset had been mended, as well.

Rebel gathered her wits. Of course the man could tell no such things, but judging by the items encased in glass before him, he was used to customers dripping

15

with diamonds and gold watchchains, not simple country girls without adornment of any sort. It didn't enter her mind that her face and her hair might be all the adornment she needed.

"Yes?" The word was stiff, withholding judgment for the moment on her acceptability.

If this was her uncle-by-marriage, Rebel thought, her heart sinking, she was probably out of luck. He looked about as merciful as a chunk of Appalachian granite.

Her voice came out sounding surprisingly confident, however. "Do I have the honor of addressing Mr. Bickford? Mr. Arlen Bickford?"

Suspicion flickered in the cold eyes. "I am Arlen Bickford, yes. What may I do for you, miss?"

She resisted the impulse to lick her lips. "I am Rebel Moran, sir."

"Moran?" He repeated the name with what could only be distaste, an inauspicious beginning. And then, as comprehension filtered across his pinched features, there was alarm. "Not the offspring of *Ned* Moran?"

"Yes! And my mother was Beryl—"

He held up a hand as soft and white as her own. "Please! Do not explain the obvious."

Nonplussed, Rebel mentally groped for the non-obvious. "You know, perhaps, that my mother died a little over a year ago, of—"

"I heard. Someone wrote to my wife with the sad news." His mouth, already thin-lipped, became more so as it flattened. "And now I presume you are the bearer of more ill tidings."

She had considered that there might be a lack of warmth in her reception here, but this was even worse than she'd imagined possible. There was no welcome here at all, no sign that the familial connection held any meaning for him. Despair pulsed through her, but Rebel kept her words steady.

16

"Yes, I'm afraid so. My father died three months ago, and as you must be aware, Aunt Winnie is my only surviving relative—"

"And you seek refuge from the impoverished state in which I am certain Ned Moran left you." Was there a note of *satisfaction* in the words? "My dear miss, ah . . ."

"Rebel," she supplied, and saw him wince.

"Rebel. Yes." His tone conveyed what he thought of her name. Well, she'd often thought, herself, that her mother had made an unfortunate choice. Perhaps in the south, where Beryl and Winnie Westin had grown up, it might have been understood. But here, among all these Yankees—

It never occurred to her that she was a Yankee, too, by birth and by upbringing. All she knew was that Arlen Bickford was not going to offer the home she had hoped for.

"I'm seventeen," she said. "No doubt marriage is in my future, but so far I've no plans, and until then . . ."

She stopped, unable to speak the words that would so demean her, not when he was looking the way he did. She could not explain that her father had been sick for so long before he died, and that his salary as a teacher in Lyons Falls had stopped when he could no longer perform his duties. She could not explain how their little house and most of their goods had gone to settle the remaining debts, nor that the founding fathers had declined her services in her father's stead, for she was adequately qualified to teach only young children. She could not add to her humiliation by admitting that her train fare to New York City had depleted her purse to the point that should someone snatch it on those dreadful streets outside, it would hardly be worth shouting "Stop, thief!"

17

Behind her, the little bell jangled cheerfully, and Rebel turned to face the newcomer. This, now, was the sort of person her uncle was used to dealing with, she thought.

The girl was rosy-cheeked from the wind, and wore her deep auburn hair in a stylish upswept coiffure, topped by a pert hat of dark fur matching the fur that trimmed her deep blue, floor-length woolen cape.

How beautiful she was! Even in her own miserable predicament, Rebel noted that. In the other girl's ears were tiny diamond chips, and though her fingers were ringless, there was the glimpse of a slender gold bracelet as she lifted a hand to adjust her hat.

"Papa, I dropped in to see if you could give me a ride home—" The girl stopped upon realizing that the man was not alone. "Oh, I'm sorry! You have a customer!"

Papa, she had said. This then must be her cousin, Rebel decided, and spoke the name without thinking. "Evelyn? You're Evelyn?"

Startled, the other girl allowed her perfect mouth— perhaps touched with some artificial color, or were her lips really that red?—to form an O. "Do I know you?" she asked, her blue eyes bright with interest.

"I'm Rebel Moran."

"Aunt Beryl's daughter? Oh, my! Papa, isn't that wonderful! After all these years! Mama will be delighted, won't she, Papa?"

"No doubt," her father said, in a manner that would have been intimidating to a lesser person than his only child.

"Have you come for a visit? Or . . . oh, Mama did say your own dear Papa was ill . . ."

Rebel swallowed hard. "My father died three months ago, after being sick for a long time."

Sympathy showed both in the perfect face and in her voice as Evelyn extended her hands to her cousin. "I'm so sorry. And now you've come to us." Her hands squeezed Rebel's. "What a lark! I've always wanted a sister, and never had one. It's too bad it has to be under such circumstances, of course, but the main thing is, you've come. Papa, are you nearly ready to leave? Or should I ask Charles to take Rebel and me home and come back for you later? I can't wait to get her to myself and exchange confidences!"

Rebel had stood thunderstruck through this. What a different attitude from her uncle's!

"Mama will be so pleased to see you! She doesn't get out much, you know, and the visitors are mostly mine these days." Evelyn laughed, as if one might have taken that for granted, as well they might. Evelyn was stunningly beautiful.

"Shall I tell Charles to come back?" she asked again, seemingly oblivious of her father's compressed lips.

"Very well. But tell him not to dally. I have another hour's work, and then I'd like my supper on time, if you don't mind."

"Of course." Evelyn gave him a sunny smile, pulled her gloves back on, and tucked an arm through Rebel's. "Come along, Cousin, and let's get acquainted."

Without a backward look, she maneuvered Rebel out the door.

Rebel didn't dare look back, either, afraid of what Arlen Bickford's face would reveal.

Was it really going to be as easy as this? The man had not intended to invite her home with him, she was certain of that. Yet he'd not objected when his daughter had taken it for granted that Rebel's place was with them.

"How did you get here?" Evelyn demanded, pausing at the edge of the sidewalk before a handsome carriage, complete with a uniformed coachman. "Do you have luggage somewhere?"

"A trunk at the train station," Rebel answered, somewhat overwhelmed by this turn of events. She was not so overcome, however, that she forgot the attractive stranger who had rescued her earlier. Unobtrusively, for she had no wish to arouse undue curiosity in her cousin, she glanced across the street. There was no tall figure before the cafe to which he had taken her. A twinge of disappointment made her aware that she had been hoping—against all logic—that Luke Kittering would have returned from his urgent errand to seek her out.

Rebel sighed involuntarily. It made her feel warmer just to remember the way he had held her foot to determine the extent of her supposed injury—but there was no tall figure there now.

She knew she was foolish. Kittering had left in a hurry to attend to business of his own. There was no reason to think he would have come back just because of her. And even if he had, what would she have done? Walked toward him as if they were old friends, renewing an acquaintance? No, of course not.

Her cousin hadn't noticed her inattention. "Do you have a baggage ticket? Ah, here, Charles—" Evelyn reached up to hand the bit of pasteboard that Rebel had given to her to the driver. "You'll take us home first, please, and then collect my cousin's baggage on the way back for Papa, who wishes to be picked up in an hour's time."

"Very good, miss," the uniformed man said. He was middle-aged, servile, smiling. Probably everyone smiled at Evelyn.

"Don't get down, Charles, we're capable of opening and closing the door by ourselves, aren't we?" A moment later Rebel sank into the plush maroon velvet seat and let out a sigh of relief.

Evelyn, on the opposite seat, was grinning at her.

"I'm so glad you've come. We're going to have a wonderful time together, I know it," she said. "We're having a party Saturday night. I hope you've brought a ball gown."

To her own astonishment, Rebel laughed. "I've never owned a ball gown."

Evelyn's eyebrows rose as if she thought Rebel was making fun of her. Then her amusement faded. "You're serious, aren't you? You really don't have a ball gown."

"There aren't many balls in Lyons Falls." Indeed, Rebel couldn't remember a single one. "We sometimes went over to Boonville to dances, but nobody wore fancy gowns, not when we had to ride back and forth in a hay wagon. Now, in a coach like this"—her hand caressed the velvet upholstery—"that would be different."

Evelyn was looking at her closely. "We're not too dissimilar in size, I think. What size is your waist?"

Rebel sighed. "Twenty-two inches."

Evelyn's face twisted in a scowl that did nothing to detract from her beauty. "Mine's twenty. Well, twenty and a half, though don't mention the extra half inch to Mama. She thinks I eat too much as it is. Maybe we can make something of mine fit, though. We've several days, perhaps Nell can let something out. Don't worry, I'm extremely clever at making things work the way I want them to."

Rebel laughed. "I'm sure you are."

She would have enjoyed simply looking out the windows at the buildings and the people they passed— not nearly as intimidating from this vantage point as they had been when she was on foot—but there was no turning her attention from her cousin.

Rebel relaxed and let Evelyn take over.

# Chapter Three

By the time the carriage drew up in front of one of the brownstone houses facing Central Park, Rebel was in a state of awe.

She had known that her uncle was well-to-do; after all, he dealt in diamonds and fine jewelry. Though her mother and Aunt Winnie had corresponded infrequently, mostly because Arlen Bickford did not approve of Beryl and her impecunious Irish husband, enough information had passed between the sisters so that Rebel had learned a few basic facts about her mother's relatives.

These houses, however, were beyond her imagination. Row upon row of stately, elegant houses lined the New York streets. The carriages rolled at a leisurely pace, most of them with uniformed drivers. The strollers were as elegant as the houses; Rebel craned her neck to watch a lady in a red velvet walking dress with a matching cape trimmed in dark fur. Red velvet, of course, was not for a girl with a head thatched in copper. But her own colors, blue or green, in such a style and fabric—Rebel inhaled slowly, willing her pulse to slow down.

Even if her relatives took her in until she found a husband and made a home of her own, it didn't mean she'd be wearing garments such as those her cousin wore. She would be only a poor relation, and if she judged her uncle rightly, he'd see that she remembered her status.

Still, it was impossible not to feel a sense of excitement when Charles opened the door of the carriage and assisted her down behind Evelyn. They crossed the sidewalk, where tiny trees grew in earthen circles at each side of their path, climbed a steep flight of steps, and entered the foyer.

Rebel knew the word foyer, but she'd never seen one. People in Lyons Falls didn't have foyers; they had woodsheds.

It was as elegant as she'd expected from the exterior of the house, and again beyond her wildest imaginings. An elaborately carved stairway rose on the wall to their right, beyond double doors that opened into a parlor with crimson settees and chairs. There were colorful rugs, and above the dark wainscoting there was wallpaper done in crimson and silvery stripes entwined with roses.

A smiling servant took their wraps. Rebel dropped her old cloak over Evelyn's fur-trimmed one with a sense of desecration, though the maid seemed not to notice how plain and out of style it was.

"Thank you, Millie. I've a wonderful surprise for Mama. Is she in her boudoir?"

There was another word Rebel knew but had never heard spoken in ordinary conversation.

"Mrs. Bickford is resting before dinner, miss," Millie said. She was younger than either of the other girls, perhaps fifteen, with a pert liveliness to her face that lent it charm in spite of its plain features. If the Bickfords turned her out, Rebel reflected, she might have to seek employment such as this, as a maid in one of these great houses.

"Come on, Rebel, let's go directly up to see her," Evelyn said, reaching for her hand to draw her toward the stairs.

The hallway stretched far back into the house, and from somewhere came the aroma of roasting meat. Rebel had time for only a quick glimpse into several other rooms, all resplendent in French wallpaper, oriental carpets, polished woods, and fabrics she would be afraid to touch.

She climbed the broad stairs covered with crimson carpeting. To her right, the wall above the paneled wood was papered in white with a gold fleur-de-lis pattern, on which were hung at regular intervals family portraits in heavy gold frames. Many of them bore an unfortunate resemblance to Arlen Bickford.

On the second floor, Evelyn led the way down a corridor lighted by gas lamps. Evelyn wiggled her fingers at them as they passed, allowing the gold bracelet to slide over her ruffled cuff.

"Everything's old fashioned here; Papa likes it this way. I'd like the new electric lights, but Papa sees no need for the additional expense, and Mama's convinced they'd burn the house down. When I have a house of my own, it shall certainly have the convenience of electricity."

Halfway along the passageway she paused, a slender hand on the knob of one of the dark paneled doors. "Of course that may be years in the future. Papa thinks every man who expresses interest in me is a fortune hunter. He can't believe anyone would want me for myself, so I'm not even courting."

This was so patently absurd, considering Evelyn's looks and her vivacious personality, that Rebel didn't reply.

Evelyn made no move to open the door. "You'll like Mama, she's a dear soul. She'll do what she can for you, I know, but don't expect too much from her, Rebel. She made her one and only major stand eighteen years ago, after I was born, in demanding the privacy of her own quarters. In everything else, she gives in meekly to Papa. She fights not even for herself, let alone for anyone else. Even I have been left to fend for myself with him, though I daresay I fare better than anyone else ever has against his autocratic ways. Don't fear, though. The only thing that sways Papa, except of course for money, is public opinion."

Upon the conclusion of that astonishing revelation, Evelyn opened the door and ushered Rebel inside.

So Evelyn had not been unaware of her father's lack of generosity of spirit. Rebel's heart warmed even more toward her cousin.

She had no time to dwell upon this at the moment, however, for there was her aunt to meet.

The girls advanced into a parlor stuffed with more objects and furniture than could be boasted by any room in Lyons Falls. There were velvet-covered chairs and small tables scattered around the room loaded with figurines and framed daguerreotypes and carved boxes.

On a chaise longue near the burning fireplace lay a woman with only a superficial resemblance to Beryl Moran. She was tiny, yet well-rounded in bosom and thighs, and her hair, which had once been the same shade as Evelyn's, was now a startling shade of pink.

25

Blue eyes lifted to meet the girls, and even before her daughter made the introduction, a small, heavily ringed hand was stretched out toward Rebel.

"Rebel! Oh, my dear, I'm so glad to finally meet you!" A genuinely welcoming smile quickly dimmed, however, when Winnie looked at her daughter. "Does your papa know . . . ?"

"That's where I met her, in his shop. He knows she's here for dinner, at least. We must keep her here, Mama," Evelyn said with a frankness Rebel found both disconcerting and endearing. "Her own papa has died, and she has no one else. And no money."

The last she had deduced on her own, though it probably hadn't taken clairvoyance to do so. Evelyn pulled up two of the dusty-pink velvet chairs close to the chaise, and the girls sat down.

Winnie's smile flickered uncertainly. "You know your papa, dear. He can be . . . difficult." She reached again for Rebel's hand. "Not that we don't want you, dear. My own sister's child, after all. I'm sure we'll do our best for you."

Rebel's voice was huskier than usual. "Thank you, Aunt Winnie. I do appreciate . . . whatever . . ."

Evelyn gave her an affectionate pat. "Don't worry about it, Rebel. As I told you, I'm an expert at getting what I want, and I want my only cousin to live with us. Mama, I think I'll leave you two to talk for a bit, while I freshen up. And then, if Charles hasn't arrived yet with your trunk, we'll see if there's anything you need to get you through supper, Rebel."

It had an ominous ring—getting through supper—as if it might be a major ordeal.

Such was not the case, however.

Millie was dispatched to prepare a room for her, and Rebel settled into it with mixed feelings. Was it fair of

26

life to expose her to heaven, and then perhaps take it away?

The room was large and beautifully furnished. Its colors were exactly right for her own coloring, in greens and white with a touch of gilt on the mirrors and picture frames—none of the family portraits here, thank heaven, but pastoral scenes that sent a surge of homesickness for Lyons Falls through her—and a chaise with a green quilted satin cover.

"I'll unpack for you after supper, miss," Millie said cheerfully. "Right now I'm needed in the kitchen."

"Oh, no." Rebel's response was immediate. "I can do it myself." She couldn't bear the thought of anyone, even a maid, seeing how meager her belongings were, noting the mended places on her underwear and the fact that some of the garments had been cut down from when her mother had worn them.

"I don't mind, miss," Millie assured her.

As soon as the girl had gone, however, Rebel opened the trunk and shook out her dresses and hung them up, and transferred her chemises, petticoats, and drawers to the standing wardrobe against one wall.

Heaven knew what Evelyn would be wearing to the table, Rebel reflected with a sigh. As for herself, she was already wearing her best, though perhaps it would not be too extravagant to put on fresh collar and cuffs.

When she was ready, she stared at herself in the full-length oval mirror, which could be tilted on its own mahogany frame. The black skirt was surely acceptable at an ordinary supper, and the white shirtwaist with its fine lace trim was nothing to be ashamed of, or so she told herself. The black armband would make clear to an observer that she was in mourning, which should diminish expectations for her to be stylishly gowned.

Her hair was the worst thing, Rebel thought. Not

27

only was it a too-bright coppery shade, it was too curly, and impossible to restrain in the styles of the day. She had tried everything with it, but it would not be smoothed out or coiled in a graceful knot at the top of her head; it persisted in escaping in tiny tendrils around her face and running riot everywhere else. She pulled a brush through it and watched it snap back into its customary ringlets.

Ah, well, she must do the best she could. She opened the door into the corridor and headed for the stairs.

Halfway down she paused in alarm, for there were masculine voices issuing from a study on the opposite side of the first-floor hallway. Company?

Evelyn emerged from the front parlor and saw her, smiling a greeting. She wore a deep green faille trimmed in fluted flounces: a simple gown for the times, but far more elaborate than anything Rebel could produce from her limited wardrobe.

Again, diamonds flashed in Evelyn's ears—different ones, it seemed—and their brilliance was matched by a brooch at her throat. Yet, oddly enough, it wasn't the jewels but Evelyn's face that drew one's attention.

"I was just coming for you. I was afraid you might be too shy to come down. Come along, Papa has brought a guest home for supper; they'll be discussing business after we've eaten." She lowered her voice and her tone took on a mischievous note. "He's quite handsome. Papa has already informed me that I'm not to make eyes at him."

"And will you obey that order?" Rebel asked, amused, and then astonished that she could feel amusement in her own uncertain circumstances.

Evelyn shrugged. "I haven't decided yet. Here, they're in the study, having a sherry, I believe."

For a moment a flicker of uncertainty made Rebel

catch her breath. Evelyn had been so welcoming, so friendly—in such contrast to her father. Could this reaction be no more than rebellion against Arlen Bickford, as opposed to a genuine sympathy and concern for an orphaned cousin? She put the suspicion aside, thinking wryly that beggars could not be choosers, and if Evelyn fought Uncle Arlen for her own reasons and therefore rescued Rebel, why, so be it.

Even Aunt Winnie was there, her round body encased in a pink flounced concoction—it had so many ruffles, ruchings and ribbons that Rebel could not quite think of it as a gown—and her fingers and throat dripped with gems that sparkled and glittered in the gaslight.

Winnie's smile flickered, disappeared as she glanced toward her husband, then flickered again. Rebel was glad Evelyn had explained her mother's inability to stand up against Uncle Arlen, or she would have thought there was something lacking in Winnie's wits. Rebel herself had never felt intimidated by her parents, nor had either of them been intimidated by the other, but Arlen Bickford was a far cry from the sort of man her father had been.

He turned from the fireplace where a fire warmed the grate, to nod at the girls and introduce them.

"Ah, Mr. Hake, I'd like you to meet my daughter, Evelyn. And, ah"—his tone changed perceptibly—"my wife's niece, Rebel Moran."

Rebel found her hand being lifted by the stranger, and an odd sensation ran through her; it was not the same as she'd felt when Luke Kittering touched her, yet not totally unlike it, either. She felt confused and flustered for the second time that day.

She had no experience with hand kissing. At home, the only males who had ever touched her were boys who'd gone to school to her father and danced with her at the rustic entertainments that were all that were offered in upstate New York.

This man was different.

He wasn't a boy, of course, but a man in his early thirties. He was tall and dark; his black eyes were oddly disturbing, though not at all in the same way that Luke Kittering had been disturbing.

Rebel stared into the darkly handsome face and felt uneasy at what she saw in his brown eyes as they appraised her. And it was not because he found her unattractive—though compared to Evelyn, she was no doubt lacking. It was as if this stranger was evaluating her in some way she could not identify, a way that had nothing to do with her looks.

"Mr. Jubal Hake," Uncle Arlen said. "A business associate. Would you young ladies care for a sherry?"

"Yes, please," Evelyn accepted for them both. "I'm happy to meet you, Mr. Hake."

He had released Rebel's hand and now took her cousin's. He smiled into her face, then turned for the glass Arlen Bickford held out to him.

"Thank you, sir."

He had an accent vaguely similar to the softly slurred speech her mother had carried with her from Georgia. Not Georgia, Rebel reflected, but somewhere south of New York, or south and west.

Luke Kittering, she thought suddenly, had sounded similar to Jubal Hake, as if they'd come from the same place. She had a sudden vivid image of her rescuer: tall and lean, with his thick mustache and hazel eyes and strong hands that had pulled her back, just in time, from the horse and wagon.

*He* had not made her uneasy in the way that Jubal Hake did now. But of course she had not been meeting *him* socially. That's all it was, Rebel told herself as she sipped at the unfamiliar sherry. She felt out of her depth in these surroundings, knew she was under-dressed beside her aunt and her cousin, and she wasn't used to meeting gentlemen who dealt in diamonds.

She sank onto the settee beside Evelyn, conscious of the velvet cushion beneath her and of the trembling hand that held the fragile glass. She must not spill the sherry. She didn't really care for the taste of it, but she saw no way out of sipping at it.

Slowly, unobtrusively, Rebel inhaled a long breath.

She was here, in New York City, and for the moment she was safe.

Consideration of the future could wait until tomorrow, she thought. For now, she would try to relax and enjoy the situation, or at least learn from it.

# Chapter Four

Dinner was as sumptuous as the house and servants had led Rebel to expect. She was ravenous; long before the meal was announced she wished she'd eaten the pie she had left untouched in the cafe.

When Millie and the cook, Mrs. Worsted, brought in the meal, Rebel's mouth began to water. She was in such awe of the dining service itself, even before the food appeared, that she'd considered not eating for fear of making some dreadful faux pas.

Real silver, delicately painted china plates with genuine gold borders, fresh flowers even at this time of year, and dozens of lighted candles instead of the gaslights or kerosene lamps—all these she had read of, but never seen.

She was in a dreamlike state, and felt like an urchin peering in from the kitchen, unworthy to share the bounty of the master. But her youthful, healthy appetite would not be denied.

There was nothing dreamlike about the savory clear soup, the platter of rare roast beef, the whole fish baked with lemon and onion slices, the mounded bowls of mashed potatoes and carrots and cabbage, and the hot, feathery biscuits. A wave of giddiness swept over Rebel, and she clenched her hands in her lap.

Her uncle bowed his head to intone a dry, perfunctory grace, and then beside her Evelyn asked, "Do you care for beef, Cousin?"

"Yes, please," Rebel murmured, and helped herself to the top slice, which was of generous proportions. Reassured by a glance at Arlen—he had taken twice as much and did not appear to notice her plate—Rebel added generously from the other dishes, glad that Evelyn was serving herself first and thereby giving her a gauge for the quantity a young lady might reasonably eat.

She forced herself to chew slowly, and she relaxed a little. The silverware was, after all, functional; a fork was used in the same manner as those she was used to at home, and a spoon still scooped up soup, nothing more. There were more pieces than she was accustomed to, but it was an easy matter to watch what the others did before she picked up each utensil.

At first she was so absorbed in easing her own hunger that she paid little attention to the other diners or their conversation. As the void within her lessened, Rebel concentrated less exclusively on the food and attempted to assess both the family and the topics apparently typical in his household.

They discussed a place called Carnegie Hall, where the family had recently attended a concert, and a building under construction that many considered an oddity because of its unconventional shape, like that of a flatiron.

"It'll be twenty-one stories, truly a skyscraper. There is building going on everywhere," Arlen Bickford stated, with a note of satisfaction, as if it were largely his own doing. The talk veered off onto politics—from the blank expression on Jubal Hake's face, he had no more knowledge of it than Rebel had—and then to a new camera that was able to take pictures that moved, rather than the old style daguerreotypes with which they were all familiar.

"I can't imagine how it does that!" Winnie exclaimed, and then blushed as all eyes fastened upon her.

"Nor I," Evelyn said, calmly slathering butter on a hot biscuit. "No doubt there'll be a demonstration of it somewhere soon, and then we shall go and find out how it works. I did see something interesting while I was out today. Not as miraculous as pictures that move, but rather intriguing. It's called a zipper, and the man who demonstrated it says it will eventually replace buttons."

Her father dismissed this absurdity with a well-bred snort. "Why should we ever need to replace buttons?"

As Evelyn explained the newly patented device, Rebel finished cleaning her plate. It was amazing how much more optimistic it was possible to be on a full stomach than on an empty one. She would take no chances on inviting her uncle's contempt or ridicule by joining the conversation, however; it was safer to remain silent.

Millie carried in tiny cups of coffee—after watching her cousin stir in generous amounts of sugar and cream, Rebel followed suit—and served slices of a rich, fruit-laden cake.

Though Rebel was no longer hungry, the cake was irresistible. This, then, was what that last fork was for;

Millie had carried away the others, leaving the single piece of silver for the dessert.

Throughout the meal, it was Arlen Bickford who directed the conversation. The others followed his lead, with Winnie, like Rebel, maintaining a prudent silence, except that Evelyn introduced several topics that appeared of interest to everyone but her father. And when his own cake was eaten, regardless of the fact that his wife was only halfway through her dessert, Bickford pushed back his chair and rose from the table.

"We'll take our brandy in the study, Mr. Hake," he announced, and led the way out of the room without further excusing the men from the ladies.

Winnie's fork fluttered over the cake as she stared after her husband, until Evelyn said gently, "Go ahead and finish it, Mama. He isn't going to know whether or not we stay at the table."

Winnie nodded gratefully, and took another bite. "Mr. Bickford says I dawdle over my food," she told Rebel with a nervous smile. "It's true, I do, but it seems to choke me when I eat quickly. Odd, it never did that when I was a girl."

Evelyn seemed to have an answer for everything. "No doubt it's a trait you developed after years of sitting across the table from Papa. When your every word and gesture is criticized, you become apprehensive, and that tends to close your throat. He used to affect me that way, too, until I decided not to allow him to intimidate me any longer."

Winnie sipped at the dregs in her cup. "You're braver than I, my dear," she admitted. She inhaled and glanced at Rebel with a frank appraisal that was not in the least offensive. "Have you thought how you're going to handle your papa in the matter of our dear Rebel, Evelyn? If I know you, you're working out some strategy. If I know what it is, I might be of some help."

It gave Rebel a disconcerting twinge in her stomach, despite the comfort of the food now filling it, to be discussed in this way, though since both women appeared firmly on her side she could hardly resent it.

"I've been thinking about it ever since we came home," Evelyn admitted. "For the time being, I think it best to act as if we take it for granted that Rebel will live with us. It is, after all, the Christian thing to do, to take in an impoverished cousin." Her smile removed any sting from the words. "I know that Aunt Beryl and Uncle Ned would have done the same for me, had I been left an orphan. And if Papa says anything to suggest that our arrangement not be a permanent one, why, we will remind him of how it would look, to turn away one's own blood relative. Papa is most susceptible to public opinion, at least among those in the business community. It might be advantageous to introduce Rebel as quickly as possible to as many of our acquaintances as we can, emphasizing to each of them how charitable dear Papa is being. That will make it harder for Papa to withdraw his charity. Mrs. Snelling will be at the party, won't she? And she's a sweet lady who will, if I drop a hint in her ear, remark to him upon her admiration for Papa's generosity."

Evelyn turned to Rebel with a laugh. "Mrs. Snelling is one of his best customers. She has a passion for diamonds and the means to indulge her passions. Oh, yes, don't worry, Cousin. We'll keep you here, won't we, Mama?"

Again the suspicion surfaced that Evelyn played a game of her own. Quite possibly it was no more than an understandable desire on Evelyn's part to best her domineering father in whatever way she could. Rebel thought that if Arlen Bickford were her parent, she would be driven to living up to her own name in dealing

36

with the man, so she couldn't hold it against her cousin if she felt the same way.

It was clear that if Rebel were allowed to remain, the credit would go to Evelyn, not to Winnie. Winnie had all the courage of a baby rabbit faced by a hungry fox.

Yet she nodded now in approval. "You're more clever than I, dear. Yes, I must remember. If your papa speaks to me on the matter, I am to remind him of how he will be regarded by society in the matter of Christian charity."

"Good." Evelyn pushed back her chair. "Shall we retire and sit by the fire? I'm afraid winter is upon us in earnest. I wouldn't be surprised if we saw some snow before long."

Rebel covered a sneeze as she followed her cousin into the passageway, trailed by her aunt. "I hope I didn't catch the sniffles while walking the streets today. It *was* very cold, and I've forgotten a handkerchief. Excuse me, while I run up and get one."

"We'll be in the back parlor," Evelyn told her. "Join us for a good talk. We want to know all about your poor papa."

Rebel climbed the stairs, grateful that Evelyn had some sympathy for her recent loss, which was more than could be said for Arlen Bickford. She heard her uncle and his visitor in the study, speaking in low voices, and wondered what Jubal Hake's business was. He was respectably garbed, but somehow he didn't have that air of prosperity and confidence that Bickford exuded, which she somehow believed a diamond merchant would have.

The gaslights burned in the upper hallway, but her room was dark when she entered it except for the faint glow of coals on the hearth. She made her way toward it and drew aside the screen, then transferred a small shovelful of coal from the scuttle to the dying fire; it would be nice to undress later in a room not gone entirely cold.

The handkerchiefs had been folded away in the top drawer of a chest near the window; she wouldn't need a light to find them. Rebel's fingers searched out one of the linen squares, and then, as she turned from the dresser, she was drawn to the window.

Evelyn was right. It was snowing, the first great white flakes of the season. They drifted slowly downward in the illumination from the gaslight on the street below.

Rebel had known heavy snows every year of her life, yet she never failed to feel a thrill at the first fall of winter. It would be different in this great city than she was used to on the hills around Lyons Falls, but no doubt here, too, it would be beautiful, at least until it was trampled by the horses and carriages.

In the shadows below something moved. Rebel, about to let the curtain fall back over the glass, paused, watching.

There was a man down there. This gave rise to no alarm; in a city the size of New York, there would be pedestrians coming and going along the walks at all hours, she supposed.

This man, however, wasn't walking along as a man might on his way home to supper after a day at the office. Indeed, his movements seemed almost surreptitious. He kept to the shadows until, as Rebel continued to observe him, he brought out a watch and held it so that the lamplight fell upon it.

Then he stepped back into the shadows; if she had not seen him move she would no longer be able to tell that he was there.

For no particular reason except that this man, too, was rather tall and broad shouldered, Rebel remembered Luke Kittering. What if he'd found her here?

38

Immediately, Rebel laughed scoffingly at herself. Her father had sometimes accused her of being overly imaginative, though since he shared the fault he was not critical.

Imagination filled many a solitary hour and had raised her spirits more than once. It wouldn't hurt to think about Luke Kittering, to imagine that he'd been so taken with her that he'd somehow discovered where she had gone.

It was a pity she'd never have a socially acceptable means of getting to know him better, she thought wistfully. She had been so strongly attracted to him, beyond all reason, really.

She remembered the scrap of paper in her purse, the one that would make another meeting possible. No, of course she wouldn't follow through on it, Rebel told herself. No decent woman would. The man would have no respect for her if she did.

"Miss? Shall I light the lamp?"

Rebel turned from the window at Millie's query. "No, I just came up for a handkerchief, and I have it. It's snowing."

"I know. I was outside a few minutes ago, taking out the refuse for the collector who'll be here at dawn. When you hear the dustbins banging then, don't be alarmed."

The young maid walked over to peer out, also, at the giant flakes that drifted past the window.

"There's a man out there," Rebel said. "Such a cold night to be on the streets."

Millie nodded, her profile barely discernible in the light that came in from the hall. "There are plenty on the streets who have nowhere to go," she said soberly. "I feared I would be one of them before Mrs. Bickford took me on. I didn't think the mister was going to let me stay. I was only thirteen and completely untrained, but Miss Evelyn, bless her, stepped in. She said I looked sturdy and healthy, and intelligent enough to learn. She even said there were advantages to training one's own servants; they learned the right ways from the beginning and didn't have to unlearn bad habits.''

She put out a hand to the opposite panel of curtain from the one Rebel still held drawn aside. "I hope he has a place to go for the night, poor man. He'll likely freeze, otherwise, before morning. There's ice on the steps.''

For some reason Rebel felt a pang of anguish for this stranger, perhaps more acute than it might otherwise have been because she'd been so close to a similar predicament herself only hours earlier. "He's just standing down there in the dark. I wonder if he's waiting for someone?''

Millie peered more closely, though there was nothing to be seen except for a figure that blended into the shadow beyond the small circle of light. "More likely he's searching through the refuse bins that are being set out, looking for something to eat.''

The excellent meal suddenly sat less well in Rebel's stomach. "Good heavens, do you think so?''

Millie shrugged. "There's plenty as do get their food that way. Mr. Bickford had one poor wretch arrested when he caught him going through our trash.''

So much for her uncle's Christian charity, Rebel thought. She bit her lip, then said quietly, "If this were my house, and the larder plentifully supplied, I'd invite the man into the kitchen for a plateful of leftovers. There was plenty left over, wasn't there?''

"Oh, my, yes. The staff didn't finish off the half of it.'' Millie's voice took on a different note. "There's plenty to spare, and the mister never eats leftovers, only the servants do. Mrs. Worsted was overtired tonight and she's already gone up to her room; I'm to

40

finish the clean-up in the kitchen. What's to stop me from just stepping out there for a minute and giving the poor man a bit of meat and bread, and maybe a mug of soup, if it's still hot?"

"Would you dare to do it?" Rebel asked hopefully. "Even if he's not starving, he's bound to be chilled through."

Millie giggled. "I daren't get caught, not by the mister, anyway. Miss Evelyn and the missus wouldn't object. I'll do it, miss, and nobody'll be the wiser."

Millie turned and hurried away, and Rebel lingered at the window until the maid's figure appeared below a few minutes later, swathed heavily in a dark cloak.

The stranger spun, startled, though he stayed too far away from the streetlight to be clearly visible from the window above. He held up a protesting hand when Millie thrust the tray at him. The maid turned toward the house, gesturing with one hand at Rebel's window, and he looked upward, though he could have seen nothing in the unlighted room.

Then he lifted the cup from the tray and drank its contents; Rebel could see the tiny wisp of steam that rose from it. Millie waited for him to finish, then handed over the meat and bread wrapped in a cloth.

When Millie dashed back toward the rear of the house, the stranger lifted a hand in salute toward Rebel's window. She wished he'd step fully into the light, so that she might see his face, but he did not. Indeed, he had already vanished completely into the night.

Rebel dropped the curtain into place, feeling a little less guilty about her own good meal, though the maid was probably right about the man outside. Though she hadn't seen him clearly, Rebel hadn't had the impression that he was anything like the derelicts she'd seen sleeping or passed out earlier that day. He had probably been amused that anyone thought he might be starving.

She herself had never been really hungry, although for a while on the New York City streets this afternoon she had envisioned the possibility. She was glad Millie had fed the man, whether he was scavenging in rubbish cans or not.

Rebel headed for the stairs, wondering why the man stood out there in the snowy night. At home she knew everyone; it was strange to think about all the thousands of people—no, millions—around her in every direction, with lives and problems of which she knew nothing. People who would have little if any concern if a young girl were turned onto the streets to shift for herself.

Yet the man outside had thanked her, in that casual gesture, for her compassionate act. It made her feel a bit less isolated to know that somewhere among the three million people was one who perhaps wished her well.

Someday, Rebel thought wistfully, descending the carpeted stairway, some man will fall in love with me, and I won't be alone anymore. It would probably only happen if he didn't see Evelyn first, though.

# Chapter Five

JUBAL HAKE AND ARLEN BICKFORD WERE STANDING IN the foyer below as Rebel descended the stairs, and Evelyn emerged from the back parlor. She looked up with a smile at her cousin as she came toward the two men.

Jubal Hake hadn't noticed Rebel. He was gazing down from his great height at Evelyn, his admiration evident.

"You're leaving, Mr. Hake?" she asked. "We enjoyed having you for the evening."

"I enjoyed being here. The dinner was delicious, Miss Evelyn." He smiled. "Much better than hotel fare. And the company was better, too."

Evelyn's eyelashes fluttered. Even Rebel, observing, was charmed by her cousin. Remembering what Evelyn had said about not being courted, Rebel slowed her steps, looking at Arlen Bickford.

Yes, there was a tightening of the muscles around his mouth. He did not approve this banter between a business associate and his only daughter, innocent though it might be. Was it only because he thought all men were fortune hunters? For a moment there was a prick of grief as Rebel thought of her own father. He hadn't worried about some scoundrel being after his money, because there was no money, but he'd loved her very much. He'd been protective because he loved her.

Give Evelyn's father credit for the same concerns, she chided herself, and moved slowly on down the stairs, uncertain whether to join the trio there or go past them to the back parlor where Aunt Winnie was probably waiting.

Evelyn solved that question by reaching out for her hand when she reached the bottom, drawing her into the group. "Have you invited Mr. Hake to the party Saturday night, Papa?" Without waiting for a reply, she spoke animatedly to their guest. "It will be a grand affair: music, dancing, salmon mousse and ices, all the ladies in their prettiest gowns—"

"No lady could be prettier than the ones already here," Jubal Hake responded. It made Rebel feel uncomfortable to be included, when she knew he really meant Evelyn. She felt like an impostor, trading on her cousin's beauty.

Hake's gaze drifted to his host. "New York can be a lonely city for someone who's only visiting. If that was an invitation, I'd be pleased to come to your party."

Rebel was watching her uncle, and she thought he hesitated, though this was nearly imperceptible.

"Of course. Do come. Supper at seven, with entertainments to follow." Bickford sounded stiff.

"It will be formal, of course," Evelyn added. "We'll look forward to seeing you then, Mr. Hake."

44

It was not until the door had closed behind their visitor that Arlen Bickford addressed his only child. Rebel, who had been peering out while the door was open, almost missed what he was saying, for she had been wondering if the other stranger—she thought of him, with an inward smile, as *her* stranger—was still standing about out there in the darkness. There had been only one figure visible through the open doorway, however, that of Jubal Hake, rapidly disappearing into the snowy night.

"Evelyn, that was most forward of you. I've told you before, a ladylike demeanor will gain you far more than this brash, ill-considered spontaneity."

For once Evelyn did not resort to charm in response to a difficult moment. She was still holding her cousin's hand, and Rebel felt the tightening reflex before Evelyn let her go. Almost, Rebel felt, as if the other girl did not want her drawn into the small pool of unpleasantness.

"Being ladylike has gotten me nothing except loneliness so far," Evelyn stated. "Since he didn't mention it, I assumed you hadn't invited him. And I wanted Mr. Hake to come to the party."

"Mr. Hake is a business acquaintance, nothing more," Arlen reminded her.

A bright spot of color formed on each of Evelyn's cheeks. "And how might I be expected to meet possible suitors?" she demanded. "Mr. Hake, and Rebel and I, will probably be the only young people at the party, except for Mrs. Henry's idiot son. I'm eighteen years old, and I've never even had a beau, Papa. Most girls are married by my age, and I never get to meet anyone who's eligible."

"Mr. Hake is in New York solely to conduct business for his firm. My impression is that he works for a salary; he has no wealth of his own."

45

Evelyn made an impatient gesture. "Is that all that matters? A man's wealth? I'm interested in the *man!* Not Mr. Hake, necessarily, though he's presentable enough. But I can't bear being practically a prisoner in this house, meeting no one except your elderly clients!"

"When the time comes, Evelyn, I'll see that you're introduced to an acceptable young man." He extended one soft, pale palm. "The earrings, please. And the brooch."

With a scarcely controlled anger, she stripped herself of the jewelry and dropped the pieces into his hand. Then, without another word, she swept past him toward the back parlor. After a moment's hesitation, Rebel followed.

Evelyn slammed the door shut behind them and leaned against it, tears glistening in her blue eyes. "Damn him!" she said, hitting one small fist against a door panel. "How have you stood it all these years, Mama? Letting him decide every detail of your life, every bloody little detail?"

Winnie, mouth sagging, stared up from her chair near the fire. "Dearest, what is it? Have you and your papa quarreled again?"

"I waited all through dinner for Papa to invite Mr. Hake to the party on Saturday, and finally did it myself. Dear heaven, what's a party if the only people there are old fogies? Where's the fun in wearing a pretty dress and jewelry if nobody sees them except prospective customers?"

She turned her attention to Rebel, standing uncertainly on the hearth. "I suppose you thought I was lucky, didn't you, to have diamond earrings and that magnificent brooch? Well, they aren't mine, you see. Papa lets me wear them when I'm out and about, to display them. It's a wonder he doesn't keep me chained

46

in the shop window like a pet monkey. That's precisely what I'll be at the party, won't I, Mama? Dressed to the teeth, dripping gems, and the old women will imagine them around their own scrawny necks, only they won't think of the wrinkles there but of *my* throat, which is still young and firm, *my* ears with the diamonds in them, *my* fingers loaded with rings. And the nasty old men, smelling of brandy and tobacco, with their watch chains stretched to the limit across their grossly fat bellies, will stand as close to me as they can get, pretending to look at the jewelry but trying to see down the front of my dress! And when they strike up the music, there won't even be any young men to dance with!"

This was a different picture from the one Rebel had formed of this household, of her cousin's life. She had no idea what to say. If Evelyn did, indeed, use her newly arrived relative in an ongoing battle of wills between herself and her father, who could blame her?

Evelyn produced a handkerchief and blew her nose vigorously. Her grin reappeared, though somewhat subdued. "Well, Mr. Hake *is* coming to the party. We can take turns dancing with him this one time, at least, Rebel."

Winnie was not reassured. "Were—were you much taken with Mr. Hake, dearest?"

Evelyn joined Rebel on the hearth, lifting her skirts to an immodest level so that the heat might better reach her legs. "Not actually, no. I mean, I'm not swooning over him or anything like that. But he's a young man, and if he looks down my dress I won't feel as if I've been ravaged by a revolting old man."

Her good humor was resurfacing. She met Rebel's troubled gaze. "Did you have gentlemen friends in Lyons Falls?"

"Boys I grew up with," Rebel said. "No suitors."

"Do you dream about it? What it would be like to fall in love? To be kissed, to be made love to?"

Conscious of her aunt only a few yards away, Rebel blushed. "Yes. Doesn't every girl?" But from now on, the man in her dreams would have a face, she thought: a wide, sensual mouth under a thick dark mustache, hazel eyes, and crisp black hair with a hint of a wave. "Everyone dreams," she said.

"I do. I have since I was twelve," Evelyn confessed. "Sometimes I see a man on the street and I want to put out my hand and say, 'Hello, I'm Evelyn Bickford'—"

"Evelyn!" Winnie protested.

"And then he'll say, 'You're the most ravishing beauty I've ever seen, and I'm a millionaire'—that's the only sort Papa would accept as a son-in-law, so he has to be rich, though I'm sure *I* wouldn't care—'and will you marry me at once because I cannot live another moment without you.' And I will accept immediately, and live happily ever after."

Rebel glanced at her aunt to see how Winnie was taking this fantasy. Her own mother would have laughed. Winnie, however, drooped.

"Living happily ever after isn't always the way it works," she said softly.

"No. But your marriage was an arranged one to begin with, and Papa—" Evelyn shook her head. "I don't intend mine to be an arranged marriage. You know what Papa said to me? That when the time came he'd see that I was introduced to an acceptable young man! *His* idea of acceptable, of course. Someone like that twit Peter Henry, who's rich but can't even stand up to his mama, let alone to someone like Papa! And when is the proper time going to come? I'm practically an old maid, for heaven's sake!"

"Soon, perhaps," Winnie soothed. She gave the

impression of fluttering nervously, though Rebel couldn't have said exactly how. "Dearest, if you really like this Mr. Hake, perhaps—"

Evelyn dropped her skirts and stepped away from the fire, finally warmed. "Oh, inviting him was more or less an act of rebellion, Mama. I didn't fall madly in love with him on first sight, so he probably isn't the right man, anyway." A mischievous quirk of the mouth lighted her face. "He isn't accustomed to moving in society. I suppose I'd be happier with a man who knew which fork to use, although if I loved him I guess I'd be willing to teach him about such things."

Winnie's mouth was sagging open again. "How do you come to the conclusion that he isn't used to moving in society?"

"Didn't you notice the way he waited to see what Papa did before he selected a fork or a spoon?" The amusement increased as she glanced at Rebel. "Rebel was uncertain, too, but she was less obtrusive about waiting for the proper usage to be demonstrated. Ah, what difference does it make whether a person knows the purpose of a large fork and a small one? Lord, I'm tired, but I suppose we'd better look at some of my gowns and see if there's one that might be made to fit Rebel for the party. Shall we go up and see what we can find, Cousin?"

They spent the next hour in Evelyn's room, where the girl brought out dress after dress to spread across her bed for Rebel's appraisal. Rebel was stunned both by their design and the number of them.

"Do you like this?" Evelyn asked, handing over a bronze satin gown which surely would expose an extraordinary amount of bosom. "I wore that last season, and it's loose now. It might fit you around the waist. Or there's this one, the purple velvet. I think you could wear purple. I'll ask Papa if you might have the little diamond pendant with it. Or maybe that ecru damask—" She held it up before Rebel and shook her head. "No, you need something with more color. Try the brown crepon, why don't you? It's less elaborate than some of the others, but it might be just the thing to set off your coloring, and you're pretty enough so you don't need much in the way of ruffles and ruchings."

It was fun but exhausting after her long trip and the kind of day she'd had. Rebel was glad when they'd decided on the crepon, which would need only minimal alterations to fit her.

The fire had died in her room, and she undressed quickly, feeling the chill. And then, for a moment before she slipped into the unfamiliar bed, she stood before the window, looking down at the street.

It was still snowing. The walk was covered, and there were no footprints visible. Her stranger had been gone for hours, no doubt. She hoped he had a good warm place to sleep, that he wasn't a vagrant as Millie had supposed. She'd have to ask the maid in the morning what he had been like, up close, and what he had said.

She was about to put out the light when impulse sent her toward the small purse atop the oak desk. Rebel opened it and took out the slip of paper Luke Kittering had left in the restaurant, staring with a quickened heartbeat at what he'd written.

There was a pen and ink before her, and she knew there was writing paper in the top drawer. He was only visiting in New York City; there was no way of knowing how long he would be at the Hoffman House.

If she didn't write at once, it might be too late.

The house was silent around her. Outside, the snow fell steadily. Somewhere a clock chimed, marking the hour, and the fire made its small sounds on the grate.

50

Rebel knew she was mad even to consider making contact with Luke Kittering.

She also knew she had never been so strongly drawn to anyone in her life. She could imagine going to her father and saying, "I met the most exciting man today. Is there any way we could have him come to dinner?" and having Ned Moran laugh and plot with her to bring it about. No wild flight of fancy could conjure up the same response from Arlen Bickford.

If Uncle Arlen learned she'd responded to this scrap of information on the paper, he might well throw her out into the street, further convinced that any daughter of Ned Moran's was not fit to live in his own great house. Even Evelyn would be shocked at such impropriety, Rebel suspected.

Rebel closed her eyes, seeing again the tanned face, the hazel eyes that had revealed such interest in a stranger. She remembered the way Mr. Kittering had taken her stockinged foot between his hands, manipulating it gently to be sure there was no serious injury.

Simply recalling the scene was enough to arouse those same sensations again. She felt as if warm liquid poured through her veins, and her lips parted in anticipation of what would have come next.

Only, of course, nothing had come next. They were in a public eating place, and he'd dashed out, and away from her forever.

Except that he'd scribbled his name, and the name of his hotel, on the paper.

Rebel opened her eyes and drew in a deep breath.

A moment later she was seated at the desk, writing in her best hand.

It had to be simple, noncommittal, noncompromising, Rebel thought. Was there really anything so terribly wrong with expressing her thanks for his help?

And in so doing, naturally, letting him know where she might be found, should he care to do so?

She made several attempts before she was satisfied with the result. She reread it in a whisper, imagining how he would react to it.

Dear Mr. Kittering:

Please accept my sincere gratitude for your assistance and your concern today. Without your intervention, I would surely have suffered grievous injury, and I thank you. I did locate my uncle, Arlen Bickford, and am now safe in his lovely home overlooking Central Park. I trust that the time you spent assisting me did not inconvenience you in your own affairs.

Sincerely,
Rebel Moran

There. Without giving the exact address, she had surely made it possible for him to locate her, as she knew her uncle could easily be traced by one determined to do so, especially once the seeker knew the house faced Central Park.

Quickly she folded and sealed the missive. Perhaps Millie, if she was still up, would know whether the note needed a more specific address than the name of the hotel.

Millie was no longer in the kitchen when Rebel reached it, however, but Charles, the coachman, was having a late-night snack of ale and meat and bread. He rose at once, and answered her question easily.

"The Hoffman House? Yes, I know it, miss. Would you like me to deliver your message? I will be passing by there on the way home after I take Mr. Bickford to the shop in the morning."

Rebel hesitated. "It's . . . rather private . . ."

Charles gave her a knowing grin. "Quite so. Nothing to worry about, miss. I've a closed lip. The only thing I ever say to the mister is 'yes, sir' and 'no, sir.'"

She handed it over, then ran back up to her room.

It was done. The moment she closed herself in the bedroom, Rebel was convinced that it had been a crazy thing to do, that she'd be found out and made to feel a fool or worse.

But maybe, just maybe, Luke Kittering would respond to it, she thought, and anticipation overwhelmed the uncertainties.

At the moment, it seemed worth the risk.

# Chapter Six

REBEL HEARD A LIGHT TAP ON HER DOOR AND ROLLED over, knowing at once that she'd slept later than she'd intended.

The door opened enough to permit Millie to peer around it. "Oh, I hope I didn't wake you, miss." She shouldered the door wider and came in balancing a covered tray. "Just stay right there, covered up, like, and I'll get your fire going."

Embarrassed, Rebel pushed herself into a sitting position against the pillows. "You needn't wait on me this way, Millie. I'm not used to, and don't expect it. I'll come down to breakfast with everyone else—"

Then she remembered the note she'd given to Charles to deliver to Luke Kittering at the Hoffman House. "Has . . . has my uncle left for work yet?" She'd get it back, Rebel thought in a wave of panic.

She'd tell Charles she'd changed her mind, and no one need ever know how foolish she'd been last night.

"Oh, I think he was leaving as I came up with your tray," Millie said cheerfully. "A bit earlier than usual, because he was angry at Miss Evelyn. He don't like it when she sasses him, but she's not like her mama." Millie lowered the tray on its little legs over Rebel's lap and lifted the cover, allowing savory aromas to escape. There were crusty brown sausages, boiled eggs and fresh bread with melted butter, and raspberry jam in a sauce dish at the side. The tray also held a pot of tea and an exquisite china cup.

Stricken, Rebel stared at the maid. If Charles ever spoke of the surreptitious note, or if anyone found out any other way . . .

Millie lowered her voice in a conspiratorial tone. "Miss Evelyn told me to bring breakfast up to you today. The missus never comes down with the others, and I don't blame her. The mister gets out of the wrong side of the bed of a morning, as the saying goes, and Mrs. Worsted says the missus gave up years ago trying to sit across the table from him. She always has breakfast in her room."

The maid flicked a snowy napkin off the tray and onto Rebel's front. "Miss Evelyn, she usually eats with her pa, but they had a row about something today. She told me you'd be more comfortable eating alone, this time."

She lifted the silverware and pulled a bit of folded newspaper from beneath the knife and fork, a sly smile touching her lips. "I reckon the mister would be really furious if he knew about this, but he's none the wiser."

Rebel stared at the newspaper. No, it wasn't a complete paper, only a bit torn from one page. "What is it?" She read the headline, disembodied because the story itself had been torn off: *Will Buck Sloan Be Number Sixty-five for the Hanging Judge?*

"Look on the inside," Millie urged, waiting expectantly.

Rebel unfolded the bit of newspaper, noting that it was part of the *Fort Smith New Era* of November 12, 1891—some two weeks old. But that scarcely registered when she unfolded one more layer and saw the penciled message, written in a strong, legible hand. A familiar hand. She was assailed by vertigo.

*Many thanks to the kind lady who took pity on a freezing, hungry man.* It was signed *L. Kittering.*

A most peculiar thrill swept through her, and Rebel's breathing was suspended until it became painful.

"I found it on the back steps this morning," Millie said. "Protected from the snow under a brick. It's a good thing the mister never goes out the back door. Nice, polite feller, wasn't he, to leave a note, even if he didn't have any proper paper but the newspaper he was carrying. Too bad you didn't get to take the tray out to him yourself, miss. Right good-looking, he was. Eat up while it's hot, miss."

It wouldn't do to make Millie suspicious, so that she would talk with the other servants. Rebel liked Millie, but she didn't know enough about the others to guess if they could be trusted, and with what Charles knew, they might put two and two together and come up with something that could endanger her entire future.

Rebel nibbled on a sausage and found that her appetite was returning. She took a bite of the boiled eggs, her mind still racing.

"He was very good looking," Millie said. "Tall, very tall. Built the way a man ought to be, you know, miss? Broad in the shoulders, slim through the middle. And dark. I always preferred dark men." She giggled. "I

56

don't know what he was doing out there, but I could tell the minute I got close to him he wasn't scavenging in the rubbish bins. He was well-dressed enough, and he spoke educated, like." She paused to consider a matter that had just struck her. "Sort of the same as Mr. Hake, come to think of it. He didn't pronounce his words the way New Yorkers do."

"From the South, or the Southwest, maybe," Rebel concurred. She wiped her hands on the napkin and picked up the scrap of newspaper again. "Fort Smith, Arkansas. That's where this newspaper came from."

Millie turned away and busied herself with getting a fire going. "That's a ways from New York, isn't it? Well, he was grateful for the soup, and the sandwich to go with it, though I don't think he was starving, by any means. For one thing, he was wearing a watch chain and fob that could have been sold for enough to keep him going for a month or two. I know a little about such things. The mister often shows such items to the family and his guests. I've heard him mention their values."

Rebel finished off the sausages and eggs and spread jam thickly on the last of the bread. There was no point in starving just because she'd acted on impulse and might get into trouble over it. It was too late now to change anything, and besides . . . besides, Luke Kittering might respond to her note. She decided that she wasn't sorry, after all, that she'd sent it.

"Well, I'm glad he wasn't really in need. Thank you, Millie, for bringing up the tray. My cousin mentioned having someone alter a dress for me to wear to the party on Saturday night, so I'd best get dressed and see if she's ready to take on that problem."

"Oh, she spoke to Nell about it, I heard her. Nell's chief housemaid, and she's clever with a needle. No doubt you'll find them in the sewing room when you're

57

ready. That's on the upper floor, straight up the back stairs. Timothy had orders to get a fire going there, so you'd all be comfortable. Fierce cold out, it is."

After Millie had gone, Rebel cleaned her plate, drank a second cup of tea laced with sugar and lemon, and got dressed in another of her dark skirts and a white shirtwaist. No doubt she should be in mourning, but she couldn't afford to buy anything new. The arm band would have to serve.

As she made up her bed—she knew Millie would have done it, but she felt uncomfortable being waited upon—she thought about the note from Luke Kittering.

Why had he been outside this house last night? He hadn't known she was here or that she was the lady who had taken pity on him, or he'd have worded his note differently, wouldn't he? He'd have called her by name, or made some reference to the matter of their having met before.

Or would that have been an error in judgment? He might not have wanted to expose her rash action in accepting his invitation to go into the cafe to anyone else who might intercept the note, although his simple thanks condemned her anyway. Could Millie have mentioned her name to him? She'd have to ask her.

Rebel folded the newspaper and put it away in a drawer, under her corset covers. The excitement remained with her, filling her veins with the new kind of fire she had discovered only yesterday.

She would see Luke Kittering again. She knew it.

Nell was a woman of forty-odd years, thin and quiet, though she often smiled at the things her young mistress said. She was not only clever with the needle, she was quick, too.

"What do you think about this one?" Evelyn would

say, bringing out gown after gown, once they'd decided the first project must be the brown crepon for the ball. "I can't wear any of them any longer, or at least I don't intend to. My cousin might as well get some good from them."

Nell smiled and nodded. "I'll take care of it, Miss Evelyn."

When Rebel tried to express her gratitude, Evelyn dismissed her with an airy gesture.

"It's going to be great fun, having someone my own age in the house," she said.

It didn't take long for Rebel to understand just why her cousin was so delighted with her company.

While Evelyn had beautiful clothes and all the stunning jewelry she wanted to wear (even though her father locked it in the safe between wearings), she had few friends. When she went out to entertainments at Carnegie Hall or private homes, it was in the company of her parents, not with young people. The two young men who had been allowed to call upon Evelyn over the past six months had not caught her fancy at all, and she'd quickly discouraged them.

"You can't imagine what they were like," Evelyn confided. "Mr. Cornfeld was insipid in the extreme, and Mr. Moulton had bad breath of such magnitude that I couldn't even concentrate on what he was saying. And so Papa decided that I was not properly appreciative. Right now he's teaching me a lesson by not inviting anyone to the house who's under the age of forty."

Arlen Bickford was a difficult man to live with. He wanted everything just so, catering to his own indulgences in lavish fashion, but as far as his family was concerned, any luxury was for show, for his own image rather than the comfort of his wife and daughter.

59

It didn't take a genius to realize that Winnie Bickford's semi-invalidism was the poor woman's sole defense against an irate, short-tempered husband. She kept to her boudoir and sitting room, except for suppertime when there were guests. On the rare occasions when Winnie was at the table, Rebel understood only too well why her aunt preferred to dine in solitary peace. Nothing Winnie did met with approval, from her clothes and her hair to her conversation—what there was of it—and her management of the house and servants.

In truth, it was Evelyn who directed the household, not her mother. She protected Winnie when she could, calmed her father's worst outbursts, and acted as his hostess when he entertained.

"All the parties," Evelyn told Rebel with a hint of bitterness, "are for the purpose of selling diamonds. Or, in the case of Mr. Hake, buying something from someone. At least Jubal Hake is different from the musty old codgers who usually sell diamonds to Papa."

Evelyn was usually good-natured and of sunny disposition, though it must have been a strain, constantly acting as a buffer between her parents and between her father and the servants, while having no buffer of her own. And now, Rebel thought guiltily, her cousin had one more person to protect: her.

Several times she approached a room only to stop, her face burning, as she heard her uncle's annoyance surface in her own direction, until it was defused by Evelyn.

"But Papa, what will people think if we don't do our best for her? Besides, she isn't costing anything. We throw out more food every day than Rebel eats, and she can wear my cast-off clothes."

Rebel felt a surge of resentful misery. It was difficult

to feel grateful for Arlen Bickford's "hospitality," knowing that it was involuntary and begrudged. Had Rebel and Evelyn's positions been reversed, Bickford's daughter would have been welcomed without reservation.

What choice did Rebel have? The few days she'd spent here proved she didn't know enough even to seek a position as a maid like Millie, and the thought of prowling through rubbish bins looking for food was a chilling one.

Yet if she lived here in this house, how would she ever escape her uncle's dominance? If Evelyn, startlingly beautiful as she was, had no beau, how was her less striking cousin to meet an eligible young man who might offer love and marriage? Unless, of course, something came of the chance meeting with Luke Kittering. That hope gave her courage.

How long would it take him to respond, if he chose to do so? The question burned in her mind. She hadn't warned him that he could not simply walk to the front door and ask for her, though surely he would realize that. How, then?

Evelyn provided a possible answer. "Come on, let's take a walk," she suggested. "It's the one thing I can do. Papa doesn't know I do it, for I'm careful never to be away when he's to be at home. There are advantages to living near Central Park."

They bundled up against the cold and set out, making their own path through several inches of snow. They were by no means the only ones doing so; children built snowmen and threw snowballs under the watchful eyes of their nursemaids or their mothers. Rebel was reminded of home. In Lyons Falls, where there were hills and woods all around, there was no need for a park. Here in this great city, Central Park's more than eight hundred acres was a reminder of what she had left behind, as long as Rebel ignored the buildings that rose to such heights around it.

There was even a small lake. "People will be skating here before long, if it stays so cold," Evelyn said with satisfaction. "I have a stunning skating costume. We'll have to see about one for you, too."

They spoke to no one, however. That, too, was different from home. Rebel had hoped that her cousin might have acquaintances that she met during these unchaperoned excursions, but though Evelyn took some outdoor exercise nearly every day, there were no illicit meetings, nor even any ordinary ones.

"Sometimes I meet the Edson sisters," Evelyn said, indicating one of the brownstones where they lived. "And Olivia Sherrington, when the weather is nice. None of them cares for the cold or the rain, though. I hope you don't mind bad weather, Rebel. It's my only chance to escape the house, except for shopping expeditions, and to have anyone my own age to talk to."

That Evelyn was starved for conversation was apparent, and Rebel was glad to oblige, though she kept her eye out constantly for a tall, wide-shouldered man with dark hair. He didn't appear.

Luke Kittering strode across the lobby of the Hoffman House late in the evening, feeling morose. He'd spent most of the day out-of-doors and he was numbed through. His dislike of the city grew by the hour, and he hoped he'd be able to head for home before much longer. He'd have no regrets at all when he finally was able to board the train heading south.

Except for the girl.

He'd memorized her features, and he'd liked her voice: low and husky. He wished he'd thought faster and figured out a way to become further acquainted with her, but she'd been so unexpected. She had taken him off guard, and he hadn't gotten his wits together quickly enough.

The lobby was empty except for an elderly gentleman reading a newspaper. Luke was past the desk, making for the stairs, when the clerk spoke his name.

"Mr. Kittering?"

Luke paused. "Yes?"

"A message, sir." The man slid a note across the desk, and Luke accepted it automatically. More orders from Fort Smith? Or a letter—he grinned, thinking of it—from his mother, telling him to dress warmly in the dreadful New York climate?

It wasn't from his mother, however, nor even from Arkansas, for there was no postage stamp. He stopped beneath the gaslight at the foot of the stairs and ripped open the letter.

*Dear Mr. Kittering . . .*

He read it twice, unaware of the observation of the clerk, who correctly interpreted the message as being from a young lady. What else would make a man look that way?

For a moment Luke forgot why he was in New York, his purpose erased by the words written on the note-paper. Rebel Moran, he thought. An unconventional name. An unconventional young woman, too. And then he sobered, because she'd given her uncle's name.

Arlen Bickford. The coincidence was incredible. Bickford, the diamond merchant, and it had to be the same one because his house fronted Central Park. Not so great a coincidence at that, he concluded, for after all, he'd been standing across the street from Bickford's shop.

Luke climbed the stairs, cursing under his breath. But nothing could hold down his spirits over Rebel Moran's response to the address he'd left her. Maybe, when this was over, he could do what he wanted to do about her.

By the time he was unlocking the door to his room, the grin was back on his face.

Two days passed, and there was no sign of Luke Kittering, nor any word from him.

On the third day, Evelyn was indisposed, but she urged Rebel to exercise on her own.

Even without Arlen Bickford there, the house was oppressive, and Rebel was happy to escape for an hour or so. Out in the open, among strangers, she didn't have to pretend to be something she was not.

It was early, shortly after breakfast, when Rebel crossed the street into the fairyland of the park. It had snowed heavily during the night, leaving trees and ground laden with a fluffy icing that sparkled in the sun. She walked briskly, enjoying the fact that the snow was as yet untouched by romping children. Rebel laughed aloud; she felt like a child herself, and bent to scoop up enough snow to make a snowball, which she flung against one of the trees.

If only Luke Kittering would come, her happiness would be complete, she thought. Yes, even living as uncertainly as she did in Arlen Bickford's house could not dampen her spirits if she had such a meeting to look forward to.

No one came, however, except the children and their nursemaids. Rebel walked at least a mile before she turned back, wishing she didn't have to re-enter the house, yet getting too cold to stay out much longer.

The postman met her at the foot of the steps. "Morning, miss." He consulted the letter in his hand. "Would you be knowing if there's a—" he squinted, not recognizing the name, "a Miss Rebel Moran at this address?"

"Yes, that's me," Rebel said. "Mrs. Bickford is my aunt."

He looked at her intently, as if by doing so he could be convinced she was telling the truth. Then he nodded and handed over several pieces of mail. "There you go, then."

Rebel stared down at the top one with her name written on it. The hand was familiar. She had seen two previous samples of it.

Rebel's heartbeat was tumultuous, her strength draining away as her fingers tore open the flap.

She was unaware of the cold, of the crunch of the snow beneath the postman's boots as he went up the walk to the adjoining house.

Miss Rebel Moran: I would like to see you again. My time is not, at present, my own. But as soon as my business in New York City is concluded, I would like permission to call upon you.

We are, I believe, old acquaintances. Such a meeting can surely take place with complete propriety, since your father and mine were friends of long standing. I look forward to seeing you again.

Sincerely,
Luke Kittering

Rebel drew a shuddering breath. The sensations were back, the tingling due to more than the cold. How cleverly he had put it, so that she might prepare the Bickfords for his appearance. They had no way of knowing who might or might not have been a close friend of her father's, and surely she would be allowed to receive him if she laid a convincing foundation for his coming.

She'd never been happier in her life. No wonder her

cousin longed to meet that special man she dreamed of, for this was surely the stuff of which ecstasy was made.

Rebel felt a measure of sorrow that Evelyn had not yet experienced this miracle. But surpassing concern for her cousin was her own flood of joy.

She would see Luke Kittering again. She wondered how she would keep everyone in the household from realizing that something momentous had happened; she was certain it shone from her face as the sunlight sparkled on the snow.

Yet when she entered the house a few minutes later, everyone assumed the color in her cheeks was from the cold, her smile from simple pleasure in her outing. Rebel hugged her memories and expectations to herself, and spoke to no one about them, not even to Evelyn.

In spite of a general uneasiness about her place in the Bickford household, it was impossible for Rebel not to feel a rising sense of anticipation as she dressed for the party the following evening. The only thing that would have made it more exciting would be to have Luke Kittering on the guest list.

She knew that Evelyn was going to be a vision in her dress of green broche satin with its deeper green velvet bodice. The fabric that had been used so sparingly in the bodice, leaving a breathtaking expanse of skin upon which to display the necklace of diamonds and emeralds that Arlen had brought home to go with it, went into the huge, exaggerated puffs of gigot sleeves, the latest in fashion. Evelyn would draw and hold every eye.

Yet Rebel was not displeased at her own appearance in the standing mirror. There was nothing she could do to shape her coppery curls into a fashionable coiffure;

Evelyn and Nell had agreed upon that after several attempts to form more conventional curls. But Rebel's figure, while regrettably not quite meeting the hourglass standards of the day, did well enough in the brown crepon, which clung to her bosom, waist, and hips, swirling out attractively about her feet.

She was even to wear diamonds.

Evelyn brought them, laughing. "I told Papa we couldn't have anyone thinking we had poor relations, and I thought this would do nicely. Unfortunately, it's already been sold to a lady who's traveling in Europe. She'd expected to take it with her but the clasp was defective, and she brought it back to Papa to be repaired. She'll never know the difference if you wear it this evening. Turn around, and I'll put it on you."

The reflection in the mirror, under the gaslights, was suddenly transformed.

The diamonds sparkled and flashed, and the topaz that nestled between her breasts went perfectly with the color of her gown.

Evelyn was grinning at her. "Like it?"

Rebel lifted a hesitant finger to touch the topaz. "It's . . . gorgeous!"

"Now the earrings to match," Evelyn said, and fastened them in place.

Rebel stared at herself, moistening her lips. "It's a shame to waste all this on anyone but a lover. Or a prospective one." Luke Kittering flashed into her mind; how she would like to have him see her now!

"Agreed," Evelyn admitted. "Well, Mr. Hake will be here. He appreciates a pretty female, I think."

"I feel a bit guilty wearing all this finery so soon after my father's death. I ought not to be going to a party at all, and certainly not dancing. Though Father didn't hold with long mourning, not the trappings of it, anyway. I suppose I'd best wear the arm band, don't you think?"

The black band didn't detract from her appearance, and it was with a breathless feeling, which made her aware of how tightly Millie had helped to lace her corset, that Rebel finally descended the stairs.

The guests were already arriving. A lady in violet bengaline was being relieved of her furs by a maid, while her formally clad husband handed over his topcoat, hat, and cane. Through the doorway into the front parlor, Rebel saw two stout matrons in lemon-colored damasse and burgundy grenadine chatting with considerable animation.

Each of the ladies was so bedecked with gems that Rebel felt her own borrowed diamonds fade into insignificance. Arlen Bickford greeted each new arrival, saw that their wraps were taken for safekeeping, and steered the gentlemen toward the study where they could partake of cigars and a pre-dinner libation.

His glance caught Rebel as she descended, and he spoke to his wife, who hovered near his elbow, without bothering to lower his voice. "Pity she couldn't do something with that hair. She looks like a child."

Winnie fluttered. "But such a pretty child, Mr. Bickford." She gave her niece what was intended to be an encouraging smile. Her own plump contours were draped in pale pink silk chiffon, with more flounces and tiny pleats than Rebel had ever seen on any one gown, the whole enhanced by a profusion of deeper pink feathers. She would not be outdone by any of the guests in the adornment department, Rebel thought, smiling back with an effort, for Winnie must be wearing a fortune in jewels: at her throat, on her bosom, in her ears, and on her fingers.

Rebel could only pretend she hadn't overheard her uncle's remark. There was, after all, nothing to be done about her hair other than to cover it, and she was too proud to allow him to see hurt or resentment.

She reached the bottom step and inhaled deeply, preparing to move into the midst of her first formal party, and hoping she would do nothing to disgrace herself.

# Chapter Seven

Evelyn murmured into her ear, "I'll introduce you to Mrs. Snelling as soon as I find her in this mob. She'll be the best one to assure Papa that his 'generosity' toward an indigent cousin will be rewarded on earth as well as in heaven."

From anyone else, being referred to in that way would have been humiliating in the extreme, Rebel thought, but curiously enough, Evelyn had a way of making outrageous remarks without being in the least insulting.

"You'll know her when you see her," Evelyn added, looking around at the gathering which now numbered at least twenty couples, with more arriving in a steady stream through the snow. "She'll be the only one wearing a bustle. I do believe she still has the gowns from her trousseau fifty years ago, but when they're all smothered in jewels, nobody remarks on the fashion. Ah, there she is, talking to Peter Henry."

Evelyn's small, perfect nose quivered in distaste, and for a moment Rebel didn't understand this reaction to the only other young person in the double parlors, where the doors had been thrown open to form one huge room.

Though Peter Henry was not overly tall, he was well built, if rather slight, and almost classically handsome. At close range, however, as Evelyn made introductions all around, his vapid manner and expression explained all. He examined Rebel through a glass that was attached to a chain, then smiled and raised her hand to his lips.

Rather, as Evelyn said later, like being kissed by a slug. One must be grateful that his lips touched only one's hand, and not one's cheek or mouth.

Mrs. Snelling was past seventy, a spry lady with a perceptive gaze that went far deeper than young Henry's scrutiny. It wasn't until much later that it occurred to Rebel that the woman's face was extremely plain, with such a large nose and wide mouth that she could never have been beautiful even in her youth. Yet it wasn't only the diamonds and rubies that gave her presence; there was intelligence and character in that wrinkled face. Rebel had a flash of conviction: Mrs. Snelling would never have turned herself into a semi-invalid to escape a domineering husband. She would have fought him on his own terms, if fighting were necessary, and probably have won.

"Lovely hair, my dear," the old lady said. "Unusual color." The wide mouth twisted in amusement. "My mother used to tell me that if I couldn't be beautiful, I could be different, and to make the most of it." She patted her bosom, her rings making tiny sounds against the magnificent necklace that was actually a collar of gems. "I did. You, of course, are pretty as well as unusual. I predict you'll go far, Miss Moran."

Uncertain what else to do, Rebel thanked her.

"If you don't mind my leaving you with Peter," Evelyn said to Rebel, tucking her arm through Mrs. Snelling's, "I want to have a word or two with Mrs. Snelling."

She didn't wait for a reply; Rebel watched them go, heads together, and suspected that once Mrs. Snelling was roped in on a plan, she would be a formidable player.

Peter Henry produced a fatuous smile. "I take it you're unacquainted with most of the guests, Miss Moran? Allow me to introduce you; I've known most of them since I was in short trousers."

After the first two or three, Rebel forgot the names. The one guest she would have known had not yet arrived; she wondered if Evelyn would be sorely disappointed if Jubal Hake didn't show up, after all.

She need not have worried. There he was now, towering over the elderly couples. Rebel spoke to the man beside her. "Excuse me, Mr. Henry. I must greet Mr. Hake. Thank you so much for your kindness."

She gave him the most dazzling smile she could manage; Mrs. Snelling's words continued to ring in her ears. If she couldn't be the most beautiful, she could play upon the qualities that made her different from the others. It gave her a small measure of confidence to realize that the advice might be perfectly viable.

Rebel was not ordinarily timid, not in her own environment, or among people of her own class. Actually, no one that she'd met this evening had intimidated her half as much as her uncle did, for all their obvious wealth. Mrs. Snelling, one of the richest, to judge by her jewelry, gave promise of being a delightful individual.

Rebel thought that Jubal Hake, too, was feeling out of his element. Upon close inspection, his formal attire seemed just a bit tight through the shoulders and short in the sleeve and trouser leg. He had, she guessed, rented it for the occasion, unlike the other guests to whom this sort of dress-up affair was commonplace.

"Miss Moran." If the light in his eyes was any indication, Mrs. Snelling was correct about there being something intriguing in her looks. Or was the man simply responding to a kindred soul, another fish out of water?

"I believe some of the gentlemen are having a drink or a smoke in the study," Rebel told him. "I'm not accustomed to this sort of thing, either; it's a real crush, isn't it?"

He smiled wryly. "Is it so obvious I'm not used to high society parties?"

"Only to another of the same persuasion, no doubt," Rebel assured him. "I've looked over the buffet that's being set out in the dining room, and the delicacies look delicious. I think that supper will be worth the rest of it."

Jubal Hake patted his pockets as though looking for something. "I must have left my cigars in my coat pocket; I just picked them up on the way here. I wonder, if it wouldn't be asking too much of you, if you'd determine where the maid put my topcoat?"

"I'll be happy to show you," Rebel agreed instantly. "They're in a bedroom upstairs."

She led the way, encountering several elderly gentlemen who looked at her in such a way as to assure her that she was, indeed, worth admiring. Whether it was because of beauty, her "differentness," or simply her youth was uncertain, but she was glad Nell had been able to make the brown crepon fit. Imagine being in this assemblage in her black skirt and a shirtwaist!

She waited in the doorway while Jubal Hake extricated the cigars from his coat pocket and dropped the garment back onto the bed with dozens of others. From the lower floor came the strains of music. He looked at Rebel as they reached the top of the stairs. "There's going to be dancing?"

"After supper, yes. They'll roll back the rugs in both parlors, I understand."

"Then may I speak now for the first dance—if it's not something so fancy this country boy doesn't know the steps?"

"Why, thank you." Her pleasure at the invitation was balanced with a mild consternation that it hadn't been Evelyn he'd asked first: Evelyn, who had invited him, who longed for the company of young people. "I'd be delighted," she said.

They descended into the festive crowd, and she glanced up at him with a smile. "I'm sorry I can't introduce you to everyone. I don't know anyone outside the family. But here comes my cousin; I'm sure she'll do the honors."

As Evelyn swept Jubal Hake away, he smiled apologetically at Rebel for abandoning her for a time. Rebel didn't really care; she didn't remember the names of most of those to whom she'd been introduced, anyway, and the old ladies had a tendency to interrogate her rather more thoroughly than she liked.

It was enough for her to stand beside Aunt Winnie and observe. The female guests might average sixty or seventy years old, but they were for the most part dressed in the height of fashion; Rebel enjoyed observing their clothes and their jewels and imagining herself, at some distant date, similarly adorned.

Once Aunt Winnie leaned over and spoke to her. "Rebel, dear, would you run into the dining room and see if the maids have set up the champagne fountain? It's nearly time to begin serving it. Mr. Bickford doesn't like the ladies to begin too soon before supper; he can't abide tipsy females. But they're so busy in the kitchen they may not be watching the time."

Rebel rose obediently, torn between amusement and irritation at her uncle. The men had been offered drinks the moment they'd entered the house, and more than one of them exhibited signs of inebriation. What made male drunks any more acceptable than female ones?

The dining room was empty except for Jubal Hake.

Rebel paused in the doorway; the man turned away from the massive breakfront, where extra plates and glasses had been stacked, smiling when he saw who it was.

"You're right about the food. It's quite a display."

"Isn't it?" she agreed. "I'm to check on the champagne fountain—it seems to be ready to go."

He withdrew his hand from his coat pocket and gestured toward the decorative device that could be made to spew its sparkling contents into the crystal goblets. "Shall I get you some?"

"No, no. My uncle has an aversion to tipsy females, I've been told, and I'm not used to spirits in the first place. I'll wait for the others, and try some when I've something to eat with it."

He nodded understanding, and they walked out of the room together to report to Aunt Winnie. "Very good," that lady said. "Mr. Hake, perhaps you'd walk in to supper with me in about ten minutes?"

"I'd be happy to, Mrs. Bickford," he assured her.

The supper was like nothing Rebel had ever eaten. Not only was the food delicious, it was colorful and decorative. She liked the champagne better than the sherry her uncle usually served in the evenings, and sipped at it with a sense of awe that she, Rebel Moran, was in this place, doing these things.

The musicians were ensconced on a raised platform set up in front of the big bay window in the front parlor. The rugs had been removed for dancing, and although most of the guests were elderly, the music was vigorous and enthusiastic. Mrs. Snelling romped through the quadrilles and the waltzes, and neither Evelyn nor Rebel lacked for partners throughout the evening.

Jubal Hake danced with the old ladies as well as the girls. He was not an especially adept dancer, but he was pleasant company. He was attentive without being cloying, and he didn't exude a musty air as some of the elderly gentlemen did, nor were his palms soft and moist.

Winnie didn't dance. She sat on one of the ivory brocade chairs that had been brought in to line the walls, watching, smiling, visiting with whomever chose to sit out with her.

Arlen Bickford didn't dance, either. He moved from one guest to another, genial, expansive, persuasive. Selling his wares, no doubt, some of which were displayed on his wife, daughter, and niece. That's what the three of them were, Rebel thought. Mannequins, hawking his merchandise.

During an intermission, when musicians and guests alike partook of punch and more champagne, Evelyn materialized at Rebel's elbow. "Have you seen Mr. Hake?"

"He said something about stepping outside for a smoke." Rebel wrinkled her nose. "It would be nice if some of the others did the same. How long will this go on?"

"Some of the guests will leave by midnight," Evelyn

predicted. "A few will linger until one or two, but we can go up to bed once the musicians leave. Have you enjoyed it? As much as one might, without a devoted suitor at one's side?"

"Yes. This is all so different from anything I've known before."

Evelyn gave her a rather sad, intuitive smile. "I suppose so. But your whole life has been different from mine. You had parents who loved you—and each other—didn't you? I've tried to imagine what that would be like, and I can't, quite. And you've had the freedom to attend gatherings of other young people."

Evelyn shrugged and laughed. "You're a great hit, Rebel. Even Papa is basking in the admiration you're getting. Mrs. Snelling, darling that she is, swooped upon him and made a big fuss over you. Told him how stunning your looks were, how beautifully you wore the diamonds. Ordered a necklace like it, except that she wants rubies instead of topazes." Her laughter bubbled over. "That should cinch it; there should be no trouble about your staying on permanently."

"Until I find a young man who wants to marry me and take me away from all this." Rebel waved a hand to take in her ostentatious surroundings.

"Ah, please, Lord, let it be soon, for both of us," Evelyn pleaded, lifting her face heavenward. "Come on, the music's beginning again. Let's see which of us gets Mr. Hake, and which of us has to settle for good old Peter."

The temperature had dropped sharply, and Luke Kittering jammed his hands into his pockets and wondered if his ears would be frostbitten by the time he got back to his hotel. Most of the time his mother's admonitions, delivered to a man past his thirtieth birthday, either amused or annoyed him. Tonight he'd have given a lot to have her press upon him one of those knitted caps she'd insisted he wear when he was a boy, and some of her warm mittens, also.

And, he thought, a hearty bowl of steaming soup would set well, too.

That reminded him of the girl who had, without recognizing him, sent food and hot soup out to him the other night. To a stranger, simply because she was kind-hearted.

He could see her face in his memory, with those half-dozen freckles on an otherwise flawless skin, the greenish eyes with the thick lashes, the cap of unfashionable but delightful coppery curls, a mouth that was the most beautifully shaped and expressive he had ever seen.

Rebel Moran had bewitched him from the moment he saw her.

Luke groaned inwardly. Of all the inconvenient and impossible times to meet the girl he'd been dreaming of all his life—though he hadn't known what she'd look like, he'd recognized her at once when she showed up—this had to be the worst.

It had been a miracle that she'd entered that cafe with him, and confounding that she'd permitted him to remove her shoe and gently examine her foot. And it made him warm, even now, to remember how strong the compulsion had been not to stop at the ankle, but to run his hand up that stockinged leg, under those black skirts.

Luke swore and stamped his feet, hoping to bring back the circulation. In his room that night, waiting to fall asleep, he'd imagined a lot more than that. Removing the stockings, removing everything. He knew beyond all doubt that Rebel Moran's body would be as perfect and as glorious as her face.

And she was in there, somewhere. Among all those

rich old people and her Bickford relatives, and the man who called himself Jubal Hake.

Once he'd settled this matter with *him* he'd be free to pursue the desire that had consumed him from the moment he looked into Rebel Moran's green eyes.

The door of the house opened, and Luke pulled back into the shadows, standing motionless. The guests were leaving. About time, before he froze his damned ears off, he thought.

Maybe tonight it would be over. Or as near over as it could be before he returned to Arkansas.

He watched the departing guests impatiently, not daring to stamp his feet now, lest he draw attention to himself.

And there he was. The one he waited for.

Jubal Hake set off at a brisk walk, and Luke fell in behind him at a discreet distance. The gas streetlights had been a help; now they were a hindrance, and he wished they could be extinguished.

Ahead of him, the man turned into a dark side street where there were no gaslights. Luke followed without hesitation. At an intersection he paused, however, for there was no figure ahead of him.

Luke's expletive was barely audible. Where the hell had he gone?

The blow came without warning. The snow was soft and it muffled the footsteps behind him; there was no time to defend himself.

Luke pitched forward in the darkness, pain obliterating all thought.

And then the pain was gone, and there was nothing.

# Chapter Eight

It was at breakfast the following morning that the world began to crumble around their ears.

Since it was a Sunday morning, breakfast was at nine rather than at seven. Having danced until past midnight, both girls had appreciated being able to sleep late, and they descended to the dining room with voracious appetites.

Mrs. Worsted rose to the occasion with hot cinnamon rolls in addition to the coddled eggs and a platter of crisp bacon to follow the chilled orange juice. Even Arlen Bickford had no criticism of the meal; indeed, he seemed in an expansive mood. No doubt last night's party had achieved its objective; Mrs. Snelling's commission alone would have made it worthwhile.

The enjoyment was diminished when the doorbell resounded throughout the ground floor. Bickford consulted his watch with a small frown. "Before ten, on a Sunday morning?"

A moment later, to the surprise of the trio at the table, an alarmed Millie ushered in a young uniformed patrolman and an older man who, though in plainclothes, was obviously the police officer's superior.

"These gentlemen have asked to speak to you on an urgent matter, Mr. Bickford," Millie said, and scuttled out of the room before she could be blamed for the intrusion.

Bickford rose. "Mr. Plummer, isn't it? Captain Plummer?"

"Of the New York City Police Department," the older man confirmed. He was Arlen Bickford's age, but there was no pot belly, no thinning hair, no glasses. Only sharp gray eyes that scanned the room and their faces, soaking up, Rebel thought, perhaps more than any guilty party would have liked to reveal. She didn't know why her heartbeat quickened. The matter, whatever it was, could have nothing to do with *her*. "I'd like to ask you some questions, Mr. Bickford."

"On the Sabbath? What's this all about?" Bickford glanced at the girls. "Excuse us, please. Come with me, sir, we can talk in the study."

The officers didn't move. "Were these young ladies present at the party in this house last evening?"

"Why, yes. They were. Captain Plummer, what—"

"And Mrs. Bickford. Was she in attendance as well? If so, we'd like to speak to her, too."

"My wife? My wife never rises before eleven on Sunday, sir."

Captain Plummer stepped to the doorway and spoke to Millie, who was hovering just out of sight. "Will you fetch Mrs. Bickford, if you please. Tell her Captain Plummer of the city police requires her presence."

81

Arlen Bickford's face took on a dangerous hue. "I say! I've just told you, sir, that my wife has not yet arisen—"

Captain Plummer was enigmatic. "We are prepared to wait until she has dressed, so that she may join us, sir."

For a moment Bickford's mouth worked like that of a fish thrown out of an overturned fishbowl, and the captain took pity on him.

"I assure you, sir, this is a matter of gravest concern. We would not trouble you otherwise. I am sure you will want to cooperate to the fullest in our investigation."

"Investigation into what?"

"We would like to avoid repeating our information or our questions, so we will wait until Mrs. Bickford puts in an appearance. If you would prefer to wait for her in some other room, we may, although this one is perfectly satisfactory for our purposes."

Clearly Arlen Bickford was not accustomed to being addressed in this fashion, but he was beginning to be apprehensive now. "Is it my shop? Has anything happened at my shop?"

The captain made no direct reply, instead addressing Evelyn across the breakfast table. "I wonder, Miss Bickford, if it would be asking too much for a cup of that coffee? It's a blustery morning, snowing again, very cold."

"Yes, of course," Evelyn said. She rose to bring two more cups and saucers from the sideboard. "Please sit down, Captain. Officer—?"

"Officer Cummings, miss," the younger man said. He was looking at Evelyn as if she were a heavenly vision in her pale blue silk mull. There were no jewels this morning, but she didn't need them.

Rebel realized her hands were clenched in her lap

and consciously relaxed them. Though this could have nothing to do with her, she was concerned for Evelyn and Aunt Winnie. What connection any of them could have with matters pertaining to the police was unimaginable.

The officers sat at the table, both using sugar and thick cream in their coffee. Evelyn offered them some of the sticky cinnamon buns, which both refused, Officer Cummings with visible regret.

After twenty minutes of waiting, Arlen Bickford said irritably, "Evelyn, go and see what's delaying your mother."

"I'm here, Mr. Bickford," Winnie said, tottering into the room as if she'd only that moment opened her eyes. Her pinkish hair had been hastily combed, and her mauve pongee morning dress had one button left undone. "What is it? What's happened?"

Bewildered, she sank onto a chair and nodded at the police officers when they were introduced. Even when she sat perfectly still, Winnie Bickford gave the impression of fluttering. Rebel saw Evelyn reach out a hand to rest it upon her mother's arm in a protective way.

Officer Cummings produced a notebook and a pencil. Captain Plummer leaned forward, addressing them as a group. "You held a party in this house last night, did you not?"

"Yes. I often hold parties," Arlen Bickford conceded impatiently. "Surely there is nothing to concern the police in that."

Plummer regarded him with deadly seriousness. "Quite so, Mr. Bickford. Under the usual circumstances, that is. But these are not usual circumstances, quite the contrary."

"For God's sake! We're all present now, surely you don't have to draw this out any longer!" Arlen

Bickford exploded, emphasizing his words by hitting the table so that the saucers jumped. "Kindly tell me, man, what's happened!"

"Certainly. Since I came on duty at seven o'clock this morning," Captain Plummer said, his gray eyes intently fixed upon Bickford's face, "my precinct has received nineteen reports of robberies. Nineteen. Now this number would not necessarily be extraordinary except for one thing. Eighteen of them were apparently engineered by the same party, or parties. Eighteen of those who called us attended your supper-dance last night, Mr. Bickford. And not one of them reported a break-in."

Baffled, Bickford allowed his mouth to sag in the manner that always so provoked him when his wife did it. "No break-in? Then how did the robberies take place? On the streets? On the way home from here?" His voice had risen and he struggled to bring it under control. "What was stolen?"

"Diamonds were stolen," Captain Plummer said quietly. "As well as various other precious gems, but mostly diamonds. And the reason there were no break-ins was that apparently the thief, or thieves, opened the doors of the houses they robbed with keys."

"Keys?" Bickford was flabbergasted. "Sir, what are you suggesting? That *I*—? Good God, you can't be thinking that *I* had anything to do with this— What was taken? From whom?"

Captain Plummer reached into an inner pocket and produced several pages which he unfolded and pushed toward the choleric diamond merchant. "Here is a list of the names, in the order in which we received their calls. You recognize them, sir?"

"Of course I recognize them! Most of them are friends and customers of years' standing!" Bickford scrutinized the list and his color went from reddish-purple to chalky. "The Empress necklace—my God! They got the Empress necklace! It's priceless!"

Bickford sputtered, running a stubby finger down the list of names, the descriptions of the items that were missing. Rebel, beside him, could read a few of them. On the other side of her, Evelyn spoke.

"No one was hurt during all these robberies?"

Officer Cummings paused in his note-taking. His face reflected recognition of the fact that she was concerned for the individuals involved, while her father's concentration was only on the jewelry. "No, ma'am. None of them saw the perpetrator."

"Ruby pendant? Since when does Lila Schaffer have a ruby pendant?" Bickford demanded of no one in particular. "She didn't get it from me. And Ernestine Snelling's pearls. They were exquisite, the finest I've ever seen. Oh, dear God, how did this happen?"

"That, of course, is what we wish to learn. We are here to ask you and your family some questions," Plummer said. "There is no doubt but what the thief had keys that opened all eighteen of those front doors. And since every one of those people were guests at your party last night, and they are not careless with their keys, we can only suppose that someone, somehow, obtained them here, in this house, last night."

Arlen Bickford was clearly in anguish; whether over the loss of the jewels or in distress that he could have been involved in any way in this catastrophe was uncertain. "Impossible. Impossible, Captain. There must be some other explanation."

"I'm afraid not," Plummer stated with chilling conviction.

"But if their keys were all missing, they'd surely have noticed when they couldn't get into their own houses on returning home!"

"Oh, they all have their keys. We are considering

several possibilities in that regard. Either the keys were borrowed long enough to make an impression of each of them, so that more keys could be quickly made, or someone was prepared with a set of master keys which could easily be altered to fit the different locks—not at all a difficult task for someone acquainted with the intricacies of locks, or having access to various keys. All this was planned well in advance, no doubt. It was carried out quite professionally. The eighteen houses were entered after the occupants had gone to sleep and before they arose this morning. Nothing else was taken, only jewels. Are any missing from your own dressing tables or jewel boxes?"

Sheer horror etched itself onto Bickford's countenance. With a strangled oath, he flung himself out of the chair and dashed for the study, the others following in various degrees of agitation. Rebel saw that Evelyn was practically supporting her mother; together they eased the older woman into one of the chairs just inside the study doorway.

Bickford tore a picture off the wall and with unsteady fingers worked the combination lock of the safe it had concealed. His howl of outrage told them as much as his words.

"Damn them to hell! Everything gone! Everything!"

Winnie was close to swooning. Millie, who had followed along, was sent to bring the smelling salts, which were waved under poor Winnie's nose. Arlen Bickford clutched at his chest, and Rebel wondered if he would drop dead on the spot.

No, she decided, he was too angry to drop dead. Profanity burst from his mouth as he slammed the door of the safe, not even hearing Captain Plummer's words.

"Can you tell me exactly what was in the safe, Mr. Bickford?"

It took some minutes for Bickford to calm down enough so that the inventory of items missing from his safe could be added to the list. His shoulders sagged; there was defeat now along with the anger. "I don't understand. I don't see how it could have happened. No one but me had that combination. No one!"

Plummer intently examined the other man's face. Convinced, Rebel hoped, that her uncle was not himself responsible for this catastrophe. For whatever she might think of the man, she could not believe him a thief, even without the evidence of his own empty safe.

"There was no written record of the safe combination numbers anywhere?" Plummer pressed. "Anywhere? Neither on your person nor at your shop?"

Arlen Bickford's complexion had taken on an unhealthy grayish tone. "I memorized the numbers years ago, when the safe was installed. There was no need to carry them written out. However, there is a copy of the numbers in my files at the shop. No one outside the immediate family could have gotten at it, however. I hire no employees except for a cleaning person, and everything is securely locked when she is there."

Rebel was trembling, a tremor she could not control. She scarcely dared look at her cousin, who sat frozen-faced in shocked rigidity. What if they thought that *she*, as a newcomer in this household, had had a hand in the matter?

No sooner had she thought that than the police captain fixed those penetrating gray eyes upon her. "You are visiting here, Miss Moran? Or are you a permanent member of the household?"

Rebel's mouth went dry. Before she could formulate a reply, Evelyn did it for her.

"My cousin makes her home with us now, since the death of her parents. You cannot have any suspicion of

Rebel, Captain. And all our servants have been with us for years. Some outsider must have done this . . . this terrible thing."

The man's mouth twitched, and Rebel felt the tremor extend from her limbs to her stomach. She hoped she wouldn't be sick.

A penniless girl, unknown to her relatives until such a short time ago—why would suspicion *not* fall upon her?

Across the room, standing in the hallway but visible through the doorway, Rebel saw Millie, listening with the others. No doubt she, too, shook in her boots, because someone was responsible for a series of awful crimes, and regardless of what Evelyn had stated so flatly, it was the servants and Rebel herself around whom the captain's investigations would center.

Plummer shifted his attention to Winnie as he slid his papers toward her, though there was no relief for Rebel in that. "Please examine this, Mrs. Bickford, and tell me if there were others, guests who were *not* robbed last night. Is this a complete list of your party guests?"

Winnie was like a frightened bird that had dashed itself against a window, stunned by the impact, terrified by the would-be rescuer who had picked it up. Rebel could almost feel the pounding of Winnie's heart.

"I . . . I . . ." Winnie looked from the paper to her husband and back again. "I don't know . . ."

Evelyn's hand closed reassuringly on her mother's arm. "Let me look at it. I'm the one who wrote out the invitations. Hmmm. The Castletons aren't on here. Nor the Medlocks. Wait—I'll get the complete list and you can take that."

She rose and moved to the breakfront, which had been cleared of all the extra dishes from last night. She opened the glass doors on the upper section and then, puzzled, she ran a hand over the shelf. "I thought I'd left it right here in plain sight, but it must have been taken away when the servants were moving dishes last night. Well, my preliminary list is upstairs in my room. Excuse me while I get it."

When she had brought the list, Plummer looked it over carefully. "This is a complete listing, is it? There was no one in attendance who is not on it? And all of these people are well known to you, Mr. Bickford? None are recent acquaintances?"

The name came to four pairs of lips at the same time. They breathed it as a chorus.

"Jubal Hake!"

The keen gray eyes scanned the list. "I don't see anyone named Hake on here. Who is he?"

"I didn't send him a written invitation," Evelyn said. "I asked him in person—"

"He's a business associate, a wholesale dealer in diamonds—" Bickford said simultaneously.

And then Rebel moaned involuntarily, bringing all eyes in her direction.

"Oh my God!"

"What is it, Miss Moran? What have you remembered?"

Her lips were so stiff it was an effort to make herself understood. "He asked me—he said he'd left his cigars in his coat pocket, and he asked me to show him where the coats had been put. I . . . I took him upstairs, to where the bed was heaped with coats and . . . and there were purses there . . . could he have . . . ?"

"Taken the keys and made the impressions, or altered a set of dummy keys, then returned the keys to pockets or purses?" Plummer asked softly. "Yes, indeed, I think he might well have done so. And the safe, Mr. Bickford. Would he have had access to your records at the shop to learn the combination to your home safe?"

Arlen Bickford looked sick. "The combination was in the other safe, the one at the office. I don't think I ever left him alone in the back of the shop . . ." His voice trailed off and it was clear that he was not as sure of that as he'd liked to have been. "And all my keys—" He choked. "They were lying in plain sight on my dresser during the entire party last evening. Oh, my God, if he got into the shop—!"

He rose so abruptly that his chair overturned. "Come with me, Plummer. Oh, God! Oh, God!"

For the first time Rebel felt compassion for her uncle. And her own guilt flooded through her, for she'd played a part in assisting the thief. Those times when he'd been "outside having a smoke," he'd actually been hurriedly making impressions of keys to be used later.

The recollection came suddenly, and she blurted out the words without further thought. "He was here . . . in the dining room . . . when I came to check on the champagne fountain. By himself. He was standing over there by the breakfront, and when he turned to face me"—she swallowed as the significance of this worked its way through her—"he—he had his hand in his pocket. He might have seen the guest list there and taken it, I suppose. So he'd have known who all those people were . . ."

Plummer's words were sharp as he addressed Evelyn. "Were the addresses on that list, as well as the names of the guests?"

Evelyn, too, had lost her normal vivid coloring. She moistened her lips. "Yes, they were."

Her father moaned and moved toward the door, with the police officers at his heels. No one said anything more.

They waited in silence for the men to return. A frightened Millie brought another pot of coffee and they drank it simply to have something to do.

They rose as one when footsteps sounded in the foyer, meeting the men there with palpitating hearts.

There was no need to ask; Arlen Bickford was ashen, shaking, a broken man, supported by Officer Cummings.

"All gone," he reported hoarsely. "Everything. And he already cashed the draft I gave him Friday afternoon for the diamonds he delivered that day, so even my bank account—"

Winnie swayed and toppled. Rebel and Evelyn caught her, but they could not keep her on her feet, lowering her instead into a chair.

"We'll have to loosen her corset," Evelyn muttered. "Please, if you'd help us get her onto the sofa in the parlor—"

It was the police officers who carried her there. Winnie's husband did not even seem to notice that his wife had fainted. He was locked in his own private hell.

Rebel knelt beside her aunt, chafing her hands while Millie waved the smelling salts and Evelyn struggled with the corset lacings.

It was going to get worse, Rebel thought numbly, before it got better.

If, indeed, it ever *did* get better.

# Chapter Nine

Winnie opened her eyes, eyes that begged to be told it had all been a horrible nightmare, but there was no such reassurance that the girls could offer her.

She struggled to sit up, then gasped, putting a hand on her bosom as if that might enable her to breathe more deeply.

"Mama, can you walk well enough to get back upstairs?" Evelyn asked, kneeling beside the sofa at her mother's feet. "If you would just take that corset off, you'd feel better."

From the foyer, they heard the men's voices. Rebel realized she'd been hearing them all along, absorbing bits and pieces of what they said while keeping her attention upon her aunt.

Arlen Bickford's voice held a stronger note now, a note of rage. "I tell you, the diamonds the man offered me were of high quality! I've been in this business all my life, and I know diamonds! If he'd actually sold me the gems, instead of taking my money and then stealing them back during the night, it would have been much to my advantage! They were high quality gems!"

Captain Plummer's words remained calm, but then of course this was not a personal thing to him.

"Do you have any explanation for it, then? This stranger approaches you with a large number of gems, which he offers at a reasonable price— The price was reasonable, I take it?"

Bickford hesitated. "Yes. A good price, though he certainly wasn't giving them away. Damn it, sir, I'm not a complete dolt! You make it sound as if the man walked in off the street offering to cheat me with inferior merchandise or to sell me stolen gems at a reduced price. That wasn't the case. He had identification, and there was a letter from his home office before he arrived. I examined the diamonds carefully, and we negotiated the price, which was good but not a give-away. It wasn't low enough to make me suspicious."

"But we must now be suspicious of everything this Hake did, must we not? Could the diamonds you say he sold you have been stolen?"

"He had credentials from a company I know by reputation," Bickford protested. "There was no reason for me to suspect he and his company had not come by them legitimately. You can't believe I'd have knowingly participated in anything illegal—I've been in business in this city since 1866—"

"I'm not suggesting anything, Mr. Bickford. Only trying to get at the truth. I'd like to see the letter you received before Mr. Hake arrived in the city, and we will, of course, check with his company."

Meanwhile, the girls got Winnie to her feet and guided her toward the stairs; it took both of them to hold her upright. The two police officers and Arlen

Bickford were still standing in the entryway, facing each other as antagonists.

"Credentials can be forged," Plummer pointed out. "Or stolen. It's difficult to run down such information on a Sunday, but tomorrow we should be able to learn the truth about that. It would not surprise me to learn that no one at the wholesale diamond merchant whose reputation reassured you has ever heard of Jubal Hake, or that there has been a large jewelry robbery somewhere else in the country recently. A clever ruse, you must admit. To offer quality merchandise, take the money for it, and then to steal it back again. And, in this case, to gain access to a house where some sixty people of considerable wealth were assembled, so that they might be fleeced, also."

The women started up the stairs. Behind them, Bickford moaned softly, burying his face in his hands.

"I'm ruined," he groaned. "They'll blame me, they'll all blame me for their losses, and there is no way I can repay them or recover their jewelry."

As the girls steered Winnie into her room, Rebel heard her uncle say, "I'll never be able to hold up my head in this city again."

She had little time to think about him, however, for her aunt's color was very poor. Even divesting her of the constricting corset—an absurd garment for one of Winnie's plump contours, since a fashionable figure was clearly impossible no matter how tightly the corset was laced—did not entirely ease the problem.

Winnie lay back on her pillows, still gasping for air, as if she could not get enough. Rebel's eyes met her cousin's. "Perhaps a doctor?" Rebel asked.

"Yes. I think so. Please ask Millie to go for Dr. Davidson. I'll stay here with Mama. A wet cloth on her forehead may help, and more of the smelling salts."

Rebel ran back down the stairs just as the police

officers were leaving. "We'll be in touch, sir," Captain Plummer said, and though his voice carried no censure, she felt that the words were as much a threat as a promise.

She hesitated at the bottom step, then walked past her uncle, who did not appear aware of her presence.

Millie was in the kitchen with the rest of the staff, and for once they were not busy. They sat around the table conversing in low voices, springing up when they realized that Rebel had entered the room.

"Is it true, miss?" Millie asked, her eyes wide. "Is the mister really ruined?"

"I couldn't say about that yet," Rebel evaded. "My aunt is having trouble breathing, and Miss Evelyn asks that you go for Dr. Davidson."

"Yes, of course, miss." Millie was already reaching for a cloak from a hook beside the back door. "He should be back from church by now." She paused and lowered her voice. "Do you think we'll be let go, miss? I'm the latest hired . . ."

Rebel opened her mouth to utter some platitude, then changed her mind. She understood only too well the position that Millie was in. "If it's as bad as it seems, it might be wise to keep your eyes open for another position."

"Mrs. Snelling told me a few weeks ago that if I ever got tired of working here, she'd make a place for me." Millie hesitated before adding, "She has a big house, and her Sophie is getting on in years. She has trouble running up and down stairs. No doubt I'd earn my keep and then some, but it'd be better than being on the streets, and they do say as Mrs. Snelling sets a good table—"

"Hurry back with the doctor," Rebel interrupted the flow of words.

"Yes, miss," Millie agreed, and was gone.

The others were silent as Rebel walked past them. She'd never known anything about servants, and until she'd come to this house had given servants very little thought. Now she saw their worried faces and would have liked to offer them reassurance, but what could she say? If her uncle truly was ruined financially, Rebel herself might be on the street before long.

She was halfway to the front stairs when she heard the shot.

The doctor was a dour, bewhiskered individual, none too happy at being drawn away from his family on the Sabbath for this stranger, who lay, unresponsive, in the hospital bed.

"Can you tell us your name, sir?" he demanded, putting the final adjustment on the cap of bandages that covered a nasty head wound.

The hazel eyes refused to focus when the doctor snapped his fingers before them, and the physician turned away in disgust. "There was no identification on him?"

The nurse, a middle-aged woman, shook her head. "They said not, Doctor; no doubt he was robbed. There was a key in his pocket, however, a hotel key. The police officer who was called when Mrs. Meldrum discovered the poor fellow in the alley said he'd run it down and that it would probably tell us who the patient is."

The physician snorted. "Fat lot of good the police are, for the most part. Didn't keep him from being hit over the head and robbed in the first place. Well, he may come around more fully within a few hours and be able to tell us who he is. Listen for him, write down what he says." He turned from the bed, having done all that he could for the unfortunate stranger. "If we're lucky, we may even get paid for our services, Mrs.

Dobbins. His clothes would seem to indicate he comes of a good family.''

"Yes, sir," Dobbins said dutifully. She lingered at the bedside after the doctor had gone, however, looking down at the man who had slipped into either sleep or coma.

What a pity, she thought. He was such a good-looking young man. Too bad he'd been struck down in such a way. She hoped he wouldn't be like that fellow they'd had six months ago; *he* had been discovered in an alley, too, and when he'd regained consciousness the pathetic creature had lost his memory. Hadn't even known who he was, and no one had ever come for him. He'd eventually died of an infection and been buried in a pauper's grave.

She sighed and turned away, still regretting the waste of handsome young manhood.


Evelyn's face appeared over the upper railing as Rebel stood rooted in place below her. "What was that?"

They both knew what it had been. Rebel gathered her wits and took a few steps to the door of the study, opening it with dread.

Her dread was justified.

Arlen Bickford was slumped over his desk, and the gun lay on the carpet just below his limp hand.

"Rebel? What—"

Rebel put out a hand to keep her cousin out of the room.

"No. Stay where you are. Millie's already gone for the doctor."

"Doctor?" Evelyn peered past her, but to Rebel's relief did not plunge past her into the room. "Papa? Oh, God. He's dead, isn't he? He's killed himself!"

"I'm afraid so. Evelyn, don't go in. The doctor will notify the police."

The house was very quiet. Mrs. Worsted and Nell and Timothy, who carried coal and ran errands and did most of the scut work, stood white-faced at the rear end of the hallway. From above, they heard Winnie's alarmed cry.

"Evelyn! What's happened?"

Evelyn moistened her lips, as pale now as her father had been earlier. "We'll have to tell her," she murmured. "But maybe we can wait for Dr. Davidson . . ."

"Evelyn, what is it?"

Winnie had actually risen from her bed and come to the railing to look down upon them.

"Is it your papa?" she demanded, knuckles white on the banister rail.

Evelyn hesitated, reluctant to impart the news without being at her mother's side for fear she would faint again and fall down the stairs.

Winnie, however, seemed to gain strength even as they watched her. "He's shot himself, hasn't he? He's killed himself."

She drew herself up and said with dignity, "Someone will have to fetch the police."

"Yes, Mama," Evelyn murmured. "We'll call the police."

Rebel had to admire her aunt's reaction.

"Very well. When Captain Plummer comes, you may tell him I'll receive him in my sitting room." She paused. "He . . . he didn't suffer, did he?"

Rebel saw her cousin's throat working, saw that she was temporarily incapable of speech, and replied to the woman above.

"No, Aunt Winnie. I don't think he did. I'm sure he died instantly."

For long moments Winnie stood there. Then, "Good," she said. She inhaled deeply, steadied herself, and walked into her boudoir, closing the door behind her.

Evelyn met Rebel's gaze, eyes swimming with tears. "Poor Papa. He must have been out of his head. Oh, Rebel, what are we going to do now?"

It was at that moment that Rebel began to take charge, though she didn't yet realize it. "The best we can," she said, and closed the door on the sight of Arlen Bickford slouched forward in a pool of blood not even the oversized blotter could soak up.

"I'm so glad you're here, Rebel," Evelyn told her, and for a minute or so they clung together, seeking and giving comfort in the only way they could.

# Chapter Ten

CAPTAIN PLUMMER HAD COME AND GONE. TIMOTHY HAD been sent with a note to Mr. Grader, the family lawyer, and he, too, had come and gone. Grader looked more like a mortician than a lawyer, Rebel thought irrelevantly: tall, cadaverous, with long bony fingers.

He had expressed his sympathies and promised to look into the financial picture as rapidly as he could. In the meantime, he said, they were not to worry unduly.

It was a tall order.

"I always thought," Evelyn said at one point, "that if anything happened to Papa, he'd leave Mama well provided for."

"Perhaps he did," Rebel told her gently. "He had a terrible loss, but it may not have been as bad as he saw it. It was loss of face, the tarnishing of his reputation, as much as anything, that drove him to it."

Though the circumstances were not the same, and

100

though she had felt no affection for Arlen Bickford, Rebel could not help being newly reminded of her own recent loss. She offered no platitudes; they had not comforted her, and she did not think they would help Evelyn and Aunt Winnie. Indeed, Rebel wondered with a touch of guilt if their loss might not be considered minimal except for the dreadful circumstances of it. Both her aunt and her cousin were so numbed that she could not accurately judge the depth of the emotional impact on them.

Luke Kittering had said he would contact her when he could. She prayed that it would be soon; she met the postman every day, but there was no letter. A few neighbors, none who had been present at the party, came to the door with offerings of casseroles or cakes. Each time the doorbell rang, Rebel flew to it before one of the maids could respond, hoping that it would be Luke Kittering. Each time, her disappointment was more keen than the time before.

She even contemplated sending him another note, explaining about her uncle's death and the predicament it had placed them in. Common sense and an intuitive conviction of what an impropriety that would constitute held her back. It was not as if Luke Kittering were really a friend of long standing. Rebel waited, and prayed.

The lawyer returned two days later. They had all just ridden through the snowy morning from the cemetery after a funeral that few outside the family attended. Rebel, dry-eyed at the gravesite, had watched Mr. Grader as he stood with the snow accumulating on his hat and shoulders, and guessed from his lack of expression that whatever news he brought, it would not benefit her relatives.

"No doubt the weather kept most people indoors,"

Winnie had observed on the carriage ride home. "Most of Mr. Bickford's friends were elderly, after all, and couldn't be expected to expose themselves to the chill."

Was that it, Rebel wondered? Or was the explanation simply that most of Bickford's friends had been robbed, and they blamed him for it.

Winnie had held up surprisingly well throughout the morning. She had not fainted, either at the church or the grave; her color was good and her voice stronger than Rebel had yet heard it, though there was a puffiness around her eyes when her veil was lifted to reveal her face.

Winnie spoke graciously to the lawyer as he mounted the front steps with them, accepting his arm because of the slippery footing. "There'll be a fire in the back parlor, and Mrs. Worsted will have tea ready for us. Come and warm up before you tell us the dreadful news. It is bad, isn't it?"

Mr. Grader sighed as they moved into the foyer, stomping snow from their feet. "I'm afraid so, Mrs. Bickford. A cup of tea does sound good, thank you."

No one had eaten breakfast before the services. Rebel was ashamed of her appetite now, but when Millie served hot buttery scones with the tea she was relieved to see that everyone else helped themselves, too, even Aunt Winnie.

Evelyn did not take a seat; instead she stood before the fire, holding her head high. "Please don't keep us in suspense any longer, Mr. Grader. Are we to be put out on the streets?"

He sighed again, and sipped at the hot, sweet tea before replying. "I pray it will not be as bad as that, Miss Evelyn. Your situation is, however, precarious. Your father had various investments that will eventually realize a moderate sum. And there is this house. However, forced sales do not usually bring the highest amounts, and I fear that is what we have come to. Perhaps the shop can be rented, perhaps sold. I will take what steps I can to make sure that it produces income, one way or another. Of cash there is precious little, I'm sorry to say. Mr. Bickford had written a bank draft to this, ah, Jubal Hake, for a considerable sum, and the man cashed it within an hour of the time he received it, so there was not much left in the bank. There are some accounts receivable, but since most of the money is owed by those who were robbed—well, perhaps we can't count on those being paid. Unless, of course, you want to take legal action to collect—"

"No, no," Evelyn said impatiently, biting her lip. "They blame us, and rightly so, I suppose. Papa shouldn't have done business with Hake, and I shouldn't have invited him to the party."

"And I shouldn't have showed him where the wraps and purses were," Rebel added quietly. The burden of that innocent act lay heavily upon her.

"Ah, well, there's no sense in trying to apportion the guilt," Mr. Grader said, helping himself to another scone. It dripped melted butter and he made a grab for his napkin. "We know that Jubal Hake—or whatever his name really is—forged his credentials, copying those he took from a man who really did work for the company Hake supposedly represented. That poor fellow he robbed is still in the hospital with a fractured skull, so Hake's victims here were fortunate, it seems."

He sipped at his tea cautiously, for it was scalding hot. "Human nature being what it is, there's little gratitude among them for having come off as well as they did, considering the alternatives. The police have no doubts that those who were robbed were lucky they didn't wake up during the robbery. Hake would have had no compunction about striking down anyone who got in his way, apparently. I've spoken to most of those who suffered losses, and they're unanimous in their resentment, though it was only Mr. Bickford whose entire financial structure was destroyed."

The lawyer looked at the scones remaining on the plate, hesitated, and helped himself to one more. "At any rate, I will do my best to salvage as much for you as I can. But I tell you frankly that I think selling this place and the shop, and disposing of all assets—this furniture is very nice and will perhaps bring several thousand—is the only way to go."

"Sell the house?" Winnie echoed. "Where would we go, then?"

"To something smaller," Evelyn said at once. "Yes, of course, Mr. Grader. Please take care of all of this for us, as quickly as you can."

Delicately, he licked his fingers and patted his mouth with the napkin. "The servants, of course, should be given notice immediately. The amount you save on their wages alone will keep you for some time. But I'm sure you'll do admirably; you are ladies of intelligence and courage."

After he had gone, Evelyn stared after him with a hint of bitterness. "Intelligence and courage. You can't eat those, can you?"

"No. But being poor isn't always fatal," Rebel said gently. "Mama and Father and I were poor all our lives, and we were very happy. Would you like me to break the news to the servants?"

Evelyn hesitated. "I suppose so. Tell them we'll give them each a month's wages—" She stopped, seeing her cousin's expression. "A half-month's wages?"

"If it's as desperate a situation as I gathered it is," Rebel told her, "I doubt you can afford that generosity. They have a week to go, I take it, to finish out this pay period? I suggest we tell them they will be paid for this coming week, but that we cannot come up with additional severance pay."

Evelyn managed a tremulous smile. "No doubt I'd impoverish us even further if I didn't have you to offer advice. Do you know that in my entire life I've never dressed all by myself?"

Rebel smiled back. "And in all my life, since I was a small child, I've never had any help with dressing. We'll do it, Evelyn."

It wasn't easy to convey the news to the staff, but Rebel undertook it at once. It was more cruel to keep them wondering than to break the news bluntly.

Tears appeared in Nell's eyes. "I've worked for Mrs. Bickford since she was a bride," she said.

"And I," Mrs. Worsted said. "I'm getting on in years to be looking for a position, but my cooking is well known in New York society. It may be that one of the wealthy ladies will take me on. I'll start asking about."

It was soon evident to Rebel that she herself would have to undertake responsibility for the trio who had survived Arlen Bickford. Dressing herself was not the only thing to which Evelyn was unaccustomed.

"Maybe we ought to keep Mrs. Worsted on, at least," she said uneasily. "How will we manage without a cook?"

"There's nothing to cooking. I've been doing it since I was eight," Rebel told her. "Mrs. Worsted's salary is the highest of the lot, so she *must* be let go. That money you're paying her will keep us all fed, and then some."

Evelyn spread her pretty hands in a helpless gesture. "The nearest thing I've done to cooking is to lift the kettle off the fire to make tea."

"I used to make the lightest biscuits," Winnie interjected unexpectedly. "Better than your mama's, Rebel. I wonder if I still could."

There was a tap on the door, and Timothy entered with a scuttle of coal, which he set upon the hearth. "I've been taken on elsewhere, miss," he told Evelyn. "I'm to begin Monday week."

"I'm glad for you, Timothy," she told him. Only after the boy had gone did the magnitude of his loss strike her. "Who's going to carry coal? And sweep the walks? Don't look at me that way, Rebel. It has taken a staff of five to run this establishment. Don't tell me three females—two of us useless—can do everything *they* did."

"No, of course not. Some things simply won't get done," Rebel explained.

Evelyn's brows rose. "Including carrying coal scuttles? In this weather?"

"No. But I think that until a buyer is found for the house and while we're still here, it would be wise to close off as much of the house as possible to conserve on coal. I've looked in the cellar and I doubt there's enough fuel to last more than a month, even if we are very careful with it and heat only the rooms we actually use. I'd suggest keeping the stove going in the kitchen and eating there so we can close off everything else on this floor except for this parlor; we'll keep a fire here, too. And it might be wise to move our beds downstairs. Perhaps Aunt Winnie could make do with the front parlor, and you and I could share the music room. It isn't a good idea to let that get too cold and damp, or it will damage your piano and harp."

Evelyn stared at her in astonishment, but Winnie was nodding. "Yes, before Charles and Timothy go, let's have them bring the beds downstairs. You're very sensible, Rebel dear."

Once the arrangements were made, everyone adjusted fairly well. Rebel set about teaching her cousin how to prepare simple meals. To everyone's amazement, including Winnie's own, Winnie took an interest and a hand in matters she had ignored for twenty years. She dusted the parlor, made her own bed, and practiced making biscuits. Her first results were somewhat below Mrs. Worsted's standards, but within a week she was blushing over the girls' compliments.

With the exception of Mrs. Snelling, they had no visitors. She, like the others, blamed Arlen Bickford for her loss. "But that doesn't mean I hold you responsible, too," she said gruffly. "You're victims as much as I. I'm glad to have your Millie, she's bright and biddable. And your young cousin is bearing out my prophecy, Evelyn: she's handling things in an intelligent manner. Is it true that Grader has sold this place to some poor relation of the Rockefellers?"

It was the first they'd heard of it. Rebel felt a chill run through her that had nothing to do with the rationing of coal. Evelyn's lips had gone white.

"Will you be using the proceeds to compensate those of us who lost so much because of your father's bad judgment?" Mrs. Snelling asked, and though Rebel liked the old lady, she wished the woman had not added yet another blow on top of those they'd already suffered.

"Why, I don't know . . ." Evelyn glanced quickly at her mother and then away. "We won't have much to live on, and we're not really equipped to go out and work as . . . as barmaids, or some such."

"It would go a long way toward clearing your father's memory," the old lady said shrewdly. "To repay them for their losses."

Evelyn sounded wooden. "Yes, I suppose it would," she said.

After their visitor had gone, she ground her teeth.

"Even if we gave them every cent, leaving ourselves destitute, we couldn't fully reimburse them. Not for all those jewels! And it's true, we *are* victims just as much as they! Damn Papa, anyway, for getting involved with that Jubal Hake! And damn him for shooting himself and leaving us to deal with all this mess!"

There had been little sorrow expressed over the master's demise. Certainly the servants had been more concerned over their own predicament than over that of the remaining family, which was natural enough. They had had no love for Arlen Bickford during his lifetime; why should they grieve for him when their own futures were so precarious?

And while Winnie and Evelyn had both wiped their eyes during the funeral, Evelyn had said later, "It's so sad, don't you think, that we didn't have a better feeling about Papa? That we are concerned more about our own future than grieving because he's gone? Your sorrow was greater, Rebel; when your papa was alive you had such love and joy with him. It makes me wonder where we all went wrong, why our family was so different from yours."

Comparing Ned Moran to Arlen Bickford was like comparing a ripe peach to last year's turnip, Rebel thought, but it hardly seemed a comforting thing to say.

Evelyn looked at her cousin with a sad smile. "What are we going to do?" she asked.

And for the moment, Rebel had no answers.

Later that night, having gone upstairs to get a few items she had not yet transferred to the makeshift bedroom below, Rebel stood at the window, looking out on the street.

Again the snow swirled in the light from the street-lamp, but this time there was no dark figure in the

108

shadows, no footprints to indicate that anyone had passed by since dusk when the snow had begun to fall.

How she wished she would hear from Luke Kittering! Not just a note, but the man, in person, so that she could discuss the situation with him. Men were prepared by their upbringing to take responsibility for the kinds of problems that faced her now. She wasn't at all prepared, and gradually during the past few days the realization had grown on Rebel that she was now faced not only with the question of how to manage her own future, but Evelyn's and Aunt Winnie's as well. She was confused and frightened, but *they* were like babes in the woods compared to her.

Not even her beloved father had advised her about what to do after he was gone. At first, she supposed, he'd expected to recover from his illness. And toward the end, when even he must have known he was dying, it had perhaps been too much for him to deal with. At any rate, he'd never said a word to her about how she might manage. Men never seemed to think it essential for the females in their lives to know anything about business or finances, even though many of the women would be orphaned or widowed and have to cope with all sorts of things beyond their knowledge. It would be humiliating to have to confess to Luke Kittering, a relative stranger, the predicament in which she found herself. Yet what was embarrassment compared to this creeping fear of the unknown?

Yes, she was convinced that Luke Kittering was the kind of man who could advise her and help her. If only he would finish his business and call upon her! With her uncle gone, she wouldn't even have to make up an elaborate story about how she came to know him.

There had been no word from Kittering, however. Rebel stared down into the cold, silent street, biting her lip. She wished she'd run downstairs herself that night and offered him the food, instead of sending the maid to do it. Who knows how differently things might have turned out?

Why had he been out there? Who had he been waiting for? Was lurking in the shadows—until now the word *lurking* hadn't entered her mind in connection with the man concealed in the shadows—somehow part of the business he had to take care of?

The suspicion came with the force of a blow.

Why hadn't it occurred to her before? He had been watching this house, and perhaps her uncle's shop as well, days before the night of the robberies. For what purpose? What had he been waiting and watching for?

"No, no," she protested aloud, her heart suddenly accelerating. "There's no reason to think he had anything to do with what happened. Besides, he was never in the house, he couldn't have been the one who duplicated the keys or got into Uncle's safe . . ."

Could he have been an accomplice, though? She suddenly remembered that she and Millie had both thought he and Jubal Hake sounded as if they'd come from the same part of the country, with those accents that reminded her of her mother's, and Aunt Winnie's soft South Carolina tones.

No, no, it was absurd.

Rebel no longer saw the empty street and the swirling snow; her vision turned inward. Illogical though it might be, she was grateful she hadn't thought of this sooner. If she had, she'd have been honor-bound to mention Luke Kittering to Captain Plummer, and she was glad she hadn't.

Rebel set down the lamp she carried—since the staff had departed, no one had lighted any of the gaslights on the second or third floor—and pulled open the

110

drawer where she had tucked the piece torn from the newspaper. She got it out and spread it on the dresser top, smoothing it with her fingers.

The penciled message was difficult to read in the soft glow of the kerosene lamp. Rebel squinted to make it out, though she remembered what it said.

Many thanks to the kind lady who took pity on a freezing, hungry man.                                    L. Kittering.

No, she told herself. An accomplice, a thief, would not have written such a message. Whatever the stranger had been doing out there, he had not been waiting for Jubal Hake to hand over impressions of eighteen keys so that he could duplicate them and later break into all those houses to steal jewels. She could not believe that. Not after the way he'd assisted her, the way his hazel eyes had looked into her own in such a straightforward manner.

There was that headline again, *Will Buck Sloan Be Number Sixty-five for the Hanging Judge?* What did that mean, anyway? She wondered idly. Her mind returned to Luke Kittering. He was the most attractive man she'd ever met, and she refused to believe he wasn't as honest and honorable as she'd thought him to be.

She wasn't thinking about the newspaper at all. Yet gradually some of the printed words impinged on her consciousness. A black border made one paragraph stand out from those above and below it, and she read the advertisement.

WANTED, AT FORT SMITH, ARKANSAS, TO TEACH IN THE BELLE GROVE SCHOOL: YOUNG LADIES QUALIFIED IN READING, WRITING, CIPHERING, HISTORY, AND

OTHER APPROPRIATE SUBJECTS. CONTACT WILLIAM FORESTER, SOUTH NINTH AND WHEELER STREETS, FORT SMITH.

Rebel felt as if electricity had surged through her. Fort Smith was a more enlightened settlement than Lyons Falls, obviously. They were willing to hire females to teach school. The only problem might be that, since the paper was several weeks old, the positions had already been filled.

Why had Luke carried a newspaper from Arkansas? Was that where he was from? Would he be returning there when his business was concluded in New York?

Rebel heard her own breathing in the quiet room and became aware of the cold. Hope grew within her breast: could this be the answer to her prayers? Not only a means to support the three of them, but perhaps to find Luke Kittering again?

On the way downstairs she put aside the encroaching notion that if Luke Kittering wanted to see her, he knew where she was. Many things could have happened to prevent his coming here to seek her out. His failure to do so didn't necessarily mean he had changed his mind, though in truth she couldn't imagine why he had not followed through on his expressed desire to further their acquaintance.

Two minutes later she burst into the back parlor where Winnie and Evelyn were conversing in low tones.

"I've just determined what we are going to do when we move out of this house," Rebel said. Her eyes were sparkling, her lips curved in a triumphant smile that hid an inner insecurity that she refused to admit.

Evelyn looked up hopefully. "Oh? What?"

112

"We're going to Fort Smith, Arkansas, to teach school. I will write to this Mr. Forester the first thing in the morning. I feel it in my bones, we will be just what he's looking for." She handed over the newspaper and pointed to the ad.

Evelyn, who had been snubbed that very afternoon by an erstwhile customer of her father's who used to give her pennies when she was a little girl, sat up straight on her stool. "It's all very well for you to speak of teaching. *You* can probably do it. But what about me? I can read and write, but I can't imagine how one goes about teaching someone else to do it."

Undaunted, Rebel smiled. "Why, you'll teach music, of course. You'll play the piano while the children sing. And art—those watercolors you did are very well done. We'll take them with us to show Mr. Forester. And when we find a place to rent, Aunt Winnie shall cook and keep house for us."

For the first time in many days, the three of them burst out laughing.

"Very well," Evelyn conceded. "If the positions are obtainable, you and I shall become teachers and Mama will cook. I shouldn't wonder but what we'll get our waists down to seventeen or eighteen inches, eating her cooking, except for the biscuits."

They laughed again and touched hands, and Rebel felt renewed, rejoicing, capable of taking on the responsibility for the three of them. In only a few short weeks, their roles had been reversed. Now she, not her aunt, became the savior.

She could hardly wait to hear from Mr. Forester in Fort Smith, Arkansas.

And if this was where Luke Kittering was from, and if he'd gone back there, why, the next time they met she would try fluttering her eyelashes, as she'd watched her cousin do—and in the meantime, she'd try to master Evelyn's seductive smile, too.

In the dark, lying beside Evelyn in bed, Rebel determinedly set aside the misgivings that kept creeping into her mind, and began to smile.

# Chapter Eleven

It was four days before Christmas when they stepped off the train in Fort Smith, Arkansas.

Excitement and anticipation trickled through Rebel as she stood on the station platform, looking about.

Fort Smith was a city, but it was nothing like New York, she saw to her relief. While the buildings were large by Lyons Falls standards, they had not the intimidating height of the skyscrapers, nor were the streets narrow and crowded.

There was a pleasant bustle of horses and carriages, as well as pedestrians. A cool breeze blew off the Arkansas River, but it was not bone-chilling like the wind in New York this time of year, and the day was bright and sunny.

It was absurd, of course, to think she'd descend from the train and spot Luke Kittering among those gathered to meet incoming friends or bid goodbye to departing ones, yet Rebel's gaze searched for a tall figure with dark hair.

She had thought about him all the way here, wondering what she would say and do when they met. There was no explanation for why he had not sought her out in New York, yet since he *had* sent her that note saying he would, she clung to the belief that he'd been as strongly attracted as she had.

Of course there was no way of knowing if he had by this time returned to Fort Smith. Surely, though, in a town of this size it would be possible to find out if he belonged here, if he were known among the townspeople. She would be circumspect about this, naturally; she wouldn't want him to hear that she'd made inquiries and think she was pursuing him.

Even though, she thought with an involuntary smile, she *was*.

Evelyn, radiant in her rich blue fur-trimmed coat even after the tiring journey, was looking around with interest. When her attention came to rest on her cousin's face her remark was perceptive.

"Rebel, what is it? Who are you looking for? Surely Mr. Forester won't be meeting us?"

"No, no, he said we were to go to . . ." Rebel groped in her reticule for the letter, ". . . Mrs. Tolman's boarding house, on . . . yes, here it is, on J Street at Tenth. He says to take the streetcar there. We'll have to get our luggage."

Evelyn was not turned aside from her observation. "You look like a girl meeting a lover."

Winnie, puffing a little after the exertion of descending from the train, straightened her hat as she joined them. "What's that? A lover?"

"No, no, Mama," Evelyn said shamelessly, "you must be getting hard of hearing. I said it's such a *bother* to have to handle all the luggage without a man. I wonder if that fellow could be persuaded to take our baggage checks and see that everything is loaded onto the streetcar, wherever that is."

She moved toward a black man wrestling with a heavy trunk as it came out of a baggage car, engaging him in conversation. Winnie stared after her in bewilderment.

"I'd have sworn she said something about a lover. How extraordinary! I didn't know I was hard of hearing. My, this is certainly different from New York, isn't it. Rather . . . rustic," she decided, but there was no condescension in her tone. "It reminds me of where we grew up, your mama and I. I *liked* living in a smaller place, where one knew one's neighbors. I guess I must be getting older," she added, "for I'm aching in every bone from those horrid seats, and you're looking as fresh as if there'd been no journey at all."

Rebel was tired, too, but not enough to dampen her enthusiasm. In this place she might again encounter Luke Kittering, the man she'd been dreaming about ever since she'd met him.

Just remembering some of the dreams, both day and night ones, brought heightened color to her face. To prevent her aunt from observing too much, Rebel swung around, looking for the streetcar. "There are the trolley tracks. I wonder how often the cars run?"

An unfamiliar male voice responded. "They meet the trains. There'll be one along in ten minutes or so, by the time the baggage handlers are finished."

Rebel, startled, looked up into a smiling face just as Evelyn returned.

"The man says—oh, excuse me!" Evelyn, too, stared at the newcomer, her lovely mouth forming a startled O.

Rebel watched it happen, the same thing that had

117

happened to her when she'd looked into Luke Kittering's face.

He was over six feet tall, with a shock of pale hair that fell forward over a high forehead as he swept off his Stetson. The luxuriant mustache was gold-tinted like his hair, striking against deeply tanned skin, and his eyes were a bright blue.

"Ma'am," he said to Evelyn, the smile broadening, and then to Rebel, "We don't stand on ceremony in Fort Smith, miss, not when a lady appears to need help. Is that small mountain of trunks and bags over there belonging to you? Where is it you're going with it?"

Evelyn appeared mesmerized, though not so much so that she overlooked the essentials. "Yes, that's ours. My cousin has the address. I'm Evelyn Bickford, sir, and this is my mama, and my cousin Rebel Moran."

"I'm Cotton Stirling," he introduced himself. "I'd be glad to help you get those things where they belong, if you'll let me have the baggage checks."

Aunt Winnie was opening her mouth to protest that they couldn't take advantage of a stranger (meaning, no doubt, that they couldn't chance having a stranger take advantage of *them*) but Rebel got her words in first.

"We'd be most grateful, Mr. Stirling. We're expected at a Mrs. Tolman's, on J Street at Tenth." She and Evelyn exchanged looks, and she knew the two of them had just been plunged into a conspiracy against the proprieties Aunt Winnie would insist upon observing. "Here are the stubs."

They watched the tall man stride toward the heap of luggage being sorted out on the platform, relieved not to have to cope with it themselves.

"He's not too old, is he?" Evelyn asked. Her lips were parted, her eyes sparkled like the tiny chip diamonds in her ears, the only jewelry she'd salvaged from the wreckage of her former life. "Twenty-eight or so, would you say?"

"Too old for what?" Winnie asked, confused. "He looks perfectly capable of lifting a trunk . . ."

"I'd guess about thirty," Rebel supplied, laughing. "Yes, Aunt Winnie, I'm sure he can handle the trunks."

"Cotton Stirling," Evelyn murmured, and Rebel wondered in amusement if she were trying it on for size, as in *Mrs.* Cotton Stirling. "Breathtaking," Evelyn added.

"What is?" Winnie demanded almost crossly. "Evelyn, I *know* I heard you say that, but I haven't the faintest idea what you're talking about. It's a nice enough town, but hardly *breathtaking.*"

"Don't you think so, Mama?" Evelyn's smile was guileless. "I think it's going to be a lovely place to live. Ah, Mr. Stirling! We're so appreciative of your help."

"I'll move everything over to the curb, there, and load it for you when the trolley comes," he offered, adjusting the trunk resting easily on his shoulder.

"That's very kind of you. I hope we aren't keeping you from your own business."

"My business will keep," he said cheerfully, and led the way to the streetcar stop. "You aren't by any chance the new school teachers, are you? Heard there was some coming in shortly."

"Why, yes, we are. I mean, the jobs aren't actually ours, yet," Evelyn told him, "because we have to be interviewed by a school board, I believe, but the letter from Mr. Forester made it sound quite positive."

He lowered the trunk to the walk and grinned at the trio who had followed. "Oh, the school board's all men," he said. "I reckon you'll get the jobs, all right."

He headed back to the platform for another load.

Winnie was frowning ever so slightly. "Evelyn, I have the feeling that Mr. Stirling is flirting with you."

"I surely hope so," Evelyn agreed, laughing. "He knows we're teachers, so we'll be at the schoolhouse, and he knows where we're boarding, and Mama, so help me, I'll throttle you if you do anything to ruin what promises to be the most exciting adventure I've ever had!"

Evelyn hugged her mother to take the sting from the words, and if Winnie still seemed dubious, she at least said nothing more.

Cotton Stirling, they learned a few minutes later, was the kind of gentleman who would see them to their destination after he had loaded the luggage onto the streetcar.

"Oh, that's not at all necessary," Winnie began, but Cotton Stirling only gave her a broad grin.

"There's no way Mrs. Tolman can help you unload all this and get it upstairs to your rooms," he said. "And Harry, here," he winked at the driver of the trolley, who had waited patiently for them to board, "has a bad back, right, Harry? He can't help, either. What you need is an able-bodied man who can do the job quickly."

There was no further argument, not even from Aunt Winnie. They took their seats, the girls facing Winnie and Cotton Stirling, and the conductor urged the mule forward; the car began to roll along the tracks.

Beneath the cover of their spreading skirts, Evelyn squeezed Rebel's hand, and Rebel squeezed back. Rebel thought Evelyn had already made a conquest; she hoped she would be equally lucky.

If Cotton Stirling had known they were coming, knew the conductor by his first name, and knew that Mrs. Tolman's rooms for rent were upstairs, he probably knew whatever there was to know about Luke

Kittering, too. Only she didn't dare ask. She had not yet even confided in her cousin so that Evelyn could help her.

The ride was a leisurely one, though too brief for Evelyn's taste, Rebel realized. She herself was only too ready to reach their destination and remedy the lack of bathing during the days they'd been on the train.

Garrison Avenue was an exceptionally wide street, lined with businesses of all sorts. "Great place for parades," Cotton Stirling told them. "Plenty of room for the floats and the bands, and standing room for the viewers. We always have a great parade on the Fourth of July."

He continued to indicate points of interest as they rode away from the train station on the riverfront, waving a large, well-shaped hand toward things beyond their sight. "The cotton compress and oil mill is back that way . . . largest one in the world," he said. "Over 40,000 bales of cotton a year come in here. Belle Grove Hospital's over that way—hope you won't have any need for that. We got us a new post office, and as handsome a courthouse as you ever saw. That was built in 1889, too."

Winnie compressed her lips, no doubt thinking this young man was altogether too forward, though when he pointed out the Grand Opera House she looked at it the same as the others.

"Not as big as the one in New York, I suppose," he admitted, "but pretty fancy all the same. That is where you're from, isn't it? New York City?"

"Yes," Evelyn answered, showing her dimples.

When they turned off from Garrison Street, Rebel became more interested. The homes were large and gracious, many as impressive as those in New York, except that these were set in their own grounds, with lawns and trees between them.

Did Luke Kittering live in one of these? Or in a place like the tiny, yet charming, Victorian cottage she had seen, with the trellis that in summer would be covered with roses?

Winnie was sagging in exhaustion by the time they reached the end of their journey.

Mrs. Tolman's house was white clapboard, a comfortable two-story structure with a veranda encircling three sides of it. In the summer there would be an expanse of green lawn, and perhaps boarders sitting on the chairs or the swing on the porch. Even now, with remnants of snow near the steps, the house had a welcoming air.

Harry brought the streetcar to a stop without being asked, and they disembarked. As Cotton Stirling lifted the trunks and bags off the back of the streetcar, he told them, "You'll like it here. Mrs. Tolman's a nice lady, widowed two years ago. That's why she takes in boarders, to make ends meet. And you're within walking distance of the school. It's down that way." He gestured with one hand, then picked up the largest trunk—Evelyn had brought virtually all her clothes, since there was little to be gained by selling them—and headed toward the front steps.

Mrs. Tolman greeted them hospitably, a woman of Winnie's age with graying hair and faded blue eyes. She limped badly on a foot that was swathed in bandages and encased in a man's slipper.

"Come in, come in!" she urged as she held the door wide for them. "Excuse me for not showing you upstairs myself, but it was the stairs that nearly did me in. Took a tumble, I did. The doctor says I didn't break any bones, but I swear the twisted muscles are just as painful. It's the two front rooms at the top of the stairs, Cotton, and bless you for taking their things up!"

Cotton paused at the foot of the stairs that rose from the entryway. "Maybe one of you would come with me and tell me what goes into which room," he suggested.

"Of course," Evelyn said at once, and ran lightly up the stairs ahead of him, giving him a tantalizing view of slender, silk-clad ankles.

"You must be worn out after that long trip," Mrs. Tolman addressed her two remaining guests. "Come into the dining room and I'll get you a cup of tea. I've a bit of pound cake left; perhaps you'd like a slice, as well?"

They followed her through the well-appointed house into a dining room with a table that could seat at least a dozen. Winnie and Rebel removed their outer wraps; when Winnie took a seat, Rebel followed Mrs. Tolman into a spacious kitchen and offered to serve the cake.

"That would be nice, dear," Mrs. Tolman said. "Saves me a few steps. The plates are in that cupboard right over there."

The others had nearly consumed their refreshments before Evelyn and Cotton Stirling joined them. Cotton waved aside a suggestion that he have a piece of cake, too.

"No, thanks, ma'am. The old man's waiting for me to show up with his parcel that came in on the train. I'll be seeing you later, ladies," he said, and from her look, Evelyn clearly took that as a promise.

She sank onto her chair when Cotton had gone, accepting her cake and tea while the others refilled their cups.

"The cake is very good. I think," Evelyn said, revealing her dimples for Mrs. Tolman, "that Mr. Forester did us a favor in arranging for us to stay here."

Mrs. Tolman sighed. "Well, I may have to apologize for the cooking for a bit, I'm afraid. I don't usually do it

123

myself, but the cook I hired up and married a tinker day before yesterday—left me high and dry, as they say. The cake's the last thing she made. Cooking was never my strong point, I must admit. When Mr. Tolman was alive, God rest him, he never said anything against my cooking, mind, but when I asked if we could afford to hire a woman, he agreed right off. So I always had a cook, until day before yesterday. Then when I was trying to cook for the others—there's two elderly ladies have the rooms beyond yours, and Mr. Sylvester has the back bedroom—he's a clerk at the American Express, and *most* reliable—as well as keep up the cleaning and such, why, I got in too big a hurry and tripped over an armload of sheets as I was at the head of the stairs. I can't stand for very long without the ankle hurting to beat fury, so you've arrived at an awkward time. I hope you can be patient with the inconvenience until the wicked ankle heals and I can find another cook."

Evelyn sipped her tea and gave the woman a sunny smile. "What a coincidence, isn't it? My mama, you see, is an excellent cook, and since we're short of money until we begin to earn our salaries at the school, how would it be if Mama filled in, to help pay our board?"

Winnie, in the act of swallowing the last of her tea, choked.

Rebel patted her on the back and, conscious of how few coins remained in her purse, added, "Yes, Aunt Winnie makes the lightest biscuits you've ever tasted. It seems an excellent solution to both your problem and ours."

"Oh, goodness, that would be a godsend! By all means, if you're a cook, Mrs. Bickford, you shall have the position! Drat, there's the door, it's probably Miss Helen again. She *will* forget her key. Excuse me."

124

Mrs. Tolman rose and limped toward the front door, while Winnie glared at her young charges.

"You're out of your minds," she said. "I haven't cooked in years, except for what Rebel supervised. She'll find out in a moment that my only talent lies in the biscuits."

"Anyone who can make good biscuits can make anything else, I should think," Rebel encouraged her. "And I'll tell you how to do it."

"It'll be a month before we get paid," Evelyn reminded, "even if they hire us. I'm not as sure as Rebel is that they will, either. Not me, anyway—not if they discover how ill-equipped I am to teach anything. You must try it, Mama, for all our sakes."

"We'll both help you at first," Rebel said earnestly. "Please try, Aunt Winnie."

There was no more time for discussion, for Mrs. Tolman ushered in another of the boarders. Miss Helen Lovell was a slender, fragile lady of some seventy years, who had been out for a walk and a ride on the streetcar, which was apparently her only diversion. She acknowledged their introductions, accepted tea and cake, and was inclined to talk about what she had seen.

Since the three newcomers knew none of the people Miss Helen mentioned, and they were anxious to settle into their new quarters, they rose to go upstairs. As they were leaving, however, Rebel's attention was caught by a name carelessly dropped; she nearly tripped on the edge of a throw rug she hadn't seen, and caught herself on the post at the foot of the stairs.

"Something going on at the Kittering place," the old lady was saying. "All sorts of people gathered there, delivery wagons and such."

"Of course, Helen, I told you. The youngest girl is being married the day after tomorrow!" Mrs. Tolman said with tolerant exasperation.

Rebel looked backward, ignoring Evelyn and Winnie, who were already climbing to the second floor. The Kittering place?

Miss Helen's forehead was furrowed in an effort to recall. "I thought Rosalie was married weeks ago."

"No, no. It was *planned* for several weeks ago, but then when Luke was hurt and Adam had to go North and fetch him home they put off the wedding, until Luke was better. I *told* you that, Helen, don't you remember?"

A physical pain, true anguish, surged through Rebel's system. Luke hurt? How? When? Was that the reason she'd never heard from him? And how was he now?

"I guess I forgot," Miss Helen muttered. "Luke's the good-looking one, isn't he? The one who refused to go into banking like his brothers?"

"That's the one. Refused to do about anything Adam wanted him to do, from what I've heard." Mrs. Tolman sighed. "Well, getting four of your five children to do what you want is better than nothing, I suppose. Was there something else you wanted, Miss Moran?"

Rebel gathered her wits. "No, no, ma'am. I caught my toe in the edge of the rug. Excuse me."

She went quickly up the stairs, her heart racing. Luke had been hurt, but he was here in Fort Smith. Miss Helen had either walked or ridden past his family home in the past hour, so it couldn't be far from here.

Tomorrow she might meet him on the street.

The electricity ran from her fingertips down to her toes as she entered the room she would share with her cousin, wondering if it would be out of the question to go out for a walk yet this afternoon. A bit of judicious interest in Miss Helen's excursion might even extract from the old lady the exact location of the Kittering house.

126

Evelyn turned from looking out the front window to flop onto the bed with its blue and white quilt in a wedding ring pattern.

"Ah, Rebel, I'm glad you talked us into coming here! This is going to be the first great adventure of my life!"

Rebel smiled down at the other girl.

"Yes," she agreed. "It's going to be a great adventure." And not only for Evelyn, she vowed.

For Luke Kittering was only a few miles away at most, and if he didn't find her, she promised herself, she would certainly find him.

# Chapter Twelve

THE EVENING AIR WAS COLD, CARRYING THE PROMISE OF snow. The wind from the Poteau River, several miles outside of town, cut through his jacket.

Behind him, his horse nickered, and Luke Kittering turned from his contemplation of the slow-moving water below, putting out a hand to the animal to quiet him.

The approaching horse and rider came at an easy lope across the grassy slope. Luke waited long enough to be sure of the rider's identity, then stepped out of the concealment of the stand of sycamores and waved his hat.

A moment later, Cotton Stirling slid out of the saddle beside him and knotted the reins around a low branch. "Gonna snow tonight," he said by way of greeting. "We'll have a white Christmas."

"You're late," Luke told him. "What held you up?"

"The new schoolteachers," Cotton said, grinning. "There they were, standing on the platform with enough baggage to fill half the railroad car, not knowing how to get to Mrs. Tolman's boardinghouse. Naturally I saw them safely there and carried their trunks upstairs."

"Naturally," Luke said, his tone dry. "How many of them are there?"

"Two. Both redheads. One for you and one for me. And the mama of mine. We wouldn't be so lucky that they wouldn't have a chaperon."

"Redheads?" A memory, sharp, poignant, rose within Luke.

"That's right. Never cared much for redheads, actually—I guess I thought of them as looking like Lucy Turner, with that carrot-colored hair and the rabbity face. But Evelyn Bickford is a different matter altogether. Gorgeous! Great big blue eyes and—"

"Bickford?" Luke felt strangled, suddenly hot instead of freezing cold. It wasn't possible, he thought, yet hope surged through him in a scalding wave. "What's the other one's name? The one that's mine?" He kept his tone casual, amused, conveying none of the tension he felt.

"Rebel Moran. She looks as unusual as her name. Curly hair the color of a new penny, a couple of freckles on a pert little nose—oh, you'll like her, Lucas my friend. Pretty little thing."

It *was* her, the girl from New York. For a few moments he didn't hear Cotton's words. He'd been in no shape to make inquiries about her in person when his father arrived to take him home; the note he'd sent by way of the young nurse who attended him had been returned, with an apology.

"I'm sorry, sir," the girl had said. "Nobody answered the door at that address, and the neighbors said the family has moved."

So that was that, he'd thought. He'd considered the possibility of going back, eventually, when the pressing matters were under control, but it was a long way, and there was little hope of success in finding her.

And now she was here in Fort Smith.

From being tired and discouraged, Luke now felt re-energized and optimistic.

"So what do you want me to do? Stay out of sight? Stay away altogether?" Cotton was asking.

Luke blinked. He hadn't heard a word of what the other man said. "What?" he asked.

"Weren't you listening? I said they're meeting Christmas Eve, and the word is they're looking to recruit a few more hired guns. Do you want to go in alone, or shall I be on hand, just in case you need me?"

Luke no longer felt the cold. "Either they'll accept me or they won't. No need for both of us to get killed if they don't," he said. "Where are they meeting?"

Cotton looked at him oddly. "I told you. The woods at the end of Free Ferry Road. Luke, you all right?"

"Never better," Luke assured him. He reached for the reins of his horse and vaulted easily into the saddle, then paused to look down at Cotton's upturned face. "You said those schoolteachers were staying at Mrs. Tolman's?"

"That's right. Just don't forget, Evelyn's mine. You can take Rebel Moran." The grin was back.

"Understood," Luke agreed, laughing. "I waited here for nearly an hour, so I'm leaving first. Freeze your own tail for ten minutes before you follow me back to town."

Cotton touched two fingers to the brim of his Stetson

in acknowledgment, and Luke wheeled the horse and urged him forward with the pressure of his heels.

He didn't think about the dangers that lay ahead of him as he rode through the dusk. He thought about Rebel Moran, and the thoughts kept him warmer than he'd been all day.

Adam Kittering looked up from his ledgers when his oldest son entered the study. He was a handsome man of fifty, with hair going silver at the temples. Even in the privacy of his own home, he was dressed as he did for business, in a dark suit, white shirt, and string tie, with the boots most men customarily wore when they rode horseback.

"Snowing yet?" he asked, putting down his pen for a moment.

"Sure to by morning," Luke said. He walked across the room to the cabinet where his father kept a stock of excellent spirits and poured himself a glass of apricot brandy. "You want some of this?"

Adam's lips tightened perceptibly. "No, thank you. Lucas, have you given any further thought to my proposal?"

"I gave it all the thought it needed when you made it." Luke stood with his back to the crackling fire, sipping the brandy, which was smooth as it went down and burned comfortably in his stomach. "You know I hate the banking business, Pa. I'd go crazy, cooped up inside that place every day."

"So what do you propose to do instead?" There was a bite in the older man's voice.

Luke shrugged, setting his empty glass on the mantel behind him. "I'll find something," he said casually. "I might take one chore off your back, though."

Adam sat very still. The offer was unexpected. "Oh? What chore is that?"

"The school board is meeting tomorrow evening, isn't it? To decide whether or not to hire those teachers came down from New York?"

Adam's manner was guarded. "Yes. One more damned thing to do in a week already too full, with Rosalie's wedding the next night. Wish it had taken place when it was originally scheduled, and we'd be past all that fuss." Was there a hint of criticism of Luke because his injury had caused the delay?

"Give me the authorization, and I'll sit in for you on the meeting," Luke proposed. "If they're adequate, you haven't any feelings against hiring them, have you?"

"No. Forester said their credentials seemed adequate. Why are you willing to sit in a meeting in my stead, all of a sudden?"

The smile Lucas flashed had won over his parent many times in the past. "I know Ma and Rosalie have you running in circles, and I thought it would be one way to ease the pressure a little."

Suspicion was etched on the older edition of Luke's face. "You haven't by any chance met these schoolteachers, have you?"

"Haven't been anywhere near 'em since they got here," Luke said honestly. "If you want to do it yourself, I've got plenty of other things I can do. Ma wants—"

He didn't have to finish. His father made an impatient gesture. "All right. It *would* help if I didn't have to attend the school board meeting. You can vote in my stead, and they can have it in writing if they want."

"Fine," Luke said, revealing none of what he felt. "Meeting's at seven, isn't it?"

As he left the room and climbed the stairway to his own room, he was smiling. But by the time he opened the bedroom door, the smile had vanished as he thought about what he'd be doing on Christmas Eve.

Winnie's first meal, its preparation presided over by Rebel in the guise of assistant, won praise from the entire household.

Mr. Sylvester was a dried up little man who seldom spoke except to say "please" or "thank you." His gaze lingered on Winnie's unusual hair, and when she looked in his direction, he produced a small, stiff smile. Miss Helen's sister, a widow everyone addressed as Miss Margaret, was as plump as Helen was thin, but with the same white hair and pale blue eyes. They all thanked the new cook, who trembled when she confronted the girls later in their room.

"Rebel told me every step of everything, except for the biscuits," she said. "How am I going to prepare three meals a day without Rebel beside me in the kitchen?"

"I'll write everything down for you ahead of time," Rebel proposed. "It's easy, Aunt Winnie, really it is. You *used* to cook, when you were a girl."

"That was so long ago," Winnie sighed. "I've forgotten so much." Her expression sharpened. "Where are you going?"

"Out for a walk. To explore the town." Evelyn's response was glib.

"But it's nearly dark! And so cold!"

"There are streetlights, Mama. We'll dress warmly, and we won't be gone long. Rebel talked to Miss Helen and learned of some of the more interesting streets to go on. The ones with the really nice houses."

Winnie's face crumpled and her eyes filled with tears. "Our house was nice, wasn't it?"

"Oh, Mama, I'm not going because I'm grieving for

our house! It's simply fun to see them, that's all. And we want to know what our new surroundings are like, don't we? We want to walk past the school, where we have to go tomorrow evening to be interviewed, so we'll know where to go."

Rebel was wrapping herself in her warmest garment, a becoming, dark green wool fur-lined cape that Evelyn had given her, and was impatient to be off before it was completely dark. It had been pathetically easy to get the information she wanted from Miss Helen; she had few people to listen to her, and she'd been only too eager to share her excursion route.

"You can turn back at the Kittering house," the old lady had bubbled. "You'll know it because it's so big and grand, and the name is on the gate. That's on Twelfth Street, and then you can circle around through the Belle Grove district, and back home. It will make a fairly strenuous walk, but then, you're young and healthy, aren't you?"

For a moment, when they let themselves out of the house a few minutes later, Rebel wondered if she were young and healthy enough to walk for an hour or two in the suddenly plunging temperature.

Evelyn looked up at the night sky. "It's going to snow," she said. "Let's walk fast so we'll stay warm."

And then, pausing under one of the streetlights, she demanded, "All right, cousin, tell me what's going on?"

Rebel maintained an air of innocence. "I don't know what you mean."

"Oh, yes, you do. We answered an ad for school teachers. Even though it may have been a legitimate reason for coming, it certainly isn't the prospect of employment that's making you glide around like an angel floating on a cloud. It's a man, isn't it?"

"I just got here," Rebel protested. "I haven't met anyone but Cotton Stirling, and he had eyes for no one but you."

"But there's someone," Evelyn insisted shrewdly. "Someone you knew was here." She linked her arm with Rebel's as they strode briskly off in the direction Miss Helen had suggested. "Of course—there was something about that paper, the one you read the ad from. If my brains hadn't been so addled over the mess we were in it would have occurred to me before: where did you get a page from a Fort Smith newspaper?"

Rebel hesitated, then gave in. After all, they were here now, and it was most likely to be Aunt Winnie who would raise objections, not Evelyn.

"I met a man in New York," she admitted softly, holding the hood of the cape tightly around her throat. "His name is Luke Kittering."

"And we're going past the Kittering house! How marvelous! Tell me everything!"

Evelyn listened with commendably few interruptions to a condensed version of the story, then squeezed Rebel's arm in delight. "It's fabulous! What do you suppose he was doing in New York, and how did he get hurt? Mrs. Tolman made it sound as if your Luke might be the black sheep of the family, not following his father's wishes. I always thought I should do nicely with a black sheep; they must be quite entertaining, don't you think?"

Rebel's mouth twisted in a wry grimace. "My father was considered a black sheep by some people because he didn't do what his family wanted and never made any money. He was a wonderful man, but perfectly ordinary in most ways. I don't know about the 'entertaining' part. All I know is that Luke Kittering is the most attractive man I ever met. What I don't know is

135

whether or not he'll be pleased or displeased to see me. After all, he didn't follow through on finding me again."

"But Mrs. Tolman said he'd been hurt, and his father had to go to New York to bring him home. Poor man, he probably couldn't search you out. Why on earth would he have written you that note if he didn't mean what it said?"

"I don't know. I'm excited, and I'm frightened, all at the same time."

"Walk faster," Evelyn said, quickening her own steps. "The school can wait until tomorrow morning, if necessary, but we must see the Kittering mansion. It will be a mansion, won't it? He's the scion of a wealthy family, and he'll be smitten with you all over again. No, he didn't abandon you, it was simply a matter of his being too badly injured to find you. And you'll get married and live happily ever after. Just as I have every intention of doing with Mr. Cotton Stirling. Then it won't matter if they want us to teach school or not."

Rebel had to laugh. "You don't even know if Cotton Stirling is unmarried and available."

"Oh, yes, I do! You're not the only one who can pry information out of old ladies. I asked Mrs. Tolman, point-blank, and she says Cotton's single, works in his father's business—they have a large plantation where they raise cotton, and a business on Garrison Avenue—and that the family is well-to-do. So it's settled."

Evelyn was absurd, but she liked it, Rebel decided. A touch of humor was welcome in her life, and what was wrong with pretending that Luke Kittering would greet her with joy and sweep her off her feet?

It was fully dark before they reached the house on Twelfth Street, but there were still buggies and horsemen on the streets; the two girls had no apprehensions about being afoot in an unfamiliar area. Most of the houses were lighted, the streetlamps kept them from getting lost, and none of the passersby intimidated them in any way.

"That must be it!" Evelyn cried suddenly. "Goodness, it *is* a handsome place, isn't it?"

Even at night the house was imposing, which immediately cast a pall over Rebel's high spirits. A family living in such a place would be most particular about whom their son married, or even formed an attachment to. A penniless orphan from a tiny village in upstate New York would hardly qualify as a desirable daughter-in-law.

The house was enormous, a three-story Victorian structure elaborately decorated with the intricate wood carving known as "gingerbread." It was on a corner lot, surrounded by a wrought-iron fence with the family name on the gate.

There were lights glowing in nearly every window. A veranda surrounded three sides of the ground floor, which had another wing at the back even wider than the front one. On the second level there was an uncovered porch above the lower veranda, and rising above the steeply pitched, gabled roof was a rectangular tower.

The overall impression was unsettling; even in a neighborhood of grand houses, this one was superior.

Evelyn made an admiring sound. "Mr. Kittering comes from one of Fort Smith's top families, it seems."

"But if we correctly interpreted what Mrs. Tolman said," Rebel added, "he's the black sheep, out of favor with his father, who undoubtedly controls the funds. Evelyn, it truly doesn't matter to me whether he's wealthy or not. He . . . excites me as a *man*."

"I know what you mean. Only now we've seen the house, and my toes are getting numb. Let's save the school to view in daylight, and go home."

The first tiny flakes began to fall as they hurriedly

retraced their steps through the darkness, and Rebel wondered how she could search out Luke Kittering without being obvious about it.

She needn't have worried.

The first person she saw the following evening when she and Evelyn were ushered into the school board meeting was Luke.

# Chapter Thirteen

REBEL'S SPINE STIFFENED IN SHOCK. SHE STOPPED MOVING so abruptly that Mr. Forester, the genial, paunchy man who headed the board, ran into her and murmured an apology.

Her eyes locked, across a broad expanse of polished table, with Luke Kittering's.

He didn't remember her! There was nothing in his face, she thought wildly, to indicate they'd ever met. He was standing, being introduced with the rest of the school board members, giving her a noncommittal smile, the same as the others.

Beside her, Rebel heard Evelyn draw in a breath when Mr. Forester announced, "Mr. Lucas Kittering. He is sitting in tonight for his father, who was unable to be here."

Rebel never heard the names of the others. She sank gratefully onto the proferred chair, knees trembling, and tried desperately to attend to what the chairman was saying.

Luckily, after his introductory remarks, Mr. Forester put the initial questions to Evelyn. Rebel knew her cousin was nervous, feeling as if she were applying for the position under false pretenses, but Rebel had drilled her well.

"Emphasize the positive things. Show them your paintings; if there's a piano available, play and sing for them. Rattle off a little French and tell them you can teach it. Don't mention anything negative, stay calm, and they'll accept you for what you *can* do," Rebel had advised.

Evelyn had absorbed the lesson well. She seemed relaxed, though not overly so, and replied readily to every question put to her. There were nods of approval over the small paintings she had brought to show them, and no one thought it necessary to wheel in a piano for a demonstration of her musical ability. It was as if they took it for granted that anyone so lovely would be talented as well.

Rebel tried to slow her breathing to normal. She *must* be hired for this teaching position, she reminded herself. She had almost no money and certainly nowhere else to go. She would pretend that Luke Kittering did not exist.

Yet there he sat, studying her thoughtfully in a way that sent chills up her spine. He was just as she remembered—tall, even when he was sitting down, with that dark hair that wanted to wave, and the perceptive hazel eyes—Rebel was certain he knew that she was trembling, that her pulse was racing, that her mind had almost deserted her.

The board members were settling back in their chairs, apparently satisfied with their examination of

Evelyn. Then Luke leaned forward, resting his forearms on the table between them.

He spoke directly to Rebel. "One of our problems in hiring and holding teachers, Miss Moran, has been that they have a tendency to leave us abruptly for romantic reasons. Six of our teachers have married since school opened last fall. May we know if you have any current attachment that might prevent your teaching through the rest of the year?"

Rebel stared directly into his eyes and responded quietly, scarcely hearing her own words over the pounding of her heart. "No, sir, I do not."

His sudden smile dazzled her as he leaned back in his chair. "Thank you. I move that we hire both these young ladies and adjourn."

A gentleman with a flourishing white mustache and a goatee frowned a little. "Really, Kittering, we haven't even heard Miss Moran's credentials."

"But they're all written out, aren't they, Forester? We know the young lady assisted a schoolteacher father, that she took over some of his duties when he fell ill. We know she reads and writes exceptionally well—her letter proves that—and she's stated her knowledge of history, geography, and arithmetic. Does someone want her to demonstrate that she can name the capital of Greece, or divide 235 by seven?"

There was a ripple of amusement around the long table. Then Mr. Forester tapped the papers before him. "Luke's right, the young ladies are qualified for the positions, and it seems obvious they are of good moral character. I second Kittering's motion. All agreed say 'aye.'"

There was a ragged chorus of response.

"Any opposed?"

There was only silence.

"Very well. We agree to hire Miss Moran and Miss Bickford to teach at the Belle Grove School, beginning the Monday after Christmas at 8:00 A.M. The salaries have already been discussed. If there is any other business—"

At that moment his words were interrupted by an explosion.

Every man in the room rose to his feet. "What in hell was that?" Forester asked.

"Sounded like dynamite," Luke observed. He walked over to a window, opened it, and leaned out to yell into the street below. "Montmorency, find out what that explosion was!"

"Yes, sir, Mr. Kittering," came the reply in a pronounced Southern accent.

"There's no legitimate reason for anyone setting off dynamite this time of night," one of the men said uncertainly, moving to the window to stand beside Luke.

Rebel was still shaking from the ordeal they'd just been through. Her eyes caught Evelyn's, and the other girl smiled in a knowing way, the message clear: *Luke Kittering is everything you said he was.*

Except that he didn't remember her. Or did he? Rebel wondered, suddenly confused. He hadn't revealed any previous acquaintance, but perhaps his control was simply very good. How well she'd done in that regard she couldn't judge, but she hoped any nervousness she'd displayed would be attributed to worry over being hired.

In the ensuing silence, as several of the board members reached for their hats and coats while the others simply waited, they heard the voice from below.

"Somebody done robbed the City National Bank, Mr. Kittering, sir! Blew the side right out o' it!"

Profane exclamations filled the air, and most of the

men moved swiftly and purposefully toward the door. Even Mr. Forester started that way, only to recall that Evelyn and Rebel were still there.

"They'll be getting up a posse and will need immediate repairs to the bank," he said to them. "Just show up as scheduled, and Mr. Florin, the superintendent, will assign your duties. Excuse me, ladies, I must see how serious this bank robbery is!"

Luke was the last one to move toward the door. His gaze rested upon Rebel, his voice still carrying the formality of a stranger. "Could I offer you a ride home, Miss Moran? Miss Bickford? I have a buggy outside."

Evelyn's dimples flashed. "Thank you, Mr. Kittering, but I believe Mr. Cotton Stirling has the intention of offering me a ride. He, too, has a buggy parked across the street."

Rebel was startled at this revelation, for she had not noticed Cotton on the way in. However, she was more concerned with Luke; he had *not* forgotten her, it seemed. She was both relieved and annoyed.

She gestured with one hand toward the other men thundering down the stairs. "I'm surprised you, too, aren't in a hurry to find out about the bank robbery."

"Chasing gunslingers isn't one of my favorite pastimes," he said. "And if there are some out there on the streets, I'd hardly let a lady walk home alone. Shall we go?"

His fingers touched her arm, flooding Rebel with the recollection of this man kneeling before her, removing her shoe, his hands gently manipulating her foot in the intimate manner that had aroused sensations she had never before experienced.

She was feeling them again now as she allowed herself to be guided out of the meeting room, down the worn stairs, and out into the night. Her heart hammered.

Evelyn was right about Cotton. He had descended from the buggy and now crossed the street toward them. They saw his welcoming grin in the soft glow of the streetlamp.

"Lots of excitement tonight," he said by way of greeting. "A bank robbery, and we've hired two new teachers. You *did* get the jobs, didn't you?"

"Yes, we did," Evelyn told him. "Mr. Kittering has offered us a ride home—"

"But you told him I got my invitation in first, I hope," Cotton said smoothly.

There had certainly been no verbal invitation—Rebel knew she could not have missed *that*—but before Evelyn could say anything Luke relieved her of the need to do so.

"And I'm driving Miss Moran. Good night, Miss Bickford, Cotton. We'll see you two later." With that, Luke guided her again, his fingers creating fire even through her heavy cloak, toward the buggy parked at the curb.

Rebel wondered briefly what Aunt Winnie would say to these arrangements, but she made no protest. She had, after all, come to Fort Smith primarily because of this man, though now the doubts were making her stomach flutter.

It was almost as if he read her mind, for he had no sooner helped her up into the buggy, placed a warm robe over her knees, and picked up the reins before he asked, "Did you by any chance follow me to Fort Smith?"

Taken aback, Rebel was glad that the buggy was covered, making it dark, so that he couldn't see her flushed face. "Follow you?" she echoed, almost in a croak. "We came because we learned there was a need for teachers, and we needed to support ourselves—"

He held the reins loosely, making no move to urge

the horse forward. "I was hoping you'd come because of me," he said.

The man was outrageous. No gentleman, Rebel thought, feeling out of her element in handling this situation, would put a lady into such an embarrassing predicament.

He leaned toward her in the sheltering dimness, the better to see her face. "I did try to find you in New York, you know. The best I could, considering they wouldn't let me out of the hospital bed until my father and the ambulance took me to the station to come home. I wrote a note to you and gave it to one of the nurses, only she couldn't find you. No one was home at your uncle's house, and as she was turning away a neighbor informed her that the Bickfords had sold the place and moved away, but she didn't know where."

So much for her own efforts to leave a clear trail, Rebel thought. Yet she still could not admit that she'd been so brazen as to attempt it, or to follow him.

"I heard you'd been hurt," she said, unable to look into his face. "It must have been serious."

"Serious enough to keep me unconscious for hours, and too groggy to remember much for several days more. By the time I might have been able to get around on my own, Pa had brought me home, and my mother called in the doctor and insisted I stay housebound for another week." His tone was dry. "That tells my story. I'd be interested in hearing yours. It's extraordinary that you wound up in Fort Smith. How did you learn about the openings at the school?"

This was not quite what she'd imagined their meeting would be like. "I . . . I read an advertisement in the newspaper," Rebel said.

"In a New York paper?" He was astonished, or pretended to be.

She could hardly claim that, not when a query to Mr.

**145**

Forester would prove her a liar. "No . . . Actually, it was . . . was in that scrap of paper you wrote the note on. The night Millie brought you the . . . the food."

There was a moment's silence and then, "You *were* the one who sent it out, weren't you? I might have known."

"Why—why were you there?" Rebel blurted. She suddenly remembered the suspicions she had had—momentary, to be sure—about his connection with Jubal Hake. She was confused, excited, and upset, all at the same time.

"I was waiting for a business acquaintance, and we got our meeting place mixed up," he said at once. "I was on the wrong block, waited until I was half-frozen, and he never did come. Seemed like that was mostly what I did in that damned place, wait around for somebody, freezing my . . . ears off. That was how I got hurt, too. I'd made a mistake when I wrote down the directions for meeting this fellow, but I didn't have any other way to contact him. I'd spent another evening standing around in the cold, finally gave up and headed back for my hotel, and someone hit me over the head. I wasn't found until morning, when a police officer was dispatched to investigate my body in the alley and saw to it I was taken to the hospital."

"It was freezing cold that night," Rebel remembered, shivering. "It's a wonder you didn't die."

"I might have, but I didn't. Are you cold now? There's another robe back here—" He swiveled on the seat, then swung back. "Damnation, there's supposed to be, but someone's removed it. Well, we'll have to make do with the one we have, and maybe an arm around you would help."

Was there no end to his audacity? Rebel knew she should not allow such familiarity, yet the protest stuck in her throat when he drew her close to his own

146

warmth, and flicked the reins lightly so that the horse began to move. Slowly, very slowly. She wondered what Aunt Winnie would say if Evelyn arrived home ahead of her.

Again he seemed to read her mind. "I shouldn't wonder if Cotton takes your cousin the long way home. There's no hurry, is there? It's only a little before eight."

What was the proper response to that? Evelyn would know—Evelyn knew things like that by instinct as well as by upbringing, but Rebel had never before shared a buggy with a good-looking man who dared to put his arm around her. It would be foolish, however, to insist that he remove it, she supposed. It *was* very cold.

"I think . . . Aunt Winnie will not expect us to be very late," she said faintly.

"Surely she won't begin to worry before nine, will she?"

The constriction in her chest made breathing difficult. Nine? An hour from now? What did he intend to do in the intervening time?

A moment later she found out.

# Chapter Fourteen

"I DREAMED ABOUT YOU," LUKE SAID. "WHEN I FINALLY woke up and realized I was in a hospital with a head injury, I thought at first that's all you were, a dream. And when I realized you were real, you were gone."

The tightness in her chest was nearly unbearable. She had deliberately sought him out, over a distance of hundreds of miles, and she'd made up dozens of fantasies about him that all ended with her in Luke Kittering's arms.

Yet now that the actuality was upon her she was terrified. She had not expected things to happen so fast; that his arm would be holding her close, that his mouth would be descending over her own . . .

She gasped and drew away, aware that the horse plodded along on its own with no particular guidance, aware of the lean male body touching her own, of the

148

hand that had somehow relinquished the reins and found one of hers beneath the robe.

"Please—" She wasn't ready for this, not yet. It was too fast, it was no longer a romantic fantasy but a situation that could quickly get out of control. In fact, she felt that it already was out of control.

Luke stopped moving, eased the pressure of his arm around her, yet continued to hold her hand. She wondered if he could feel the pulse pounding in it.

"I'm sorry. I've frightened you, and I didn't mean to do that. Rebel, I thought you felt it, too, the same thing I did."

Suffocating, she could make no response, but the hand she'd lifted free of the robe to fend him off was still rigid against his chest.

Reluctantly, Luke let her go. "Too much, too soon. All right. I hadn't realized you were so . . . inexperienced. Didn't any man ever kiss you before?" Luckily he didn't wait for an answer to that. "How old are you?"

That brought her out of her panic. "I'm not a child," she said stiffly. "I'm seventeen. And it has nothing to do with my age. I simply find it . . . inappropriate . . . to allow intimacies when we are practically strangers."

For a moment he made no response, and then he laughed. Under other circumstances, she might have thought it a delicious chuckle.

"Oh, no, Rebel Moran, we're not strangers," he told her softly. "We were destined for each other; you just haven't admitted it yet. But you will. And in the meantime, I'll observe the proprieties. I'll take you home, unscathed, unravished."

He was making fun of her, and anger took some of the edge off the other things she was feeling. "Thank you," she acknowledged, and hated herself for allowing her voice to waver.

It was not until he had walked her to the door and they stood together on the deeply shadowed porch as Rebel groped for her key that Luke broke his self-imposed reserve.

"Before you go in—you'll have to wait a moment, anyway, because Cotton's buggy is just coming down the street, and you won't want to explain why you arrived ahead of your cousin, will you?—I want you to know what you've missed tonight."

And then, to her total astonishment and consternation, Luke drew her into his arms and lowered his mouth to cover hers.

Fireworks on the Fourth of July. Christmas morning when she was a little girl. A storm in summer, with lightning flashing and thunder reverberating across the heavens. And something more, far more.

The awakening of sensations that her previous encounter with Luke had only hinted at; liquid fire in her limbs, culminating in an explosion in the secret parts of her body that robbed her of the will to resist.

My God, Rebel thought dimly, lost in rapture, if his kiss does this to me, what can follow the kiss?

Luke released her slowly, his breath still warm against her skin in the cold air.

"Miss Moran, ma'am, if you want to be courted slowly and properly, that's what you shall have. Just remember, though, that you're only delaying the inevitable . . . and depriving both of us in the meantime."

She felt deprived already. She was glad it was so dark that he couldn't tell how successful he had been in accomplishing that.

The other buggy had drawn up behind Luke's, and Evelyn and Cotton got out and came slowly up the walk. Luke no longer lingered on the porch.

"Good night, Rebel Moran," he told her softly, and murmured to the pair he passed on the steps.

"Do you have your key, Rebel?" Evelyn asked. She, too, sounded breathless, though less in a state of shock than her cousin.

"Key . . . uh, yes, right here," Rebel said, and a moment later let them into the entryway.

The house was warm and redolent with the aroma of gingerbread. They followed the sounds of low voices and discovered Winnie and Mrs. Tolman and the other female boarders in the parlor, having tea and cake.

Winnie looked up anxiously, then interpreted their bright eyes, pink cheeks, and smiling mouths to be the direct result of their interview. "It went all right? They hired you?"

For a moment Rebel couldn't make out what her aunt was talking about. Fortunately Evelyn was still functioning mentally.

"Oh, yes, there was no trouble about that at all." She pulled off her outer wraps, turning her back momentarily on her mother so that the words were muffled. "Several of the gentlemen gave us a ride home, thank goodness. It's so *cold* out there!" She spun around again, looking radiant. "Did you hear about the bank robbery?"

"Mr. Sylvester just came back with the news," Mrs. Tolman reported, as Winnie got up to cut them each a slice of the warm gingerbread, "Cleaned out the vault at the City National Bank, they did." She clucked her disapproval. "Second bank robbery in two months, it is. Well, they caught the robbers the last time, and no doubt they'll catch these, as well. Judge Parker will see to it they're brought to justice."

Rebel joined Evelyn on an elegant but stiffly uncomfortable sofa opposite the fire. She didn't want the gingerbread, or the tea that their hostess poured, but she ate because she didn't want Aunt Winnie to question such a peculiarity. She would have liked nothing better than to go upstairs and relive the events of this evening, sort out her mixed feelings, and rekindle, perhaps, the emotions she had experienced. There was no way she could do that, however. She tried to force her brain to behave normally, her tongue to speak.

"I remember seeing his name in that newspaper. The headline said, 'Will Buck Sloan be number something-or-other for the hanging judge?' and I wondered what it meant," Rebel managed to say.

"Hanging judge?" Winnie echoed uneasily.

"Oh, my, yes," Mrs. Tolman replied. "You've never heard of Judge Parker? I'm surprised. He's been written up in papers all over the country because he's hanged as many as half a dozen scoundrels at a time. You'll see the gallows when you go over by the courthouse and the jail—only one in the country, they say, where the hangman can do six at a time."

Winnie lost her appetite for the last bite of ginger-bread on her plate. "They hanged six poor souls at a time?"

Mrs. Tolman's pleasure in the cake was undiminished. "Well, I'd hardly call them poor souls. Murderers and rapists, they were. I tell you, when Mr. Tolman and I came here to Fort Smith back in 1870, a more unlawful lot you never saw. We didn't live in this house, we had a little cottage over on Third Street, near the brewery then. I was absolutely terrified whenever Mr. Tolman went off and left me there, expecting to be murdered in my bed, or worse."

Miss Helen nodded. "Bank robberies once a week, in those days," she agreed. "Margaret and I didn't know if we'd be scalped by the Indians or kidnapped by the bandits. Neither of them happened," she added, almost with a note of disappointment.

Miss Margaret sipped at her tea from a cup with hand-painted forget-me-nots. "This was a wild frontier in those days," she agreed.

"It sounds as if it still is," Winnie murmured.

"Oh, there's nothing like the crime there used to be," Mrs. Tolman assured her earnestly. "And it wasn't only the gunslingers that were the problem. The judges and the marshals weren't much better. They took bribes and never punished anybody who had the money to pay them off. Graft and corruption made this territory the hell-hole of America, before Judge Parker came. That was in '75, wasn't it, Margaret?"

"That's right. Fine, good-looking young man he was, come with his wife and two little boys, and it wasn't long before everybody found out *he* couldn't be bribed, and he intended to enforce the laws."

"Was only here a week or so," Miss Helen contributed, rocking in her chair close to the fire, helping herself to a second square of gingerbread, "when the judge showed everybody what he was made of. First day he mounted the bench he heard eighteen murderers, and fifteen of 'em were convicted. That had never happened before in history! He sentenced eight of 'em to die on the gallows, and the people came from all over the territory to see it happen, and newspapermen from St. Louis and Kansas City, mind you. Pa figured there was more than five thousand people packed in the jail yard to see it. Margaret and I wanted to go watch, too, but nobody'd let us, even though we were grown women by then. Pa said it was no place for females, though there were plenty of women in the crowd."

Winnie patted her lips with a napkin. "I should think your father was right."

"Well, hanging six of them at once made everybody

sit up and take notice," Mrs. Tolman continued. "A woman could walk the streets in Fort Smith in daylight without being afraid she'd be attacked. They still rob banks once in a while, and of course there're still murders and robberies, but it's nothing like it was in the old days. They may call him 'Bloody Parker,' or 'Butcher Parker' or 'the Hanging Judge,' but he's made this territory safer for white folks and Indians alike, he has. If it wasn't for him, I reckon I'd have gone back East when Mr. Tolman died. This was no place for an unprotected female before Judge Parker took over the bench."

Winnie rose, pressing a hand to her bosom. "I had no idea what sort of place this is," she said. "My, that was pretty good gingerbread for my first try—with that new recipe, I mean—wasn't it? But I don't believe I care for any more. I think I'll go on up to bed. You'd best come along shortly too, girls; it's getting late."

Rebel was on her feet at once. "Yes, I'll go up with you, Aunt Winnie. Hold my arm going up the stairs, why don't you? We don't want any more accidents like Mrs. Tolman's."

At the top of the stairs, hearing Evelyn making her good nights below, Winnie pressed her fingers into Rebel's arm. "Do you think it was a mistake to come here?" she asked. "I lived so many years in New York, where it was civilized . . ."

"Crimes are committed in New York, too," Rebel told her. "And you heard what they said. Law and order has come to Fort Smith. There's nothing to worry about. Evelyn and I both have paychecks coming within the month; we have a place to live; and so far your cooking has been a roaring success. We're going to be fine here, Aunt Winnie, really we are."

Inside her room, glad that for the moment she was alone, Rebel stood before the mirror and stared at her own face, astonished that it revealed none of the turmoil within her. How could it be the same—oval and pale now that the cold-generated rosiness had faded, the eyes gray-green and thickly lashed, the mouth no different from what it had always been . . . ?

But it was, of course, different. Her lips still felt scorched from Luke's kiss. And just remembering sent the same heat flooding through her.

She wished they had enough money so that she didn't have to share a room with her cousin. She wanted to go to bed and lie there in the dark, reliving everything from the moment she'd walked into the meeting room and faced Luke Kittering. She wanted to brush her mouth with her fingertips and imagine his lips there once more; to touch the places where the fire had been the greatest, the places he had made her aware of with no more contact than that kiss.

Evelyn glided in and leaned against the door she had closed behind her. Her color remained high, her eyes bright in the lamplight. "I think I'm in love, Rebel. Do you think it's possible to fall in love at first sight?"

Rebel turned from the mirror, unbuttoning her shirt-waist in preparation for going to bed. "Yes, I think so," she said quietly, reluctant to be drawn away from her own musings. She folded her garments over the chair, turning her back to her cousin, reaching for the flannel gown that was one of the few things remaining from the wardrobe she'd brought from Lyons Falls.

Evelyn didn't bother to fold her own clothes before she dropped them on the opposite chair, oblivious of the wrinkles she was setting in them, forgetting that there was no longer a maid to press them. "I don't think I've ever been so happy in my whole life. He kissed me, Rebel. On the mouth, a proper romantic kiss. Do you think me an awful hussy to have allowed him to do it?"

The few coals in the grate were already dying down; the room was chilled. Rebel tugged the nightshift over her head and crawled into bed; the sheets were icy, for the room had not been heated during the day, but she hoped Evelyn would not want to snuggle up for warmth. She wanted to be separate, apart, private, for this very important night. She wanted to let her imagination run riot as best it might within the boundaries of her limited knowledge about such matters as romance and love and physical pleasures.

Evelyn stood looking down at her, exquisite in her own lacy gown, her auburn hair let down and flowing loosely about her shoulders. "Rebel?"

Unwillingly, Rebel allowed her thoughts to be pushed aside. "Yes?"

"Was he nice, Mr. Kittering? Did he . . . try to kiss you?"

Rebel didn't want to talk about it, not even to Evelyn. Nor did she want to hear every detail of her cousin's ride home.

"I have a splitting headache," she lied. "Please put out the light, Evelyn."

"Oh, dear. Here I've been rattling on about my own bliss, and not thinking that you might have had a disappointing evening. I'm sorry, Rebel, really I am."

She lifted the lamp and blew into the chimney. Rebel heard the soft sound as the lamp was set upon the table, and then felt the bed give beneath her cousin's weight.

"Good night," Evelyn whispered.

Feeling churlish but able to control it, Rebel murmured, "Good night."

Evelyn stayed on her own side of the bed, and after a few minutes her breathing slowed and became regular. Only then did the tension begin to go out of Rebel.

Only then did she allow herself the luxury of going over the evening in her mind, allow the happiness to swell within her, regardless of the accompanying doubts.

"Before you go in," he'd said, "I want you to know what you've missed tonight."

And then, "Miss Moran, ma'am, if you want to be courted slowly and properly, that's what you shall have. Just remember, though, that you're only delaying the inevitable . . . and depriving both of us in the meantime."

As she drifted toward sleep, Rebel's mouth curved in a smile. Perhaps the next time she would not deprive either of them quite so much.

# Chapter Fifteen

On Christmas Eve all of Mrs. Tolman's boarders gathered in the parlor after an excellent supper (Rebel hoped her list of recipes didn't run out before Aunt Winnie got the hang of cooking) and sang carols. Miss Margaret played the spinet and led the singing in a clear contralto.

Later, before a cheerful fire, they exchanged gifts. Most of these were small things: a handkerchief, a pressed flower, a pen. There was little money to buy anything that wasn't a necessity. Aunt Winnie had baked fruitcakes as gifts for everyone in an agony over what to do if they turned out badly. Thanks to Rebel's expertise, the cakes were warmly received, and Mrs. Tolman insisted on sharing hers for the holiday celebration.

Rebel had embroidered initials on handkerchiefs for

each of them, a simple project, and she was completely unprepared to open the small box from her cousin.

Inside the deep blue, velvet-lined container sparkled a pair of earrings that were surely genuine diamonds.

Stunned, Rebel stared at them, then at Evelyn. "But how . . . where . . . ?"

Evelyn laughed with delight. "I knew you'd like them. I saved them from the things that had to be sold, just as I did those I kept for myself. We couldn't raise enough to pay off all the debts anyway, so what did a couple pairs of earrings matter? Put them on, Rebel."

Neither the Lovell sisters nor Mrs. Tolman had ever owned diamonds; they admired them endlessly when Rebel looked at her own image in the mirror in the dining room. Would Luke be impressed by them, she wondered? They made her feel as if not only the gems in her ears glittered, but that her entire person sparkled with energy and beauty in a way she had never known before, not even the night of the disastrous party. That time the jewels had been borrowed; these were her own, and it made all the difference.

As the evening grew late, they debated adding another log to the fire. "Maybe we'd best just call it a night," Miss Margaret sighed. "Tomorrow will be a busy day, too."

Rebel was not reluctant to see this day end. Each day that went by brought her that much closer to the time when she would see Luke again; although no specific engagement had been made, she'd taken it for granted that she would not see him until after the holidays were over. His younger sister was having a big wedding, and naturally Luke would be with his family for Christmas. But after that . . .

Mr. Sylvester, who had scarcely said a word all evening except to thank the others for his handkerchiefs and hand-knit socks, stepped to the door and looked out into the night. "Snowing again," he said with satisfaction. "Always did like a white Christmas. Peace on earth, good will towards men."

At that moment, sounding anything but peaceful, there was a volley of shots.

"Good heavens, what now?" Mrs. Tolman peered out over her boarder's shoulder.

"Maybe the Daltons robbed another bank," Miss Margaret said hopefully. Rebel had already decided that the sisters' lives were so dull that they looked forward from one catastrophe to the next as a means of livening things up.

"No way to say it was the Daltons robbed the last one," Mr. Sylvester grunted. There was nothing to be seen out there, though a moment later there were two more pistol shots, sharp and clear in the cold air. "Might be somebody robbing a bank, though, at that." Shivering, he withdrew from the open doorway. "Maybe I'll just put on my coat and hat and mosey over toward Garrison Avenue and see what's going on."

Winnie watched him go in mingled curiosity and dismay. "If there was shooting going on, it's the last place *I'd* head for," she observed.

"Oh, Mr. Sylvester always keeps us informed," Miss Helen said, unworried. "I think I'll have another cup of tea and wait up until he comes back."

Winnie decided she didn't want to hear about it, whatever the ruckus was. Rebel joined her as they went up to bed, but she was unable to sleep. The precious earrings in their velvet box sat on her bedside table, and she wondered if the courting Luke had mentioned would include taking her anywhere that she could wear the midnight-blue velvet gown that was her favorite of those altered for her from Evelyn's cast-offs. The diamonds would be the perfect finishing touch to the most beautiful dress Rebel had ever owned.

It was nearly an hour later when Evelyn finally came up. Rebel was still awake.

"Did he find out what was going on?"

The fire had gone out, and Evelyn shivered as she began to undress. "More or less. There was some sort of shoot-out at one of the saloons. One man was hurt badly enough to be taken to the hospital. Saloon—the very word has a wild western frontier sound, doesn't it? It's like being set down in the pages of one of those penny dreadful novels—it's rather exciting!"

"I suppose so, if you aren't the one who was shot," Rebel said, burrowing deeper under the quilts.

Christmas morning, as they all prepared to go to church, the doorbell rang. Rebel was coming down the stairs when she heard Mrs. Tolman's excited voice. "Miss Rebel, it's for you!"

As she reached the foot of the stairs, Rebel was astonished to be presented with a bouquet of red and white roses, secured with a wide crimson satin ribbon.

"Imagine, the florist coming out on Christmas morning to make the delivery! And that was old Gunder himself! You must have an ardent admirer, indeed! Imagine the price of roses in the dead of winter!"

Rebel accepted the flowers, blushing at this public announcement of intent. She read the card that accompanied them. "Merry Christmas," it said, and was signed in the hand she had first seen weeks ago in New York City.

"Rebel! Whoever—oh!" Evelyn teetered on the stairs above. "From Luke Kittering? You lucky girl!"

Winnie appeared behind her. "Who's Mr. Kittering?"

"He's one of the men who interviewed us for the

161

school position," Evelyn informed her. "One of the handsomest ones, actually. And he's from a good family, isn't he, Mrs. Tolman?"

The mistress of the house displayed mixed feelings. "Oh, that he is. The family is most respected." Was there a faint emphasis on the word *family?*

If so, only Rebel seemed to hear it.

"I'll get you a vase for them," Mrs. Tolman offered, heading for the kitchen.

Rebel quickly followed her, to press upon her a question after they were out of Winnie's hearing range.

"Mr. Kittering *is* respectable, isn't he, Mrs. Tolman? I mean, I only just met him, and he seemed very . . . nice."

The older woman reached high onto a shelf for a vase, her expression mildly troubled. "Well, as a boy, he got into one scrape after another. Him and that Cotton Stirling. You wouldn't believe some of the tricks those two got up to, until Judge Parker finally took them in hand and pointed out to them where they were headed if they didn't mend their ways. Straightened Cotton right out, he did, but Luke didn't ever come all the way around.

"Not that he's done anything terrible in recent years," she added quickly, seeing Rebel's alarm. "But the whole town knows Adam Kittering, his father, has been on the verge of throwing him out of the house a few times. Adam heads his own bank, and the other boys followed him into it, but Luke won't set foot inside the place except to make a deposit or a withdrawal. Word is he even threatened to take his banking business elsewhere if Adam didn't let up on him, though his mama stood up for him and held off *that* shame to his father. Luke's the oldest and should be setting an example for the others, but . . . well, dear, I wouldn't be doing my duty if I didn't tell you that Luke hasn't always kept the best company. That bunch that was involved in the shooting last night—Luke's been known to drink with them from time to time."

Rebel wondered if she looked as upset as she felt. "You aren't saying Luke Kittering is a . . . a criminal, are you?"

"No, no," Mrs. Tolman said hastily, though there was indecision on her pleasant countenance. "Only that he's careless of the company he keeps. He and Cotton used to be best friends all the time they were growing up, but they don't hardly speak to each other any more, they say. Going their separate ways, you know."

Odd. Rebel hadn't had that impression the night of the school board meeting, not at all. Yet perhaps the young men had been on their best behavior to impress her and Evelyn.

Mrs. Tolman filled the vase with water, and Rebel put the flowers into it, her fingers feeling stiff and clumsy. Her heart was beating at an accelerated rate.

"Mrs. Tolman, I'd appreciate your candor. I'm a stranger here, and I've no wish to . . . to get myself into an unfortunate situation. Do you think I might damage my own reputation and jeopardize my position at the school by allowing Mr. Kittering to . . . call upon me?"

"Oh, my stars, that does put me on the spot," Mrs. Tolman said, dampening Rebel's spirits even further. Then she smiled and patted the girl's shoulder.

"Well, I'm no oracle, Miss Rebel, but I'll tell you this: Was I forty years younger, and a man as attractive as Luke Kittering wanted to shower attentions on me, I'd let 'im. More'n one man was a bit wild in his youth, including my own Mr. Tolman. And there's nothing better to settle a man down than a good woman, that's common knowledge. Could you settle Luke and bring him around to his pa's way of thinking, no doubt the entire community would be grateful to you. Not to mention the Kitterings."

It sounded like a monumental responsibility, and one Rebel wasn't at all sure she wanted to undertake. Settle him down, yes, she'd be delighted to do that, but her own feeling was that working in a bank, even one owned by one's father, would be a less than satisfying way to spend a lifetime. On that score her sympathies were with Luke.

Mrs. Tolman was smiling encouragingly. "If he's attracted to you, he's showing uncommon good sense. It's plain to see you're a young lady of good breeding, and I shouldn't wonder his folks would be delighted to see him march down the aisle with such an acceptable female. Now, no need to blush—I know that's getting the cart before the horse, so to speak, but when a man sends a girl hothouse roses on Christmas Day, why, I'd say he's been smitten. Just you keep him in line, and I've no doubt it will all come out splendidly."

That, it appeared, was the sum total of the older woman's advice. Carrying the vase of flowers back toward the front of the house, Rebel wondered how exactly to do that—to keep Lucas in line. She didn't even know what acceptable behavior was in that regard. Not kissing on such slight acquaintance, probably, though she couldn't be sure of that. She knew perfectly well that many people preached one thing and practiced something else, and that her own parents had fallen in love almost at first sight. She'd heard the story, laughingly told, of how they'd been caught kissing when Ned Moran had walked Beryl Westin home from choir practice two days after they'd met.

And she knew, by the way Luke had touched her, that what he had in mind was not simply a few stolen kisses. She herself was torn between fear of what came next and an overwhelming desire to find out.

164

Evelyn had had no more experience in romance than she had. Yet Rebel thought her cousin would have the proper instincts. Yes, she thought, placing the roses on the dining room table until they could be carried upstairs after church, she might have to confide in Evelyn simply to get the advice she needed on how far a properly brought-up young lady allowed a gentleman to go when she wanted to wind up at the altar.

For a few more hours, though, she would bask in her private thoughts, and hope that when the time came Evelyn would say nothing to dispel her illusions.

# Chapter Sixteen

ADAM KITTERING STOOD IN THE SPACIOUS ENTRYWAY AS his wife descended the stairway, his mouth tightening as he saw that she was alone. "Where's Luke?"

Frances Kittering smoothed on her gloves, smiling. "I don't think he's going to church with us." There was a touch of gray in her brown hair, but no one would have looked at her and thought *old*. She was still too pretty, too vivacious, and too stylish.

Her husband enjoyed looking at her now as much as he had over three decades earlier, when they'd met, but even her loveliness did not erase his frown. "He can't be bothered, even on Christmas?"

"I think he was out rather late last night," Frances said, reaching the parquet floor and putting her fingertips on her husband's sleeve. "He's young, Adam. There'll be time for church-going one of these days. He's a good boy, really he is, darling. It's only that he's as stubborn as his father, and the two of you together don't always mix."

"Never is more like it," Adam grunted, but as usual her touch had a soothing effect. "Well, come on, let's go then."

Upstairs, Luke stood at the window overlooking the drive. When the buggy had departed, he turned to stare at himself in the floor-length mirror, but there was nothing of vanity in the action.

He wore only dark trousers. His pale torso was firmly muscled, broad through the shoulders, tapering at the waist. But he wasn't looking at his musculature; his attention was on the improvised bandage on his left shoulder, through which blood had seeped and then dried.

He supposed the dressing ought to be changed. Bloody wounds were not unfamiliar to him, and as a rule he didn't shrink from them, but he suspected it was going to hurt like hell to uncover this one.

A fire blazed on the hearth, and steam rose lazily from the tub of hot water before it. Luke sighed and bent over to scoop up enough water to drench the bulky dressing, hoping it would soak loose enough so that when he pulled it off the whole thing wouldn't start bleeding again.

He'd let it soak while he bathed, he decided, but before he got into the tub there was one more chore to take care of, in case a servant showed up before he was finished.

He reached for the shirt he'd dropped on the floor last night and threw it into the flames. Eventually someone might notice that it was missing, but it couldn't be helped. Better missing than seen with a bullet hole.

He lowered himself into the hot water with caution, slopping more of it over the bandaging.

167

Then, with the evidence disposed of and the situation as much under control as he could manage at the moment, Luke relaxed in his bath and imagined Rebel Moran's face when old Gunder delivered the roses.

After awhile he forgot the ache in his shoulder, and when he finally stripped off the dressing and examined the wound in the mirror, he decided it wasn't as bad as he'd feared.

If he wore a coat to dinner, chances were nobody would notice that his left shoulder was bulkier than his right one.

For a few minutes more, he allowed himself the luxury of daydreaming about Rebel Moran before it was time to ride out of town for his rendezvous with Cotton.

Rebel had pinned one of the rosebuds on the lapel of her dark green worsted coat in the hope that Luke might show up at services and see it.

He did not, however. She had trouble concentrating on the service, and noticed that Evelyn, too, kept scanning the congregation.

There were only strangers. When the churchgoers poured out through the double doors into the brilliant sunshine, Rebel was still hoping, though Mrs. Tolman had told her that the Kitterings attended a different church. She was sure Luke would have guessed that the newcomers would attend church with their landlady, and after those roses she thought he would have enough initiative to determine which church that would be.

The sun glittered off the snow that had fallen the previous night, making it hard to see for the glare. No one seemed in a hurry to depart for their Christmas dinners, and they milled about, talking.

There were numerous exchanges of holiday best wishes, but the overriding subject was of the shooting the previous night. "That's the fourth shooting at the Ox Bow in as many weeks," one woman asserted. "If you ask me, they ought to close it down."

Someone else, obviously a friend of the proprietor, protested, "You can't blame John Sykes because his customers get out of hand. He's only trying to make a living, same as anyone else."

"Well, whose fault is it he draws that kind of customer, I'd like to know? There's plenty of saloons in Fort Smith, and not all of 'em are the scene of shoot-outs, one after the other! Bessie lives right next door, and she said there was men running in all directions before the marshals got there. There was blood in the snow right beside Bessie's porch! What kind of thing is that for young'uns to see on Christmas Eve?"

Rebel held up a hand to shield her eyes, but there was no tall figure on the edge of the crowd. No buggy waiting on the street. Beside her, Evelyn murmured knowingly, "Well, what do we expect? They both have families. Today is a day for families."

Though this was true, it was disappointing all the same. No doubt, Rebel comforted herself, Luke had sent the flowers because he'd known he couldn't be with her.

She held that thought as she helped with the dinner preparations—Winnie had long since forgotten what was involved in stuffing and roasting a turkey, which had gone into the oven earlier, and she kept giving Rebel grateful smiles as they worked together in the kitchen—and during the meal, which was so heavy that afterward everyone but Rebel and Evelyn needed to nap.

"I think I'll take a walk," Evelyn decided, and Rebel was quick to join her.

Their path, inevitably, led past the Kittering house.

It was even more impressive in daylight than it had been at night. There were holly wreaths at all the ground-floor windows, and buggies parked in the circular drive. Luke was the last of the Kittering offspring to remain single, and it appeared the others had all come home for the holiday.

Rebel felt a twinge of grief, remembering past Christmases with her parents, and then with only her father. This year there was no one except Winnie and Evelyn. She was grateful for them, but it wasn't the same.

"Let's cut over to G Street," Evelyn suggested. There was a note in her voice that brought Rebel immediately out of her own reverie.

"Why G Street?" And then, glancing at her cousin's laughing face, set off so vividly by the deep crimson outfit that redheads weren't supposed to be able to wear, Rebel guessed. "Cotton's house? You've learned where he lives?"

"It's easy to learn anything from Miss Helen, and the poor old soul doesn't even know she's telling you. There's no name on the gate at the Stirlings, but it's large and brick and there's a huge birdbath in the front yard."

Rebel cast a final look at the Kittering place as they veered away from it. A curtain dropped back into place on the second floor and she wondered, flustered, if Luke had noticed her. "I'd hate to end up like Miss Helen. I wonder if she ever had a suitor."

"She says she had several," Evelyn replied. "The only one she really cared about went off to California during the gold rush and she never even heard what

170

happened to him. She has one last precious letter, saying he'd staked a claim, and that he'd send for her when he found the gold. And nothing more. She waited and waited, and never heard from him again. Isn't that sad?"

Rebel shivered. "And she never found anyone else. Yes, it is sad."

It was impossible to stay depressed, however, over someone else's lost love of nearly fifty years ago. Not when they were young, and had met attractive men who were clearly drawn to them.

"I wonder," Evelyn speculated, "how quickly Mama would allow me to become engaged."

This was the opportunity Rebel had both anticipated and dreaded to introduce her own dilemma. She could not plunge directly into it, however.

"You think Cotton will propose? After only two meetings?"

"Well, not immediately, perhaps. But before long." Evelyn's smile took on a sensuality Rebel had not previously seen. "He's made it clear that he wants me . . . *that way* . . . and I certainly won't allow any improprieties before an engagement."

Rebel moistened her lips and then was sorry, because in this cold they would only chap. "How do you decide," she had to clear her throat, "what *is* an impropriety?" She flushed in embarrassment. "I mean, I know I must sound incredibly stupid, but my own mama died without giving me any . . . advice about such matters, and I don't think it ever occurred to Father that I was old enough to be concerned about courting and . . . and marriage."

Evelyn laughed. "Oh, Mama's been giving me advice since I was twelve. Not that I intend to take it all, you understand, or I'd never have let Cotton kiss me when

171

he brought me home the other night. 'Kissing is for betrothed couples,' Mama said, but good heavens. How are you going to know if you want to become engaged if you've never kissed a man? I didn't even know if I'd like it."

"But you did," Rebel guessed, eliciting another peal of laughter.

"Of course! I think even Mama would allow holding hands, though probably not while unchaperoned in a buggy." She imitated Winnie's speech. "'But a lady goes no further than that.' Unless, of course, she wants to keep the man interested and coming back for more."

"But how much more do you allow?" Rebel asked, trying not to sound as desperate as she felt.

"Well, never *all the way,* of course. If a man gets everything that he wants, why would he need to marry a girl?"

"Because he loves her? Because he wants to live with her, and raise a family with her?" Rebel suggested uncertainly.

"Of course. But Mama says he often doesn't know he wants those things until he's been driven mad with desire first."

Rebel had lost interest in the handsome houses they were passing, was no longer aware of the snow crunching under her feet. "Did she really say that? Mad with desire?"

"More or less. Perhaps she phrased it more discreetly, but that was what she meant. She cautioned me against allowing liberties, but she made them sound deliciously tempting."

Evelyn came to such an abrupt halt that Rebel ran into her. "You know, I can't help but wonder how she knows all that. I never had the impression that she and Papa were ever passionately in love. Theirs was an arranged marriage, and he was considerably older than

172

she. Good heavens, do you suppose *Mama* once had a real lover? A romantic one, before Papa?"

Rebel did not know much more about what to do than before she had begun this conversation. "So what do you intend to allow Cotton to do? Besides kiss you?"

Evelyn began to walk again. "Well, certainly that. I must say it was an extraordinarily pleasant experience. I sort of . . . tingled, all over, if you can imagine that."

Rebel could imagine it only too well.

"I rather think that . . . that anything one does without removing any of one's clothes should be acceptable—with a man one has every intention of marrying, I mean."

Still not entirely certain what this would entail, Rebel was reluctant to further expose her own ignorance. "I suppose you're right."

"And there is the object of my affections now," Evelyn said gaily, lifting a gloved hand to wave. "My, that is a nice house, isn't it? Not quite as grand as the Kittering place, but very elegant and gracious. Every bit as nice as our house in New York."

Cotton Stirling was just arriving; with unmistakable pleasure he dismounted and dropped the reins around a corner post on the fence in order to greet them.

"Good afternoon! I knew I was going to be lucky today, and here you are." The words were said to Evelyn before he even seemed to notice that Rebel was with her; then he nodded in her direction as well. "Exploring the town, are you?"

"Oh yes. We thought we might not have much time for that, once school starts. Is this where you live?"

"This is it. The Stirling homestead. You look cold. Why don't you come in and have a hot drink, meet my mother and my sisters, if they've recovered from their Christmas dinner?"

Rebel shrank back at once, but Evelyn was already tugging at her sleeve. "Of course, we'd love to meet your family, wouldn't we, Rebel?"

And so, a moment later, Rebel found herself in the foyer of a decidedly handsome house, being introduced to the blonde Mrs. Stirling and her three equally blonde and lovely daughters.

They were ushered into a drawing room, where tea was served and the Stirlings made them welcome. Rebel didn't *feel* welcome; she felt uncomfortable and out of place. It was clear that Cotton favored Evelyn, and it was she upon whom the Stirling females centered their attention, though the younger daughter, Elsie, gazed with frank curiosity upon Rebel.

Cotton's mother was smiling, gracious, and friendly. "We're happy to meet our new teachers," she said. "It is so difficult to keep them for long."

The words had been directed primarily at Evelyn, but it was Rebel who responded. "Oh? Why is that? Is the position difficult, then? Or the pay insufficient to live on?"

For a moment Mrs. Stirling's composure wavered. "Why, I should imagine a thrifty young woman could manage on the salary. And of course not all children are cooperative and satisfying to work with, I suppose." She beamed at her own brood as if they were naturally the exceptions. "But I think it is mostly a matter of Fort Smith being very nearly a frontier town. Oh, we have many modern conveniences, but we *are* on the edge of Indian territory, and unattached females of sensitivity may not feel safe here."

One of the sisters—what was her name, Gertrude?—interjected, "Either the teachers get married and have babies, or if they're from back East they go home because of all the shooting. Even Judge Parker can't make the men stop drinking and shooting."

"Trudy!" her mother exclaimed in mild reproach.

"Am I not supposed to mention babies? But that's what happens when a woman gets married, is it not?"

The youngest sister, the giggly one, changed the subject. "I think Fort Smith is an exciting town. Mostly the bandits shoot each other—only once in a while a marshal or a regular citizen gets shot. Did Luke Kittering get hurt in that fracas last night, Cotton?"

Rebel stiffened, her breathing suspended.

She had the curious impression that, just for a moment, Cotton, too, went rigid. Then he leaned back casually in his chair and crossed one booted foot over the opposite knee. "What gives you the idea Luke was anywhere near the Ox Bow last night?"

"Pooley saw him. Yes, he did, Cotton, he mentioned it to me this morning. He was just going past there on his way home—Pooley's our stableman," she said in an aside to the visitors, "and he swore he saw Luke running through the back alley."

Cotton laughed. "That only goes to prove it wasn't Luke. I never saw him run from anything except his pa's bank. Pooley's getting old; his eyesight is poor. I can assure you Luke was nowhere near the Ox Bow. I saw him half an hour after the shooting at Bill's place, playing poker. He'd been there all evening."

"On Christmas Eve?" There was a note of censure in Mrs. Stirling's tone.

Cotton shrugged. "He'd probably had all he could stand of family company after Rosalie's big wedding, and the Kitterings always make a big day of Christmas itself."

The giggly sister, Charlotte, gave her brother a soulful look. "I wish you were still friends with Luke. I think he's the handsomest man I ever saw. I wish he still came over here all the time, the way he did when I was little."

Rebel's senses were heightened by the very mention of Luke. She caught the nearly imperceptible tightening of Mrs. Stirling's mouth, and wondered if she imagined that Cotton was not nearly as relaxed as he appeared. There was something in his eyes that belied the way he sprawled in the chair and the off-handed manner in which he spoke.

"He'd never look at you, Charly, he likes grown-up women with a little meat on them, not scrawny fourteen-year-olds."

"I'm not scrawny!" Charlotte protested. "And how do you know what he likes? You haven't been best friends for ever so long."

"But we were best friends for a good many years," Cotton said in a level tone, leaning forward to strike a match on the sole of his boot and light a cheroot he had taken from his pocket. "We used to talk about—"

Mrs. Stirling rose abruptly. "We don't care to hear what you used to talk about. For myself, I'm relieved you finally severed that relationship, since it seemed to promote nothing but mischief. It was one thing when you were children, but past adolescence such irresponsibility can only cause trouble." She turned a brilliant smile on their guests. "Perhaps you young ladies would like to see our Christmas tree? It's one of the finest we've ever had, fourteen feet high, and the girls did a lovely job of decorating it."

Rebel was aware that Evelyn carefully refrained from looking in her direction. Cotton didn't look at her, either, as they all trooped into the parlor where the massive tree took up one entire end of the room, and the Stirling sisters eagerly displayed their Christmas gifts.

Rebel wasn't thinking about any of this. Her heart was still thudding at the idea that Luke might have been involved in the shooting the previous night, and she was not reassured by Cotton's assertion that he'd seen his former friend elsewhere. Nor did she comprehend what the present relationship was between the two men. The only thing she was convinced of was that there was more to this situation than so far met the eye, and it made her uneasy.

It was Rebel who finally looked out the window at the gathering dusk and remarked, "I think we'd best get on home, Evelyn, before it's dark, or Aunt Winnie will worry."

Cotton rose at once. "I'll bring out the buggy and pick you up in front in five minutes," he said at once. "I'm still full from dinner, Ma, don't expect me back for supper."

Which meant, Rebel thought with a grim little smile as Cotton helped her into the buggy, that when they reached Mrs. Tolman's she herself would be escorted to the door, and Cotton and Evelyn would find a way to spend some time together. Alone, if possible.

She didn't really care about that. What bothered her was the suggestion that Luke had been involved in the shooting, and that Cotton was lying about Luke's whereabouts.

She had no idea why or how she had come to this conclusion. She only knew that she feared for Luke—and for her own dreams of a future with him.

# Chapter Seventeen

THEIR FIRST DAY OF TEACHING WENT WELL ENOUGH. FOR all her previous confidence, Rebel was trembling with a nervousness she strove to conceal from her cousin. Evelyn was openly a bundle of nerves.

"Pretend," Rebel advised. "You can play the piano, you can sing beautifully, you can paint. No one will expect more of you than you can do. So pretend that you are securely in control, and you *will* be."

This was easier said than done by either of them, but for the most part the children were receptive and well-behaved. Rebel knew her subject matter—Ned Moran had drilled her well, and she had helped him correct papers and taken over for him in the classroom a few times—so no questions were put to her that she could not answer.

The Belle Grove School was a far cry from the little

one-room schoolhouse in Lyons Falls where her father had taught. This building was modern, built of brick, and huge by comparison. It was well-equipped with blackboards and chalk, neat rows of desks, and books, maps, and globes that would have sent Ned Moran into spasms of delight.

There was considerable talk during recess and the lunch period about both the bank robbery and the confrontation at the Ox Bow Saloon. Rumor abounded, and there were many theories.

Rebel listened more intently now, after Charlotte Stirling's assertion that Luke Kittering had been present at the saloon when the shooting took place. Certainly he could have had nothing to do with the bank robbery, for he had been with the others at the school board meeting, yet she was appalled that the idea even occurred to her. It was absurd. Why would a young man from a prominent, wealthy family take up with bank robbers or ruffians in a saloon? Yet the concern would not go away.

She wished vehemently that she and Evelyn had never strolled past the Stirling house, that they'd never been invited inside. She did not want to know that Cotton's little sister adored Luke from afar, that Mrs. Stirling felt he was a troublemaker, that a servant claimed to have seen him running from the tavern after the shooting, or that Cotton had provided Luke with an alibi she suspected was false. Why would he do that, if he and Luke were no longer friends? And why had she felt no animosity between the two men on the brief occasions when they had met and spoken in her presence? In fact, her impression had been to the contrary, that they knew each other well and respected one another.

She and Evelyn compared notes as they ate their sack

179

lunches at noon and ostensibly supervised their young charges, some of whom were no more than a few years their juniors.

Having gotten through the first morning, Evelyn was more confident of getting through the rest of the day, but never had Rebel seen her cousin as unsure of herself as here.

"Thank heaven Mama made me practice at the piano all those tedious hours, and that she persuaded Papa I must have voice lessons as well," she observed. "I never thought of myself as useless until Papa died, and then I saw that there was little of value I could do for anyone. This morning we concentrated on music, and I *am* knowledgeable there—I wonder if Mr. Florin would be amenable to a music appreciation class? I could play the music and tell the children about the composers. You might have to help me there, because my knowledge is scanty; I didn't pay as much attention to that part of my own instruction, but surely it's only a matter of reading about each composer the night before the class, if I can find the proper books."

"By all means, suggest it," Rebel agreed, hungrily eating her roast beef sandwich. Now that the tension was relieved, at least for an hour, she was ravenous.

"This afternoon we have art. I'm not as skillful there as with the music."

"You'll do fine," Rebel assured her. "Here, boys! Stop that until you go out to the playground!"

Rather to her astonishment, the boys ceased throwing the eraser back and forth; she began to feel that perhaps she was natural schoolteacher material.

Throughout the day, dealing with the children, doing her best to be the teacher she had been hired to be, Rebel thought about Luke. If she had been torn before between eagerness at meeting him again and fear of not knowing what to do when she did, she was doubly so now.

That she was physically drawn to him was undeniable. That she was perturbed about the things she'd heard—innuendo only, yet disturbing nevertheless—was no less indisputable.

She tried to draw some solace from the knowledge that her parents had been regarded by some as foolish, as failing to live up to family and community expectations. Even Beryl had laughingly admitted that she had married "below" her father's standards, that her sister Winnie had been the one to "marry well" to a diamond merchant.

"But oh," she had cried once, "how much more *fun* it has been to live with Ned Moran!"

Certainly there had been little if any fun in living with Arlen Bickford, for all his money and position and his big house.

I wouldn't mind living in a simple cottage, with the right man, Rebel told herself. The love and the laughter are more important than the outward signs of success.

Yet Luke Kittering was not Ned Moran. And she would be foolish in the extreme to be drawn into a marriage that would, in the long run, break her heart.

How could she know which way to turn?

She turned, inevitably, in the direction of her heart.

For when, after that first day, Rebel left her classroom on the second floor and descended to the street, her pulse leaped to find Luke Kittering there, speaking to the superintendent, Mr. Florin.

Florin was older than Luke by some ten years, and still trim and attractive. He had peered in on the new teachers several times during the day, but never with the attitude that made Rebel feel he was looking for

181

some shortcoming to reveal itself, though admittedly she felt better when he wasn't there.

He greeted her now with a smile, asking how her day had gone, and then asked, "Have you met Mr. Kittering? His father is on our school board, and Luke's delivering a message from him."

"Yes," Rebel said demurely, "we have been introduced."

She didn't *feel* demure. Her heart was beating like a caged wild bird, until it was painful to breathe. Even her hearing was affected as the blood pounded in her ears.

She allowed herself to look at him, and he was even more devilishly attractive than he'd seemed before. His dark good looks, the lean length of him, the graceful way he moved, all conspired to work against her judgment.

"Maybe I could walk you home, Miss Moran," Luke offered formally, though there was a glint in his eye that suggested an intimacy between them, one that could exist so far only in their imaginations. "I'll tell you about my mother's excellent idea to acquaint our new teachers with the community."

Mr. Florin was smiling, as if he found this perfectly reasonable. Surely if Luke's reputation was disreputable, he would not allow his newest teacher to walk off with the man?

Rebel forgot about Evelyn, falling into step with Luke as they moved away from the school, being jostled by children as eager to depart as they were.

She tried to affect her cousin's light, playful tone, then wondered if, on her, it sounded inane. "What is this fabulous idea?"

"Well, since the two of you are new in Fort Smith, and the community as a whole wishes to judge whether or not you are worthy of teaching their precious brats," Luke said, "—or, since they've already heard of your striking beauty, they may simply want to see for themselves—there will be a potluck dinner in your honor Saturday evening at six. And to make it a more festive affair, Ma's offered our house for it; that will encourage people who wouldn't attend if it were held at the school."

Blind panic surged through her. A little boy, running past in pursuit of a friend, careened into her, throwing Rebel off balance.

At once Luke's arm was around her waist, steadying her, holding her very close to him. The effect was electrifying; for a moment she forgot what had caused her consternation a moment earlier.

"All right?" Luke asked, and when she nodded, breathless, he released her from the embrace but drew her hand into a hold on his arm.

"You said . . . at *your* house?"

"That's right. You know where it is, don't you?" He didn't give her time to react to his assumption that she would have made it a point to find out—or perhaps he'd seen her walking past? "I told Ma I'd met you, and I want you to meet her, too." He raised his free hand and laid it over hers, curled at his elbow. "Your aunt will be included in the invitation, of course. And once we've met, and she's met my family, there's no reason why the courtship can't begin in earnest, is there?"

Rebel brought her gaze up swiftly to see the amusement in his face. "You take it for granted—" she began, but he interrupted her.

"Don't tell me you don't want to be courted. I won't believe it. And don't borrow feminine tricks from your cousin; you aren't the type to be coy any more than I am."

Rebel swallowed. It was ludicrous to imagine Luke as coy. Yet he kept throwing her off balance with his unexpected remarks; she didn't know how to handle them.

There was so much she wanted to know about him, but she didn't know how to ask. One thing she decided she could probe, and she did so as subtly as possible.

"We met Mrs. Stirling and Cotton's sisters," she said. "I understand you and Cotton were good friends as boys."

He grinned. "Best friends and occasionally bitter enemies, until someone else started picking on one or the other of us. Then we'd stand off all comers."

"But . . . you aren't that close any more?" she asked.

"Oh, we've grown up and gone our separate ways," Luke told her with a careless air, unnecessarily tightening his hold on her as they stepped off a curb. "Cotton's a good sort, went into the family business, became a respectable citizen."

Her nerve ends tingled. "And you didn't?"

"My pa's a banker. I can't imagine a duller life than sitting all day in a bank, can you?"

"What do you want to do?" She lifted troubled eyes to look once more directly into his, and then wondered if that had been a mistake. He was too close, he was touching her hand where it rested on his arm; the combination constricted her breathing.

"I have a little money, inherited from my maternal grandmother, and some land my grandfather owned. There was a house on it once. It burned down when I was a boy, and nobody ever rebuilt it. I'm getting started raising cotton and a few cattle; that appeals to me more than counting someone else's money. I'm thinking of building a new house this spring."

Again her pulse accelerated. "Doesn't your family approve of that? Of being a farmer or a rancher?"

"Pa thinks that as the oldest I ought to be in the bank. Ma backs me in doing what I want, though she refuses to quarrel with him about it. How do you feel about living in the country as opposed to the convenience of city life?"

"Until my father died I never knew anything about the convenience of city life," she said truthfully. "I grew up in a small town, and I liked it very much." Was the query a personal one? Concluding that it was, Rebel found it even more difficult to draw enough air. If she were going to be around Luke very often, she decided, she'd have to stop lacing her corset so tightly.

"I thought quite a large house," Luke said. He had forgotten that he'd been limiting his strides to make it easier for Rebel to keep up; now she was practically swept along at a trot because his legs were so much longer than hers. "I've always wanted a big family. You were an only child, I take it."

"Not from choice," Rebel admitted, and then felt the heat climb into her face. Surely this was not a topic that unmarried people discussed?

"There's a grove of cottonwoods around the site of the old house, and the foundation is still there," Luke went on, unaware of what his words were doing to her. "Or there's another place, upriver on the Poteau, that would be a good building site. How about riding out there with me on Sunday afternoon to take a look at it? Tell me which you'd choose?"

"A . . . a ride in the country sounds like a pleasant way to spend a Sunday afternoon," she agreed, and heard again that tantalizing chuckle.

"I'll pick you up right after church. How are you at picnic baskets?"

"Very good, I think," Rebel said, and somehow now she felt a bit easier with him. "Although isn't it a bit chilly for sitting on the ground?"

"We'll eat in the buggy if it's too cold. Ah, I see your cousin and Cotton are going to beat us home."

The now familiar buggy rolled past them, with Evelyn lifting a hand to wave at them. Rebel was glad Luke hadn't brought the buggy; she felt less insecure walking along the street with him, and besides, it gave them more time together.

It was only after he'd left her at the front door that Rebel allowed the doubts to creep in again. Not about Luke this time; she was reassured by what he said about becoming a rancher or cotton farmer and building a house, respectable goals.

That he was considering her wishes in the matter of a house had been perfectly clear. The very idea sent a thrill through her, unmatched by anything except his touch.

But before Sunday, before the future that suddenly seemed to stretch before her in glorious promise, there was the matter of meeting his family.

Remembering Mrs. Stirling and her opinion of Luke, Rebel could not entirely dismiss all of her uncertainties. How would the Kitterings feel about a simple schoolteacher as a wife for their son? A girl with no money, no breeding that would mean anything to people of their class, no family except an impoverished aunt and cousin?

Saturday night loomed ahead of her, terrifying in its implications.

# Chapter Eighteen

THE SCHOOL BUZZED WITH NEWS AND RUMOR. THE BANK robbers had been caught. Some of the robbers had been caught. A marshal had been shot. He had died. He was still alive but in critical condition. He had killed one of the bank robbers before he went down.

It was difficult to get the students sufficiently calm to consider nouns and verbs and participles. When asked to construct a sentence to be diagrammed, one boy responded, "Judge Parker will see that everybody that wasn't shot dead by the marshal will hang."

Rebel struggled to control the class; the students were too intrigued by the events of the real world in Fort Smith, Arkansas, to care about anything in a textbook.

At recess the games all involved violence: the U.S. marshals pursued the gang members, and the air re-

187

sounded with imitation gunshots. Shirts were dirtied and torn, limbs scratched, and again it took extra effort to settle them down enough to concentrate on their studies. Even the girls were infected with the sense of drama.

The fracas at the Ox Bow Saloon cropped up again, too.

"My uncle says it was a gang meeting there to plan a job," one small boy reported with an air of importance. "They saw a couple of marshals coming and thought they was surrounded, and they fought their way out. The marshals was just going to have a drink together, but they sure scared off them robbers! They know they winged a couple of 'em because they found the blood afterward!"

It was impossible not to remember the report about Luke being on that scene. Was the Stirlings' stableman mistaken, or had Luke actually been there? She recalled distinctly that when everyone else headed out to join the posse after the bank robbery, Luke had said that chasing after gunslingers was not a favored pastime. So why, then, would he have been in the company of such ruffians in the saloon?

By evening some of the speculation had been confirmed. Mr. Sylvester came home to dinner to impart the news in his dry manner over Winnie's beef stew and Rebel's dumplings.

"Got two of the robbers locked up at the jail," he said. "Going to try 'em on Tuesday next and hang 'em a week from Saturday." The verdict, Rebel noted, was a foregone conclusion.

"Who are they?" Miss Margaret asked. "Anybody we know?"

"No, they moved over from Muskogee area. One feller they knew about before. He murdered that Whipple and his Cherokee wife over at Sapulpa last fall, had a shoot-out with Marshal Knox and got clean away, but Knox recognized him this time. The other one they caught is a kid, not but seventeen years old, and he's told 'em who else to look for. If they find 'em fast enough, might hang all four of 'em come a week from Saturday."

It was a grisly recital, Rebel thought. Winnie's lips were pale, and even Evelyn, floating in a dream world since she was finding an excuse and a way to see Cotton almost every day, temporarily lost her ebullience.

Mrs. Tolman noticed their faces and reached out to pat Winnie's hand beside hers on the table. "Don't you worry, dear, it'll all be taken care of. Oh, Fort Smith used to be a wild place, but it's getting more civilized all the time. Was no law here at all, in the whole of the Indiana territory, when we first came. There's still a few bad apples thinks to take on Judge Parker and his marshals, but they don't get away with much, they don't." She turned to her male boarder. "Did they recover any of the money that was stolen?"

"It had been divided up, and they got what these two was carrying," Mr. Sylvester said, helping himself to another serving of the savory stew. "Now they know who else they're looking for, and every marshal, all two hundred of 'em, will be after the culprits. No need to worry, ladies."

In truth, Rebel was far more worried about the dinner for the new teachers Saturday night. She changed her mind half a dozen times about what to wear. It wasn't the proper occasion for the blue velvet, nor the brown crepon. In fact, almost all of the hand-me-downs from Evelyn seemed too elaborate for a simple schoolteacher.

Evelyn herself was not bothered by this. "There's nothing shameful in being in reduced circumstances since Papa's death," she said, examining her own wardrobe. "I think the green foulard, it sets off my hair and skin as well as anything, doesn't it?" She didn't wait for a reply. "After all, they can't expect us, on the pathetic salaries they're paying us, to go out and buy new clothes, can they?"

Rebel had her own viewpoint on that. "If we dress too well, they'll likely figure we don't need the salaries we have, and reduce them. I want to look my best, yet without putting on airs. I've noticed that the styles in Fort Smith are a bit behind those in New York City. I don't think the way to win over the women of this community is to outshine them." That meant, she sighed inwardly, not wearing the precious diamond earrings, either. "I wonder if I should wear the same kind of thing I wear to school every day."

Evelyn gave her a shocked glance. "A shirtwaist and a black skirt?"

"Well, yes. My best shirtwaist, the one with the lace and the tucks. With Mama's brooch—it's the only other jewelry I have, and it's not valuable. It would probably make the most modest impression."

Evelyn tossed her head, the light glimmering on her auburn hair. "Modest! Who cares about modest? I want to impress them with my appearance, so maybe they won't pay too much attention to the fact that I don't know what I'm doing at school."

In spite of herself, Rebel laughed. "I'm not sure it works that way. I mean, a woman who is too beautiful is a threat, and those who resent you might look for flaws."

Evelyn echoed her laughter. "As long as the school board consists entirely of males, I should be safe."

"They're mostly married men, though. And wives have a way of influencing their men-folk."

Evelyn leaned forward toward the mirror, frowning as she touched a tiny blemish on one cheek. "I hope that's cleared up by Saturday. Of all times to look like an adolescent!"

At that Rebel exploded in mirth. "I can't imagine anyone taking you for an adolescent! Not with that figure! Not to mention your hair, your eyes, your skin, and the way you speak! Seriously, though, you might antagonize a lot of people by putting on too many airs, Evelyn."

"I'm not putting on airs. I'm being myself. But if you think I should wear sack cloth and ashes . . ."

"The green foulard is probably all right, since you really don't have anything more suitable," Rebel relented. "But perhaps if you had other earrings, not diamonds."

"My earrings didn't have a negative effect on Mrs. Stirling. In fact, she complimented me on them."

"Mrs. Stirling has diamonds of her own," Rebel said gently. "Most of the women here don't. Anyway, it's really Cotton you want to impress, isn't it, and he probably won't even be there, since it's at the Kitterings'."

"Oh, but he will! He's already promised to come, though I think none of his family will be present. He said it would be worth any awkwardness to be with me. He hasn't been in that house in several years, I take it. I don't understand what happened between Cotton and Luke. Do you?"

Rebel shook her head. "No. But it would be a pity to marry men who were enemies, wouldn't it?"

Evelyn almost pounced on her. "Has Luke proposed?"

"Not in so many words, no." She hadn't told her cousin about the proposed excursion to look at a site for a house on Luke's land. "But you aren't the only one who's dreaming."

Evelyn gave her a cousinly hug. "It's fun, isn't it?

191

After all those years of imagining a lover, making up a face and a name, it's wonderful to have a real face, a real name. And," her grin became mischievous, "real arms and lips."

Rebel always felt embarrassed and uncomfortable when Evelyn talked this way, though she was glad to be included in her cousin's world and sharing similar experiences. She brought the subject back to the important matter. "Don't wear the diamonds, Evelyn. Seriously."

"All right. I'll be a mousy little creature too timid to open my mouth," she agreed, and once more they went off into fits of giggles at the impossibility of such a scenario.

"Such a nice hospitable idea," Winnie said of the welcoming dinner. "Mrs. Kittering must be a very kind lady to think of such a thing."

Rebel was by no means sure that the idea belonged to Mrs. Kittering. She suspected Luke had planted the seed for it; how unwillingly his mother had followed through they would soon know.

She had expected Luke to come for them in the buggy, but it was a smiling black man who arrived at the door to collect them.

"Mr. Luke sends his apologies, ma'am," he addressed Rebel. "He had urgent business to take care of, so he sent me. I'm Montmorency, and you be safe in my hands, I promise you."

It wasn't safety she was concerned with. What urgent business did a man have, she wondered as all three of them were assisted into the buggy, at a time of year when a cotton grower could do almost nothing on the land?

But she was more concerned with her imminent

meeting with Luke's family to dwell on it. At the last moment, seeing Evelyn looking so splendid in her dark green foulard with its matching fur-trimmed wrap and the jaunty little hat perched on her auburn curls, Rebel had wavered about her own dress. She would be totally overshadowed by her cousin, she knew that.

Yet instinct told her that for herself, at least, the course she had decided upon was the best.

There was a string of buggies and horses outside the Kittering mansion. It *was* a mansion, she thought, so nervous now that her hands were icy and trembling a little.

Lights were on throughout the lower floor, and several ladies carrying covered dishes scurried ahead of them through the dusk to the front door. Rebel glanced at Winnie, who was composed and smiling; she had presided over many elegant dinners in a house nearly as grand as this one, and she would be quite at ease.

Evelyn, too, gazed up at the house with anticipation, her lips slightly parted, the dimples deepening when she caught Rebel's eye. This, her look said, was going to be fun.

Rebel wished she could be as confident of that as her cousin. She stood to one side of the door with its brilliantly colored glass, allowing Evelyn to be the one to twist the bell handle.

She waited for a servant to answer, but she knew at once that the lady who opened the door was no servant.

Frances Kittering was tall and regal, fashionably gowned in deep blue cashmere with cascades of white lace at her throat. Her brown hair was simply styled—with her looks she didn't need an elaborate coiffure—and the hazel eyes that swept over them were Luke's eyes.

Mrs. Kittering greeted Winnie first, in a soft, charming voice, and then rested briefly on Evelyn's face as she shook her hand. But it was upon Rebel that her attention settled in unmistakable interest.

"Miss Moran. I'm so happy you could come," she said, and did not release Rebel's hand at once. Frances studied the younger woman. It was as if they were the only ones there, as if Winnie and Evelyn had dissolved away, as if there were no laughing, chattering guests behind her beneath the brilliantly lighted crystal chandelier.

She knows about Luke and me, Rebel thought. He's told her . . . something . . . about me.

And yet her apprehensions faded away as she looked into the replicas of Luke's eyes. For she read only kindness there, acceptance, approval. Frances smiled, squeezed her hand once more, and released her.

"My son was sorry not to be here to greet you, but he'll join us for supper. I understand you're recently orphaned, without family except for the Bickfords."

"Yes, that's right." Rebel's mouth was dry; obviously there had been considerable talk about the newcomers to Fort Smith.

"I was lucky enough to keep my parents until only a few years ago," Frances said. "Mama and I were very close, and I grieve for a young girl who doesn't have her mother to guide her through the critical years of her early life."

She gave a little laugh. "Now Papa, he was a different matter. Not that he and I did not get along, because we doted on one another. Perhaps that was why, when I grew up, he felt that no man was good enough for me. He was quite opposed to my marrying Adam Kittering, you see. But Adam swept me off my feet in spite of Papa's objections. That was thirty-two years ago, and the marriage has worn very well."

There was a twinkle in the hazel eyes as she looked at

Rebel. "Both of them would deny it, but there is a good deal of Adam in Lucas, Miss Moran. And now, come along, I want you to meet my husband, and of course our other guests."

The next hour was a blur. Rebel was uncertain about Adam Kittering; though he gave no indication that he realized she had attracted his son, he was affable and hospitable. There was an underlying reserve about him that put her on guard; he exuded self-confidence and authority, and from what Luke had said about him, she had gathered he had little patience with people whose opinions differed from his own. "Always nice to know we have competent teachers," he said, leaving her to wonder how he could judge that by their looks.

The Kitterings were the only ones she remembered clearly and could attach names to. Dozens of parents of her pupils introduced themselves; some of them expressed their children's satisfaction with their new teachers, though Rebel was inclined to take most of that with a grain of salt. What children told their parents and what they really thought might be worlds apart.

It was not until Luke finally showed up that the evening began to come into sharp focus.

He materialized at her elbow just as Mrs. Kittering had announced that supper had been set out in the dining room and had requested the guests to begin serving themselves in buffet fashion.

Luke spoke into her left ear. "There's a table for two set up in the upstairs study," he murmured, taking her elbow to propel her gently toward the overladen table.

She kept her voice low, though excitement trickled through her like wildfire. "I hardly think that would be appropriate for one of the new teachers. I suggest a table in the drawing room, where everybody will get the look at me that they came for."

He gave an exaggerated sigh. "Yes, teacher."

She scarcely remembered what she ate. She tried a spoonful of virtually everything, knowing that she was being closely observed, that she might well be judged by whether or not she had taken some of Mrs. Elkhorn's candied sweet potatoes or Mrs. Blackmore's baked beans. The food was immaterial, anyway; what mattered was Luke.

Cotton had appeared shortly before supper, too, and been greeted in apparent good humor by their hostess; Evelyn introduced him to her mother with great vivacity, and the two of them gathered Winnie up to eat with them a short time later.

After supper the rugs were rolled back for dancing. The musicians were two fiddle players and a guitarist; the music was lively, and the rooms grew warm with all the energy being expended.

Rebel danced with nearly every man present, but only the dances with Luke seemed real. Her hand felt small in his large one; her feet as nimble as they had ever been as they romped through the same dances she'd been accustomed to at home.

"Let's get out of here and get some air," Luke said at last, whirling her off the floor into a darkened passageway. "Don't worry, nobody's paying any attention to us, and even if they were, they'd expect a pretty teacher to stir up some excitement among the young bucks."

"I don't think—" Rebel began, but the words were stopped by Luke's.

"Good. Don't. Just feel," he suggested, and drew her into his arms.

His mouth was warm and gentle, and then, as he guided her into an unlighted room, she felt passion stirring within him, a passion matched within herself. The kiss consumed her, depriving her of strength and the will to resist.

Oh, God, Rebel thought. It was half prayer, half exultation. Her arms crept up around his neck, and she heard that delicious chuckle.

"I knew you were a woman of fire. Nobody with hair the color of yours could be anything else," he murmured, lips tracing a line from her ear down her throat to the pulsing at the base of it.

In another moment she would faint, she thought. *Damn* this corset that wouldn't allow her lungs to expand when she needed more air!

"Lucas?"

Frances Kittering's voice brought Rebel out of her near-swoon as if she'd been doused with ice water.

"In here, Ma. I was just showing Miss Moran the library," Luke said, sounding perfectly unruffled.

"In the dark?" Mrs. Kittering asked dryly, but when they stepped out into the dimly lighted corridor there was a faint smile on her patrician lips. "People will be leaving shortly. I thought Miss Moran would want to bid them all good-bye. And then, if you wouldn't mind driving Miss Moran home? I believe Cotton has offered a similar service for Miss Bickford and her mama. He would take all three," she added with a droll expression, "but he brought the small buggy, and there isn't room for four."

Luke still held her arm, or Rebel was convinced that she would have wobbled. How did he recover so quickly after those compelling moments? Was he simply more used to it, or hadn't it affected him the way it had her?

"By all means, bid them all good-bye," Luke said, smiling down on her. "I'll bring the buggy around in ten minutes."

He was gone in long strides, leaving Rebel alone with his mother. Rebel was flustered, embarrassed. How could she account for having been in a darkened room with Luke? She felt as if this woman could look into her very soul and read what was written there.

Frances still wore a hint of a smile. "My son is quite taken with you, Miss Moran."

How did one reply to that? While she floundered, unable to produce a coherent response, Frances's smile grew.

"Would I guess correctly that you return the interest?"

Rebel swallowed. "I find Mr. Kittering . . . very attractive," she managed. Dear heaven, why hadn't Evelyn prepared her for something like this?

The smile grew warm and friendly, and Frances patted her arm as she drew Rebel toward the lighted, noisy drawing room.

"I think, Miss Moran, that you may well be the making of Lucas. I've been telling his father for years that all he lacked was the affections of a good woman, and I suspect that now you are about to prove that. I always like having my judgments borne out."

With that mind-boggling speech, she led the way back to the party, where Rebel went through the motions of saying good night to dozens of people whom she later could not remember at all.

Luke had made it clear, at least to his mother, that he found Rebel very attractive. And, miracle of miracles, his mother approved! Rebel was stunned and almost dizzy with the unexpected delight of it.

The last of the guests had departed by the time Luke drew up to the front door with the buggy. She was settled into it beside him, warmly wrapped in the heavy robe, and felt her spirits rising. This was the next time, and she had already decided that Evelyn was right about kissing a man; how could she know whether or not this was what she wanted, unless she knew how she was affected by his kiss?

This time, when he allowed the horse to pick its own way through the crisp, clear winter night, she didn't hesitate to lift her lips when he put an arm around her.

The danger signals were there, deep inside her, in the secret places that came alive with liquid fire that cried out for quenching. Yet Rebel cast aside her fears; what could happen riding along a public street in a buggy on her way home?

She had thought herself already introduced to ecstasy, but when they came to a stop before the boarding house Luke made no move to descend. Instead he drew her into an even closer embrace, and his kiss deepened; the fire spread, melting her so that she yielded to mouth and hands and whispered words that didn't really register on her benumbed mind.

There was no decision to make. It would not be tonight, but when Luke Kittering wanted her, Rebel realized dimly, she would be his for the taking.

# Chapter Nineteen

Sunday dawned sunny and thawing. The icicles dripped from the eaves, and by the time they'd returned from church, which Rebel later hardly remembered having attended, there was no ice left at all. They walked with their wraps open to a decidedly springlike breeze, spirits buoyant.

Rebel and Evelyn, of course, were buoyed by more than the weather.

At the gathering last night, Cotton had monopolized Evelyn to an extent that amounted to a public declaration: he was courting her.

And Luke's intentions, though not quite so openly made to the world at large, also seemed clear. The passion of his kisses lingered in Rebel's senses, making her reckless with happiness.

She dressed sensibly for her outing in a simple

shirtwaist and skirt, and took a warm wrap as well, though by the time they rode out of Fort Smith she no longer felt the need of more than a light shawl.

Aunt Winnie was bewildered by the sudden romantic entanglements, but pleasantly so. How nice that young men of good families should so quickly be drawn to her charges, and since all the proprieties of proper introductions and behavior, as she saw it, were being observed, there was no reason why the courting should not be encouraged.

Rebel's spirits rose even higher as they headed south along the Poteau. Luke indicated points of interest and asked her opinion on everything from music and literature to the theater, of which she knew nothing.

"We'll go see some of the productions at the Opera House," he assured her. "I grew to like it when I used to go with Ma, years ago, when Pa was either too busy or couldn't be bothered." A grin flashed in his dark face. "He doesn't really like that 'screeching kind of singing,' as he puts it."

Rebel's gaze rested upon him with extreme pleasure. Today he looked more like a cowboy than an opera-goer. His jean trousers, scuffed boots, plaid shirt, and leather vest contributed to the air of virility about him. Even in winter he had retained some tan, and today he had rolled up his shirt cuffs, displaying powerful wrists that handled the reins in a casual, competent way.

Her attention rested on his hands, the hands that had held her so firmly last night, that had touched her throat and jaw, sending spasms of delight through her entire body.

He would touch her again, today, she thought. And because of the almost miraculous change in the weather, she would not be bundled in a heavy wrap and a lap robe.

Anything one does that doesn't involve removing one's clothes should be acceptable between couples who were courting, Evelyn had opined.

The mere thought made her nipples tingle. Rebel drew her shawl more closely around her bosom, as if to conceal this extraordinary phenomenon. How had she lived for seventeen years without encountering it before?

Luke saw her motion and asked quickly, "Are you cold?"

"No, no. It's such a glorious day! When we get out of the wind it's perfect." He was too perceptive; she would have to be more careful, she warned herself. It wouldn't do to have him know what she was thinking and feeling, not when she couldn't control those thoughts and sensations.

The breeze cooled her hot cheeks, and she laughed in sheer exhilaration. "It must be lovely out here, when it all begins to turn green."

"It is. I like knowing there's no one else around for four miles back toward Fort Smith, and farther than that in the other directions. Nobody but you and me."

It sent another delicious shiver down her spine, followed by a shadow of doubt. "It isn't dangerous, is it? To be out here alone? We've been hearing such tales about desperados . . ."

Luke was unperturbed. "My grandparents lived out here for forty years. They kept a loaded rifle over the mantel, and they used it a few times to run off riffraff, but that was a long time ago. Once, when my mother was about to be born, actually, and Grandma was there alone, an Osage came to the door. It scared her pretty badly when the Indian appeared in the doorway. But when he understood that she was about to give birth, he went away. He came back a short time later with his squaw, who stayed with her through the whole thing, wrapped the baby up, smiled at it. Grandma said she was never afraid of an Indian again, after that."

It hadn't been Indians she'd meant, but the sort of men who robbed and murdered and raped. Miss Helen and Miss Margaret seemed almost to enjoy relating wild tales of past horrors.

Yet there was nothing menacing to see this afternoon. The hills rolled away before them. A flock of wild geese rose suddenly and they watched, entranced, as the magnificent birds soared over their heads. And once a deer appeared briefly along the riverbank, watching curiously as they went by.

Finally Luke lifted an arm to point to a clump of cottonwoods farther along the Poteau. "There's where Grandpa built his house. It has the advantage of trees already planted nearby, cottonwoods to shade the house, and a small orchard for fruit. We'll stop there to eat. It should be warm in the protection of the old barn walls. Then I'll show you the other place I thought might be a good one to build."

Rebel liked the site at once. The fire had been so long ago there were no bitter reminders of it remaining. A lilac bush would bloom in a few more months, and perhaps there would be hollyhocks along the path. The trees were now bare, but if this weather lasted they would soon be leafing out, providing color and shade against the summer heat to come.

All that remained of the house was a stone fireplace and crumbling bits of the foundation. The barn, two hundred yards away, sagged dangerously.

"Every time I ride out here after a storm, I expect to see the weight of the snow on the roof has combined with a strong wind to push it over," Luke commented, drawing up beside the barn. "But it's still a good windbreak. I think I've been smelling chicken in that basket you brought, right? I'll spread the buffalo robe out right there, and let's eat."

It was a lovely picnic. It amazed her that Luke was so easy to talk to about any subject. For a time the overwhelming physical sensations subsided while they ate and Luke talked about the house he wanted to build.

"I like the house I grew up in," he said. "I have four brothers and two sisters, so the place was always full of laughter and noise." He was stretched out on one side of the buffalo robe, propped on an elbow. He shot her a probing look that put her suddenly back on guard. "You want kids, don't you?"

"I missed having brothers and sisters," she admitted. "Yes, certainly I hope someday to have a family."

Her heartbeat quickened, for there was something in his eyes, something strong and compelling.

He reached out to capture her hand with his. "My children, Rebel. I want you to have my children. I want you to marry me, to help me build my big house, to live in it with me. To grow old with me in it, if we're that lucky." For a moment she thought she detected a shadow passing over his face, but it was gone so swiftly that she decided she must have imagined it.

The sun was warm on her back, as warm as the masculine hand that covered hers. But not as warm as the heat that spread through her in response to his words. She felt almost suffocated with it, yet it was not at all unpleasant not to be able to breathe. She had, in expectation of this, daringly left off the confining corset this morning when she changed her clothes after church; she had thought her figure sufficiently concealed under her wraps so that no one would notice. Yet even without that constricting garment, breathing became difficult.

"Will you marry me, Rebel? Will you?"

She never recalled exactly how they came together, but she would always, for the rest of her life, remember how it had felt to be in his arms, to surrender her lips.

She thought she had already probed the depths of passion, when he'd kissed her last night. Yet it was nothing compared to this.

She felt as if Luke touched her very soul, as if her body no longer belonged to her but was a vessel waiting to be filled, and though she knew not with what, she was more than ready to find out.

His lips traced her jaw, her throat, and moved downward to where his fingers expertly took care of buttons and laces. Rebel gasped as he took possession of first one exposed breast and then the other, arching her back as if to help him further.

She had a moment's warning, far back in the depths of her consciousness, about the removal of clothing—did undoing one's buttons and laces constitute *removal?*—but she surged forward on the tide of ecstasy, euphoric, unable to summon the will to stop him. She would grant him these privileges as his wife, so what difference did a few weeks make if they were already committed to one another? Especially when her body had lost all will to resist?

Somehow she was lying on her back, seeing Luke's face suspended over her against the cool blue of the sky. For an instant he hesitated, his breath touching her skin. "Rebel?"

Did she truly know what he was asking, or did she not want to know?

Rebel moaned and lifted her arms to encircle his neck, drawing his mouth down to hers.

And then there was no turning back. Dimly she recognized that her skirts were in disorder, her lower limbs exposed, yet the cold spring air was not enough to bring her to her senses. Indeed, she thought later, she had had no sense, had made no attempt to regain control, content instead to float on the sea of rapture for however long it might last, even to drown in it.

She cried out in surprise and pain when he entered her, but Luke was fully in command now and there was no stopping. Rebel clung to him, torn between the pain and the paroxysms of jubilation.

She knew at last what it meant to be a woman.

The feelings that followed were unexpected.

Rebel scrambled around, adjusting her garments, face burning. She could not bear to look at Luke, who already seemed composed and recovered from the experience, except for the languorous way his lean body reclined on the buffalo hide. He was watching her, she knew that, but she could not bring herself to see what his expression was.

She jerked at a button and it came off in her hand.

Rebel stared at it in consternation, the symbol of her dismaying lapse of judgment. Eyes stinging, she struggled not to cry.

"Rebel?"

He put out a hand toward her, brushing her arm as she jerked away, unable now to endure the touch that had so thrilled her only moments earlier. Shame scalded her entire body.

"Rebel, what is it?" He rolled over and came to his knees beside her, drawing her into his arms against her will. "Darling, what's the matter? Did I hurt you? I'm sorry, I guess it's always a little painful the first time, but that's quickly forgotten. From now on it'll be easier, and better. You didn't climax this time, but you will. Believe me, the next time—"

The next time, Rebel thought wildly. He expected to

do this again and again, and as for it getting *better*—up to the last few moments it had been as wonderful as anything she could have imagined—no, had surpassed anything she could have envisioned. She pushed against his chest with both hands, but he didn't let her go; she was powerless against his strength, just as she'd been powerless in pitting her will against his.

No, a part of her mind contributed; in all fairness, she had not willed herself to resist him. The tears spilled over, running in hot trails down her flaming cheeks.

"Rebel, don't! Don't cry! Was it really so bad as that? I thought it was wonderful, I thought you enjoyed it too!"

He was determined to draw her close; Rebel was determined to escape, but he was by far the stronger of the two.

"Rebel, good God, what have I done to you? I thought you *wanted* me to make love to you!"

"I did!" she sobbed. "But I didn't know . . . I didn't know it would be so . . . so *undignified!*"

To her astonishment and momentary rage, Luke began to laugh.

"Honey, dignity isn't something a man and his wife need to maintain between them! Listen to me, now calm down, tell me the truth . . . you did enjoy it, didn't you?"

At this point she wasn't sure whether she had or not. One of the big hands forced her chin upward so that he could look into her woebegone face, and with a gentle thumb he wiped away a remaining tear.

"Rebel, I love you so much. I loved you from the minute I saw you. I wouldn't hurt you for the world."

The moment his mouth touched hers, Rebel trembled, shuddering, for it all came to life again, the spreading liquid fire, the melting of her bones. She moaned and tore her lips away.

"Oh, please, Luke, no, I can't do it again, not so soon!"

His laughter sent shivers up her spine as he drew her close in a tender embrace. "No, I'm not quite ready again, either. But let me hold you, Rebel. That's all I'll do, I promise, but let me hold you."

She leaned into him, fingers digging into his chest, and to her amazement he jerked back, yelping.

"Luke?" What was it? Surely, for just a moment, there had been pain in his face.

And then she saw it. A damp, reddening spot on his plaid shirt.

"Luke! You're bleeding! How could I have . . . ?"

"It's all right. You didn't do it, I just hurt myself the other night and I guess we knocked against it and reopened the wound—"

Her fingers went to his shirt buttons, and he reached up to hold them.

"No. It's all right, Rebel, it's nothing to worry about. See, it isn't spreading."

"I want to see it." She had forgotten the passion, the embarrassment, of the past few minutes. Her tone was level and firm, and when he released her hands she opened the shirt, winced at the blood-soaked bandage, and lifted her eyes to his.

"What happened?"

"Nothing, I was working in the barn and stabbed myself on a nail that was sticking out. It's healing, we just knocked the scab off it."

Decisively, Luke put her hand aside and rebuttoned the shirt.

A terrible disquiet crept through Rebel as she

watched. She thought, if she'd insisted, that even now he might have let her remove the dressing and see the wound, but she was afraid to do it.

She was terrified that if she did, she would discover a puncture wound not from a nail, but from a bullet.

# Chapter Twenty

"COME ON," LUKE SAID, "AND LET ME SHOW YOU WHAT I thought I'd do about the house, if I rebuilt it on the site of the old one."

He drew Rebel to her feet, leaving her to finish the buttons on her shirtwaist as he pulled her along.

If he felt any embarrassment about what had occurred between them, she couldn't tell. He had kissed her tenderly, with amusement as well as love, and though a part of her resented the laughter in his eyes she succumbed to the caresses as if she were a slave to them.

She felt bruised, walking was moderately uncomfortable, and the whole thing had been disconcertingly messy, as well. Yet she went with Luke, standing encircled by his arm as he pointed out where the old kitchen and the double parlors had been, and described the bedrooms and the drawing room and how he'd improve on *this* house with the installation of a bathroom with a real porcelain tub, ordered from Little Rock.

Rebel tried to listen, tried to think of something beyond the arm around her and her own newly awakened body. And she tried not to think of the wound that might be a bullet hole.

He had finished explaining what he wanted to do here, and she had scarcely retained any of it. He looked hopefully down into her face, then steered her toward the buggy. "Let's go see the other place, in case you like that better. It's on the bluff over there, and there aren't as many trees yet, but willows and cottonwoods grow pretty fast."

He didn't seem to notice her benumbed state. Perhaps he assumed that her silence stemmed from disappointment over his plans for building the new house. Yet she was not so bemused that she failed to notice when he swung himself up into the buggy beside her that putting his weight even momentarily on his left arm made him grimace involuntarily.

If he had been shot, what were the circumstances of the shooting? Was he one of those who had bled onto the snow outside the Ox Bow Saloon? And if so, who had shot him? The gang members supposedly plotting there, or the U.S. marshals? If he had been simply an innocent bystander, why not admit it? And if that were the case, why would Cotton, who was no longer a close friend, create an alibi for Luke about being at some poker game on the other side of town?

Rebel struggled with pain of her own, only a small part of it physical. A part of her wanted to reach out and touch him, to rest her hand on one bronzed forearm. Another part of her ached at the possibilities a bullet wound brought to mind.

Luke obviously thought she was subdued because of

her first romantic experience. He felt a little guilty about it, but not enough to allow it to dampen his own exuberance. He glanced over and saw her face, shifted the reins to his left hand and reached over to graze her chin with his knuckles.

"Honey, making love is supposed to be *fun*. And it's nothing to be ashamed of; everybody does it."

Nothing to be ashamed of, even when they were not married? The world would not look at it that way, Rebel thought. And then, as the images rose in her mind of various people in the extremely undignified positions they had assumed during their lovemaking, an uncontrollable giggle rose in her throat.

It verged on hysteria, but Luke did not know that. He gave her an encouraging grin, patted her knee—another spot that seemed to generate sensations she had never known there before—and urged the horse to a faster pace.

"See, there, right on the bluff. You can see all the way to the Arkansas if you climb that one tree. What do you think?"

It was a pretty spot, though not as ideal overall as the one where Luke's grandfather had built his house. Rebel swallowed her uncertainties and glanced back the way they had come.

"It's nicer back there, really. The shade trees are already up, and the orchard is there . . ."

"And the place where we first made love," Luke added, hazel eyes dancing. "Shall we build there, then?"

She made no reply; she was, for a few moments, incapable of speech, for the ache in her throat. What was she to make of an injury that might be a bullet wound? Did he simply seek to spare her distress, or was there a deception more ominous than that?

"I'll order the lumber tomorrow," Luke said, happily

212

unaware of her inner turmoil. "Get the men started on it next week, if the weather holds. And we'll be married as soon as possible." He reached for her hand and examined it. "I'd say you might be able to wear my grandmother's wedding ring without altering the size of it. I'll get it and see; as the oldest grandson, I was the one who inherited it."

Rebel felt as if things were moving too fast, as if she'd fallen into a swollen river that was rushing her, helpless, toward unseen but thunderous falls. Yet she was powerless to stop her progress.

When Luke kissed her, at first with tenderness and then with rising passion, she closed her eyes and let the current grow swifter and swifter, to dizzying speed, pushing the doubts far into the deepest recess of her mind.

Rebel felt certain, the moment she walked up the steps and into the boarding house, that everyone who saw her would know immediately what had happened to her that day.

She knew her coloring was high; she could feel its warmth. Would the others attribute it to the exposure to sunshine and wind? Or would they correctly interpret it as a measure of how far her relationship with Luke had progressed in a matter of hours?

Unfortunately the entire household was assembled and had to be faced. Rebel hesitated on the threshold of the parlor; if Luke hadn't come inside with her, she would have fled up the stairs without talking to any of them.

There was no chance of that. Winnie looked up with a smile and saw them. "Ah, here they are, no doubt with good appetites after a day in the open. You've missed supper, but there are remains of the ham and some spiced peaches."

Luke spoke. "Sounds good. There's nothing to make a man ravenous like getting engaged to a beautiful lady and planning a future together."

There was a moment of stunned surprise, and then everyone but Mr. Sylvester came out of their chairs exclaiming in delight. Evelyn gave a squeal and hugged her cousin, laughing up at Luke in approval, and Winnie was next in line to bestow a kiss.

Even the landlady, who had only a few days earlier expressed a few doubts about Luke, smilingly offered congratulations to the couple.

Rebel was taken almost as unaware as the others. It had never occurred to her that Luke would walk in and make such an announcement; she had taken it for granted that she would do it herself, in her own good time, after she had conquered some of her misgivings; now it was too late for that.

Not that she had any doubts about what she felt for Luke. On the contrary. It was only that she could not help recalling how she had met him and later seen him outside her uncle's house on the very night that terrible series of robberies had taken place; all this now came back to her with vivid clarity. And there was the injury to Luke's shoulder, which she could not believe was the result of colliding with a protruding nail in the barn.

She was given no time to dwell upon the matter. Mrs. Tolman, laughing and giving Rebel a broad wink, said she would cut them each a slice of the fruitcake and get out a bottle of wine she had been saving for a special occasion.

She bent to whisper to Rebel as she poured the sweet red wine into her best glasses. "You'll see, miss, a good woman will be the making of him, just as I said. He'll be on the straight and narrow, with you beside him."

If it hadn't been for the bloody bandage under Luke's shirt, safely concealed now under his leather vest, Rebel might have been considerably more reassured than she was.

Yet there was no denying that she enjoyed being the center of attention, being kissed and congratulated and blessed.

"My dear, I'm so happy for you," Winnie told her, not once but several times.

It was not until she lay in the darkness, unable to fall immediately into sleep, that Rebel had time for her own thoughts. They continued to be turbulent.

In the cold light of logic that was possible only when Luke was not touching her, she knew perfectly well that surrendering to passion had been a foolish and dangerous thing, even if he had proposed marriage within minutes after the sin had been committed.

That it was a sin she could not deny. Aunt Winnie would think so, Mrs. Tolman and the boarders would think so, probably even Evelyn would agree.

Beside her, Evelyn turned in her sleep, throwing out an arm that rested warmly against her own. The heat of the other girl's skin reminded her of how Luke had felt against her, his cheek, his hands, his mouth. It was embarrassing even when she was alone, and the night did not cool the remembered fervor. Rebel withdrew carefully from her cousin and let her thoughts drift back through this day that was ending.

Undignified she had unquestionably been, yet how could anyone, once knowing the thrill of making love, care? Just thinking about it was enough to engorge her breasts, to send the hot sweetness through her loins. It was true that there had been a few moments of pain, but she believed Luke's assurances that it would not be so from now on.

From now on. The words hung in her mind, and despite her concerns, they made her smile.

She was no longer alone. She would have Luke.

Perhaps there was a reasonable explanation for each of the matters that disturbed her. And even if there wasn't, why, they were already set aside, left behind, were they not?

Whatever Luke might have done in the past, he would now feel responsible for her as well as himself, and he was intelligent and caring. He might have come close to disaster in the past, but there was no reason to think he would continue to flirt with danger. Perhaps he and Cotton might even become friends again.

Everything, Rebel told herself, was going to be wonderful, marvelous, from now on.

Her happiness lasted until the following afternoon when, on an excursion to a shop on Garrison Avenue, she looked out through a window display of books and maps and saw Jubal Hake.

# Chapter Twenty-one

REBEL CAUGHT HER BREATH AND THE SLENDER VOLUME OF poetry she had been examining slid from her fingers onto the floor with an audible thud.

Evelyn, having won permission to add music appreciation to her classes ("I know so little to teach!" she had cried out to her cousin in dismay after a few days on the job), had asked Rebel to accompany her to a local store to search out material for the new venture. She was now in the back of the store, haggling with the proprietor over the price of a book on the lives of famous composers. Even when Rebel dropped the book, spinning around to call out to her cousin, no one noticed. In fact, they were so engrossed in their discussion that calling Evelyn's name in a strangled sort of voice brought no response.

Rebel stepped quickly to the door, looking out after the tall masculine figure rapidly striding past the shop.

It was Jubal Hake, she thought numbly, surely it was, although this man was fully bearded, not clean shaven as he had been in New York.

Yet he had the same height and breadth of shoulder, the same carriage, the same walk she had observed as Jubal Hake walked away into the snow that fateful night.

In a moment it would be too late; he would have vanished along the street, and she could not allow that to happen.

Rebel gave one more wild glance at Evelyn, discovering that her cousin and the proprietor had gone into a back room, leaving her alone in the shop.

She swore in an unladylike manner and reached for the door handle, plunging out into late afternoon sunshine that nearly blinded her for a few seconds until her eyes adjusted to the brilliance.

Her heart lurched uncomfortably in her chest. There! There he was, nearly a block away already, but still looking like the man who had changed their lives.

Rebel hurried after him, attracting attention from several curious ladies who stared at her; she was only peripherally aware of them. Her own attention was fixed on the man ahead of her.

After a minute or so, dodging a dog and an old fellow with a peg leg and a crutch—damn them, she thought, frustrated because they slowed her down—Rebel realized that one of the reasons the man she was pursuing looked different, besides the new growth of beard, was that he was dressed in the casual attire so many of the men at Fort Smith affected—a plaid shirt and jean trousers, with the pointed-toed boots of those who spent half their lives in the saddle.

Still, she was convinced it *was* Jubal Hake. Rebel stepped off a sidewalk to cross a street and twisted an ankle. She hurried on, ignoring the pain. She couldn't let him escape.

Yet he did. He rounded a corner, from Garrison Avenue onto Fifth Street. And in the minute or two it took her to reach that intersection, Jubal Hake vanished.

Rebel muttered another profane oath, not conscious of doing so. Where had he gone? Into one of the small shops, or one of the houses just beyond them?

Jubal Hake was here in Fort Smith. She hadn't imagined the similarity of his speech to Luke's, and only now did the full implications strike her: had Hake and Lucas both grown up here? How, in a town the size of Fort Smith, could they fail to know each other if that were the case?

And if they knew each other, she thought, her heart pounding both from her exertions and from her speculations, could it be merely a coincidence that both men would have been in distant New York City at the same time, on the very night when Arlen Bickford and his wealthy clients had all been robbed?

What was she doing? Confused and frightened, Rebel looked around at the pedestrians, all of them strangers, and at the drivers of a pair of wagons drawn up in the middle of the street for a conversation. She was trying to connect Luke and Jubal Hake, and there could be no connection. Luke was not the same kind of man as Hake.

She knew with a deep inner conviction that the man she'd fallen in love with was honorable, sincere, and honest. She'd only to look into his face, into his eyes—for a moment she remembered his eyes staring down into hers when he'd breathlessly said her name, "Rebel?"—to know that he loved her. And, loving her, he could not betray her by any conspiracy with a man such as Jubal Hake, could he?

She had a stitch in her side from practically running after the villain, and again the tight lacings inhibited her breathing. Just thinking about it after she'd returned home Sunday, she'd been embarrassed by having left off her confining undergarments on her excursion; what had Luke thought of a supposedly respectable school ma'am who didn't bother with corsets? Further reflection had allowed some sense of humor to surface; the lack of it had certainly made it easier for him to make love to her. Now she wished she could be rid of the confounded corset forever; it seemed she was always needing more air than was available when she was laced to a fashionably narrow waist.

She stood there long enough for the stitch to subside, to regain control of her breathing. It was no use staying here; Hake had entered one of these buildings, or deliberately hidden from her by ducking between two of them. Had he seen her? She didn't think so. He'd passed the bookshop without looking toward her, and he'd never looked over his shoulder.

Rebel made her way slowly back to the shop where she'd left her cousin, to find Evelyn concluding her transaction.

"What happened to you?" Evelyn asked, and then, looking more closely, "Is something wrong?"

"I thought I saw . . . an acquaintance," Rebel responded. And then she addressed the proprietor of the shop, a small elderly man with a dusty air about him. "Are you a long-time resident of Fort Smith, sir?"

"All my life. Born here in 1832," he told her, adjusting his wire-framed glasses to see her more clearly. "Wasn't but a village in those days, no railroad, as many Indians as white folks."

"You'd know most everyone who lived here, then. Do you know anyone by the name of Hake?"

Evelyn shot her a startled look, but the old man was shaking his head. "No, can't say as the name's familiar. Some Hakes over at Caddo, Choctaw Nation. Judge Parker strung one of 'em up here a couple of years ago for horse theft and murder, I do believe." He pushed the glasses up on his nose. "Not friends of yours, I trust."

"No. No, just . . . it's a name I'd heard from around these parts. I thought the man I met might have come from Fort Smith."

He shook his head. "Well, there's new folks coming in all the time, o' course. But no old-time family name of Hake, I'm sure o' that."

Rebel managed a wavering smile. "I see. Well, thank you."

Evelyn couldn't wait to get her outside. "Rebel, did you see Jubal Hake? Is he *here?*"

"Yes. I'm positive it was him, though he's disguised himself with a full beard. I tried to follow him, but he went around the corner and by the time I got there he was gone."

"What were you going to do if you'd caught up with him?" Evelyn demanded.

"I don't know. I hadn't thought that far. Evelyn, if it *is* him, shouldn't we notify the authorities? I mean, maybe even Captain Plummer of the New York police? Mightn't they send someone down here to capture him?"

Evelyn was holding her lower lip between her teeth, relinquishing it slowly. "First we'd better make sure it really is Hake. We'd feel perfect fools asking anyone to come so far and then having it turn out to be a mistake."

"I suppose you're right. But how do we make certain? We can go on looking for him, but he's just as likely to spot us, and then where will we be? He can't

221

assume we won't recognize him because he's grown a beard."

"It might even be dangerous for him to know we're here," Evelyn agreed thoughtfully. "Perhaps you ought to tell Luke. Men are better at handling some things, and this may be one of them."

"No, not Luke," Rebel said quickly, and then had to qualify that, because she could not reveal her true uncertainties. "He has so much to do right now, I don't want to add this to his problems. What about Cotton? He knows everybody, too, and would have ways of finding out about Jubal Hake more easily than we would."

Did Evelyn give her a peculiar look? Rebel couldn't be sure.

"Well, I can consult with him this evening," Evelyn offered. "He'll be coming over to the school with me after supper to practice some of the new music I bought today. He's going to move the piano across the hall and turn the pages for me."

This seemed an innocent subterfuge to allow the two of them to spend some time together. Rebel nodded. "He can make discreet inquiries. And then, if it *is* Hake, we must send a telegram to Captain Plummer."

Evelyn shifted her heavy book from one arm to the other as they walked toward home. "I wonder if he's already disposed of all the jewelry, or if there's any chance of recovering any of it. I've no real desire to return to New York, but I'd like to feel that we could, if we wanted to. If those people were repaid it would show our good faith and go a long way toward clearing Papa's name. I know it would make Mama feel much better."

Hours after Jubal Hake had ceased to be the topic of conversation, Rebel was unable to put aside her misgivings. Her heart told her that Luke was all she had ever wanted in a man; yet she was distraught and perplexed.

If only Luke and Jubal Hake hadn't both been in New York City when the jewels had been stolen. If only the two men didn't speak as if they came from the same part of the country. If only Luke were not concealing an injury that she suspected was the result of a gunshot.

If only, if only.

Yet when Luke turned up just after Evelyn and Cotton had left for the school, it took only his lingering kiss in the shadowed hallway to reassure her that he could have no complicity in any of Hake's skullduggery.

At least it reassured her as long as Luke was beside her.

Later, trying to warm up the cold bed with a couple of heated bricks and her own shivering body, the anxieties returned. Rebel knew that she would have no peace of mind until the riddles were solved and Jubal Hake was safely in the custody of the legal authorities.

# Chapter Twenty-two

"You're late again," Luke said out of the darkness. Cotton stepped into the alley behind the Ox Bow Saloon, drawing his mount with him into the concealing blackness. His tone was rich with humor. "You ought to try romancing an eager young lady and see how fast you get away from her on a night when everybody's kind enough to leave the two of you alone in the front parlor. They even had a fire going for our benefit, though I'll admit we forgot to put more logs on it."

"I'll trade you problems," Luke offered, and immediately Cotton sobered.

"What's up? Something happen tonight?"

"Yeah. While you were cozying up to Evelyn I was involved in some long-range planning."

Cotton lowered his voice so that it could have carried no more than a few feet. "Is it going to happen, then?"

"I think so. The time hasn't been set yet, but soon."

Cotton's words were so soft that Luke leaned toward him to hear better. "There may be a complication. Evelyn told me tonight that Rebel thinks she saw Jubal Hake this afternoon."

For a moment there was silence, and then Luke exhaled in a whistle. "She's not sure?"

"Well, she said he'd grown a beard, but she was practically positive it was him. She chased him—doesn't that sound like her—and he went into someplace on Fifth Street, just off Garrison. She hung around for a few minutes, but he didn't show up again."

Luke considered that at length. "Have they done anything about it yet?"

"No. But they're thinking about contacting the New York authorities if they can find out for certain it's him. They asked me to make 'subtle' inquiries and see if I can find out anything. You're going to have to be careful, Luke."

Luke's chuckle was dry and held little humor. "Thanks for pointing that out. Well, try to convince them they shouldn't do anything without telling you first. Persuade them it's dangerous to go poking around themselves. I'll meet you here again tomorrow night, same time."

Cotton slapped him lightly on the shoulder in response, then wheeled and mounted, riding out of the alley lurching sideways in the saddle. Anyone watching would have assumed he'd just come from the Ox Bow with more than a drink or two inside him.

Though Luke was cold and tired, he waited a few minutes before emerging from the alley. He felt uneasy. He had given Rebel a ride home from school that afternoon, and she hadn't said a word about Jubal

Hake. Why? What did she know, or suspect, that had kept her quiet, when Evelyn had spoken freely to Cotton about the man?

His horse nickered softly when he reached for the reins. There were no answers here, not tonight, and he headed for home through the quiet streets, thinking of a petite girl with copper-colored hair and green eyes and the silkiest skin he'd ever imagined. His thoughts were not unalloyed pleasure, however.

Why hadn't Rebel mentioned that she thought she'd seen Jubal Hake?

Rebel enjoyed teaching school. Her father had loved doing it, and had passed on to her many of his own attitudes and a few little tricks to keep the students interested and enthusiastic. It was a good thing she'd had some hints, too, about discipline, for some of her charges were nearly as old as she was, and several of the boys towered a head taller.

She liked them, however, and for the most part they responded to this in kind.

It was Evelyn they fell in love with, though. This was obvious from the start. Youths with no previous interest whatever in art or music suddenly became models of deportment in order to be in her classes. They brought her small gifts; they found excuses to hang around between classes and consult with her on trumped-up matters. The girls were in awe at her beauty and fascinated by the fashionable clothes she wore; the boys were stricken with puppy-love. If Evelyn was less than an experienced instructor, no one seemed to notice.

Evelyn herself gradually gained confidence, even though she was only hours ahead of the students in the appreciation courses. No one knew that except Rebel, who was getting an education of her own because

Evelyn practiced by conveying her recently acquired information to Rebel the night before she presented it to her classes.

The important thing for Rebel, however, was the quickening of excitement she felt at the end of each school day. She would delay strolling over to look out the window until the last of the children had left, unless one of them dawdled interminably. And then she would learn if Luke was waiting there with the buggy to take her home.

On the days when he was not there, disappointment was crushing, though temporary. For if he did not see her after school, he might come to the house after supper. If she didn't see him at all that day, there would be a delivery of hothouse flowers. While the flowers didn't make up for not seeing Luke, they made her feel warm and wanted. He was, indeed, courting her, and she couldn't think of anything nicer. Except, perhaps, being married to him.

She put down the doubts, for there was no more to suggest that Luke was anything but what he seemed: a considerate and ardent suitor, eager to see the house that they would share built, concerned with expanding his farming operations to assure he would be able to take care of her in the comfortable manner in which his parents lived.

Deeply hidden in the back of her mind, however, remained a niggling uncertainty that made her refrain from mentioning Jubal Hake to Luke.

He was all that any woman could have asked for as a suitor. The flowers were the least of it. He was considerate, courteous, and, when they were alone, passionate. In the front parlor on the evenings when Cotton didn't call on Evelyn, on their buggy rides to and from school and during a delightful evening at the Opera

House, their kisses were sweet and prolonged. Luke's touch evoked all those wild new sensations that both frightened and excited her.

For that reason Rebel had mixed emotions when Luke announced, two weeks after the searing experience that left her torn between guilt and ecstasy, that he wanted to drive out again to the building site on his ranch.

"We'll take a lunch, if this weather holds it'll be perfect for a picnic." He seemed not to notice what the very word "picnic" did to her. "I want you to see how far the workmen have come already. And I want to have you to myself for the afternoon, without Aunt Winnie or Mrs. Tolman hovering on the other side of the door, listening. Some things a man wants to say without being overheard."

Only to *say?* Rebel wondered, and shivered.

She was afraid of what would happen during those hours alone with Luke. Yet she knew she would go. There was never any question about that.

He escorted her to church that morning. Mrs. Tolman gave her a beaming smile and said from behind one plump hand, "See? I told you, all he needs is a good woman to change his wild ways!"

Rebel subdued the desire to laugh. If Mrs. Tolman only knew what had happened last time!

Aunt Winnie was pleased, too. Of course there were so many things Winnie didn't know; she was the living proof that ignorance is bliss. "He's such a nice young man," she told Rebel, smiling. "Polite, intelligent, handsome. And he comes from such a fine family, and has that property and a private income. I'm happy for you, dear."

Rebel intercepted her cousin's speculative gaze upon her and wondered how much was revealed in her own face. She wasn't skilled at deception, as Evelyn was, and she expected any moment to be confronted with questions she didn't choose to answer. It wouldn't matter; if Evelyn saw her face, she'd know the answers, whether Rebel spoke or not.

Luckily, Evelyn was more concerned with her own romance than with Rebel's. Cotton was attentive, and somehow it worked out naturally that he and Luke came courting on different evenings, so that each couple had their turns at the privacy of the front parlor. It never occurred to either of them that this might be the result of collusion between Cotton and Luke; when the men met accidentally, coming or going, they were courteous rather than cordial, and disinclined to make conversation.

Mrs. Tolman had commented on that, shaking her head. "Too bad they aren't friends anymore. You ought to have seen them when they were boys! The talk of Fort Smith, they were! Once, when they were about twelve, I suppose, they'd been forbidden to attend a hanging. Four men were being executed at once, a more disreputable lot of murderers as Judge Parker ever sentenced, and the boys wanted to see it. They'd each told their mamas they were spending the night together at the other one's house, so nobody was looking for them that morning. They spent the night in the open, then at dawn climbed a tree that would give them a good view of the gallows. Trouble was, they'd hardly slept that night, and one of 'em was so tired he fell asleep before the prisoners were even brought out of the jail. He fell out of the tree, and the other one fell trying to save him, and they landed on somebody's wagon down below. Cotton broke an arm, and Luke knocked himself out, and they spooked the horses, so they went charging through the crowd. Nearly trampled a few people before the farmer got his team under control. Both boys probably would have gotten a licking that time if their folks hadn't been scared they'd killed themselves. They never did get to see the hangings."

She smiled at the recollection, though the tale made Rebel shudder. "Always together, those two were. If there was mischief, they were right in the middle of it, every time."

That was when Luke was a child, Rebel told herself. The mischief was behind him. He was a grown man, responsible and too intelligent to do anything so foolish now.

Yet he'd never told her what he'd been doing in New York. He had been injured because he'd been robbed, he'd said that much, but there had never been an explanation of who he was meeting that night, or for what purpose. It was a measure of Rebel's state of mind that she had never been able to ask him, point-blank, about those things.

She was acutely aware of Luke at her side in church, aware too of the glances in their direction, even the comments whispered behind gloved hands. Luke paid no attention. He sang the hymns and recited the Lord's Prayer from memory, and he appeared attentive during the lengthy sermon. Only Rebel knew that, under the cover of her fur muff on the seat between them, he captured her hand and held it. That would have been sufficient to distract her from the perils of sin as disseminated from the pulpit even if he hadn't casually stroked her palm with a thumb from time to time. Rebel felt as if she'd explode if he didn't stop, yet she made no move to withdraw her hand, at least not forcefully enough to succeed.

Virtually everyone made it a point to speak to Luke

and Rebel after the services. She sensed his impatience, yet he remained genial, introducing her to those she hadn't met, including, to Rebel's surprise, the famous, or infamous, Judge Isaac Parker.

Rebel had noticed him, a big imposing man in his early fifties, because he and Luke both stood at least half a head above all the other men. Parker had a shock of thick white hair and a matching mustache and goatee; a gold watch chain drew attention to an expanding waistline. In turning away from an old lady who was beginning to irritate him with personal questions asked in a strident voice, Luke nearly ran into the judge.

The two men stopped. Hazel eyes met blazing blue ones, the latter flickering with curiosity at Rebel, then back to Luke's.

"Well," the older man said in a dry tone, "hello, Luke."

"Good morning, Judge."

"It's been a long time."

"That it has."

"Behaving yourself these days." It wasn't a question, and Rebel thought there was a glint of amusement in the eyes, which seemed so much younger than the rest of the man. She knew at once who he had to be; there was only one "Judge" in Fort Smith.

"More or less," Luke said carelessly, and the judge's full lips twitched. "I don't think you've met Judge Parker, have you, Rebel? My fiancée, sir, Miss Rebel Moran."

The leonine head bowed slightly. "Miss Moran. My pleasure. Welcome to Fort Smith."

"Thank you, sir. I've heard a great deal about you."

This time there was no mistaking the humor. "I'll bet you have, young lady. Well, don't believe anything this scalawag tells you about me. He would have to admit to prejudice."

A large woman in a plain blue bonnet appeared at the judge's elbow. "Isaac, there you are. We'd best get home to check on the roast."

He submitted good-naturedly. "Certainly, my dear. Nice to have met you, Miss Moran. Best wishes to you both."

Luke's hand was firm on her arm. "Let's get out of this crowd. Feel that sunshine! It's going to be a beautiful afternoon. Let's go."

Rebel looked after the departing Judge Parker. "He looks so . . . so nice."

Luke's laughter was so robust that heads turned to look at him.

"He *is* nice. He's a decent family man. He's cleaned up Arkansas and the Indian Territory, made it safe— most of the time—for women and children. The only way to do it was to get rid of the criminals, which the law-abiding citizens approve of by about one hundred percent."

They had reached the buggy and he helped her up into it, then walked around to climb up beside her and take the reins. Rebel stared into his face. "Does that include you?"

"Among the ones who approve of what he's doing? Certainly. Just because he had occasion to see me in front of his bench a few times, years ago, doesn't mean I don't like and respect him."

"Were you really as . . . as much of a renegade as I've heard?"

He laughed again. "Probably. What have people been telling you? About the time Cotton and I broke into the school and decorated it for Halloween? Or when we accidentally broke a window at Adelaide Hall

232

when they were having an important political meeting, and they set the marshals on us? Or the time my dog took after Mrs. Shibley's cat and chased it into Reutzel's Grocery?"

Rebel sounded faint. "I hadn't heard of any of *those* episodes." They didn't sound all that serious, though. Boyish pranks, her father would have said.

"Oh, there's a whole string of them," Luke admitted. "Most of them didn't land us in court. The third time they did, Judge Parker looked down on us—he's six foot two, and was a lot bigger than we were at that time—and told us if we didn't straighten out we were going to wind up out there on the gallows along with somebody like the man they were hanging that Saturday. Made us think a bit." He flashed her a grin that had the power to melt her insides, even when she feared he might be glossing over incidents of more significance. "Newspapers from out-of-town make it sound like the Hanging Judge is a monster, but don't you believe it. He's done what had to be done, in a territory covering 74,000 square miles, with only two hundred marshals to help him keep the peace and bring in the fugitives."

He flicked the reins so the horse would quicken its pace, taking them away from the after-church crowd. "Outsiders think he's a cruel man, without a heart or a soul. It's not so. I saw him once with tears in his eyes when he sentenced two men to die. He looked down from behind that high bench and said, 'I do not desire to hang you men, but it is the law.' And that's what matters to him. The men in charge before he came to Fort Smith ignored the law; they took bribes and were guilty of conspiracies worse than those committed by the criminals, but all that stopped when Parker showed up. Arkansas is safe, now, for men and their families.

We've got nothing to worry about, living out there beside the river. It doesn't frighten you, does it, to think of living so far from town?"

"No," Rebel told him, and it was true. As long as she lived with Luke, she didn't think anything would frighten her.

Except for this afternoon. Would he expect a repetition of the lovemaking that had taken place when they'd been here the first time?

She both wanted it and told herself that she would not allow it to happen again. Not until they were married.

The day was warm and fine with the promise of an early spring. Luke was at his most amusing, relating stories of his childhood with four brothers and two sisters.

"Since I was the oldest, I was usually the one who got the blame when anything went awry," he told her. "It established a level of communication with Pa—or, rather, a lack of it—that I've never been able to overcome. All he talks about is banking, banking—and I hate figures, except when it's the tally of cotton bales off my own land, or the numbers on the checks I get for them."

He did most of the talking; Rebel was content to let him, responding only when he paused for an answer.

The ride went more swiftly than the previous one. Rebel was astonished to see that the foundation and flooring had been laid, and framework was etched against the surrounding trees which were already showing tiny green buds.

"It . . . it looks huge!" she murmured as Luke swung down and lifted his arms for her.

For a moment she was crushed against his chest, setting her pulse to racing, and then he turned her around to inspect the work.

"Come see what we've done. See, this will be the kitchen, and beyond that the pantry, and over here the formal dining room."

Rebel walked beside him, admiring the skeleton of the house they would one day share. At a far corner of the house, Luke stopped. Partial walls were up here, holding in the warmth of the sun, though the top was open to the sky.

"This is the downstairs bedroom. Ma says there should always be one on the ground floor, so that if anyone's sick the whole staff doesn't wear out their legs running up and down stairs. We'll have a room on the top floor, with a view out over the river and the fields, but for now this will have to do."

Rebel's throat nearly closed. "Have to do for . . . what?"

He didn't answer that directly, but reached into a pocket and drew out a ring.

"This is my grandmother's engagement ring. There's a plain gold band to go with it, but for now I want you to wear this, if it fits."

He lifted her hand and slid the slender golden circle onto the third finger of her left hand. It was set with a simple small diamond, and Rebel thought it was the most beautiful ring she had ever seen.

"Is it too loose?" Luke asked, lifting her hand to inspect it.

"No. No, it's fine. It makes me feel so strange to wear your grandmother's ring. To wonder how she felt when your grandfather put it on her finger."

"About the same as you're feeling now, I expect. I *hope*. They loved each other very much. I love you very much, Rebel."

She supposed that eventually she would get used to being so close to him, to his hands drawing her close, to his mouth claiming hers. Her hesitation, her resolve to abstain from anything but the most chaste gestures of affection, dissolved as soon as she moved into his arms.

"I want to do it right this time," Luke said huskily into her hair, his lips brushing her ear. "I want it to be as beautiful for you as it is for me."

He drew back, looking into her face with a tenderness that brought inexplicable tears to her eyes. "Wait here. Don't do anything, just wait."

The things she had planned to say at such a moment died on her tongue, unsayable. He was back so quickly she knew he had planned this very carefully, but still the words to put an end to it would not come.

The buffalo robe was spread on the newly planed oak flooring; its twin was draped over a pair of sawhorses to wall off this private corner.

Protest rose in Rebel's throat as Luke began to unbutton her bodice, but she could not voice it. The love was there so plainly, so strong, in his eyes, his longing for her was no more than hers for him.

Luke paused to lift her hand and kiss the ring he had just placed on her finger. "My wife," he told her. "You are my wife, as much a part of me now as you'll be when the preacher says the words over us. Love me, Rebel, and let me love you the way it should be done."

Numbed yet tingling, awash in emotion and sensation, she allowed him to remove her clothes. She had deliberately worn the corset this time, thinking it would resist any unseemly activity. Luke disposed of it as easily as he did everything else. She had never revealed her entire body to any man, and she felt anxiety rising, that it might not be as perfect as Luke deserved. Yet when she stood at last, naked before him with the sunlight playing on curve of thigh and hip and breast, there was nothing in his face to suggest that anything about her was less than perfection.

He had taken his time in removing her garments; he

divested himself of his own far more quickly. Rebel's breath came in soft little gasps at the masculinity of him, the breadth of chest, the narrowness of hips and waist, the strength of thigh and calf, the maleness that almost made her breathing cease altogether. There was an angry scar on his shoulder, but she was too enthralled with the magnificence of the rest of him to dwell on a nearly-healed wound. When he touched her, it was possible to believe that everything he had told her was true, because she wanted to believe it.

And then he drew her onto the buffalo robe and into his arms, nuzzling her neck, exploring her mouth and body in ways beyond anything she had ever dreamed of.

There was no haste this time; there was, she sensed, a controlled urgency in Luke, but he was determined that he should give her the full measure of delight, and he knew how to do it.

He was right. This time far surpassed their first joining. There was only a brief flash of pain, and then there was only joy, spreading, enveloping, until she exploded with the unbearable wonder of it.

# Chapter Twenty-three

EVEN EVELYN, ABSORBED THOUGH SHE WAS IN HER OWN happy relationship with Cotton Stirling, could not fail to notice the glow about Rebel.

She exclaimed over the engagement ring, then looked with a disconcertingly penetrating gaze into her cousin's eyes. "He's made love to you, hasn't he? You couldn't possibly look that euphoric unless he had."

Rebel laughed, blushing, making no denial. She only hoped that information wasn't written so clearly on her countenance that *everyone* could read it.

They were dressing for school, and from the aromas that drifted up the stairway, Rebel judged that Winnie must have breakfast nearly ready. Evelyn sank onto the edge of the bed and caught Rebel's hand to pull her down, too. There was both awe and excitement in her eyes.

"What was it like? No, really, Rebel, I mean it! I'm

dying to know! Did it . . . did it hurt? Or was it wonderful?"

"A little of each, I suppose," Rebel admitted. "Evelyn, it's impossible to describe. Do you think everyone's guessed? I won't be able to face anyone without turning red . . ."

"I doubt anyone else attributes the way you float around on a rosy cloud to anything but being engaged to marry Luke. It's only someone like me—someone close to you, someone who's also involved romantically —who's likely to realize the truth. Cotton and I have gotten so close a few times—if we had a truly private place to meet God knows what would have taken place by now—but he hasn't proposed yet. I feel as if I'm walking on a razor's edge, and I don't know which way I'll fall when the time comes. The way he makes me feel is . . ."

Evelyn broke off, searching for words, which made Rebel giggle in spite of her own embarrassment. "You see? I told you, it's impossible to describe even that much, let alone what follows."

Evelyn squeezed her hand and spoke with a rare intensity. "Oh, Rebel, I've dreamed about meeting the right man all my life, and now it's happened, and it both thrills and terrifies me. I suspect that even Mama's warnings won't save me when the time comes, but what if it's before Cotton proposes? What if he *doesn't* ask me to marry him? I've been run out of New York City because people thought Papa was ill-advised in his dealings with that miserable jewel thief, and I've no wish to be banished from Fort Smith as an unwed mother!"

Rebel froze. She had never for a moment considered such a possibility, and the idea was daunting even though she wore Luke's ring and he was building her a house. What if something happened to him before the

239

wedding took place, and she then discovered she was carrying Luke's child?

Now, instead of flaming, her face had gone white. How could she have been so stupid? Luke had mentioned wanting to have children, but she had somehow blithely assumed that they would come only during marriage. Aunt Winnie might have driven Evelyn crazy with her rules and admonitions, but perhaps that was better than having had no motherly injunctions at all.

Evelyn didn't seem to notice. She dropped Rebel's hand and stood up, checking her rich auburn hair in the mirror over the bureau. "Come on, let's go or we'll be late. I don't know if you've made me feel better or worse, Rebel."

Rebel felt shaken, disturbed. There had been a few unwed mothers in Lyons Falls, girls who had been ostracized by most of the villagers, some who left their homes in disgrace and were never heard from again.

Of course that wasn't likely to happen to *her*. She and Luke were to be married, and soon, though the actual date had not yet been set. Though she remembered belatedly how some of the women had counted out the months from wedding to the birth of the first child, she didn't think they could tell to the exact day when conception had taken place. On second thought, however, she wasn't positive of that.

At any rate, there wouldn't be an opportunity for another risky session of lovemaking for a week or so. Luke was leaving town today to travel to Little Rock, where he would be taking care of some business for his father—"Pa's pleased to think I'm even carrying papers to the bank over there; it's the closest I've ever gotten to participating in the banking business," Luke had said, grinning—as well as selecting the supplies that would be needed to finish their house.

"I'll bear up under being away from you for that

long," he had told her, kissing her on the nose, "because I know that the sooner that house is done, the sooner we'll be together forever."

The time apart would give her time to strengthen her resolve, Rebel thought. She already knew what she should do, and that was to avoid further intimacies until the marriage vows had actually been taken. It was a matter now of marshaling a firm will and a determination that Luke could not shake, and in a week's time she told herself that she would think of unshakable replies to any persuasions he might muster.

Still, the week stretched emptily ahead of her. Teaching took up only a part of her mind and her time, and it was no easier to deal with her own loneliness now than it had ever been. Especially when Cotton came over in the evening and he and Evelyn (with the door open between the parlors, though only a single lamp with the wick turned low illuminated the front one) sat together and talked in low voices.

By midweek Cotton, too, announced his departure from town for a few days. "Pa wants me to take the Eureka Springs Stage out to Frank Gibson's place and negotiate for this year's cotton crop, and some of his land. Frank's getting old, and he has no sons to pass the land on to. Pa's interested in it, and Adam Kittering's bank will finance it if we can work anything out."

It made for a depressing week for Evelyn and Rebel. With no suitors around, and teaching having fallen into a comfortable routine, they missed the excitement they'd so quickly become accustomed to. Their primary diversion came from a new romance in their midst, which amused and entertained them.

Mr. Sylvester, the American Express clerk who had the room at the very back of the second floor, had scarcely said two words to any of them the first weeks they were in the house, except for his reports on the

241

bank robbery and other such matters on which he had more information than any of the others.

Now, with more time to pay attention to what went on around them, the girls became aware that Mr. Sylvester was doing and saying small things to draw Winnie's attention to himself.

"I don't think Mama's even noticed, yet, that what he does is for her benefit," Evelyn observed. "I wonder if he'll get brave enough to speak out eventually."

"Poor Aunt Winnie, she's so recently widowed that the idea of a gentleman friend has never entered her mind. Mrs. Tolman says he owns a house, over on F Street, which he rented out after his wife died. Wouldn't it be marvelous if your mama married again and had a home of her own and someone to look after? I think she could do it by herself, now, after all the practice she's been getting in the kitchen here."

"Mr. Sylvester's so different from Papa," Evelyn reflected. "I don't think he'd dominate her the way Papa did. He seems such a quiet, gentle man. Do you suppose if he married her he'd want to go to bed with her? Mama hadn't slept with Papa since I was born, and I don't know how she'd feel about that."

Only a month or two ago Rebel might have felt that a marriage without physical intimacies, particularly between people as old as Aunt Winnie and Mr. Sylvester, could be perfectly satisfactory. Now she wasn't so sure. Was it possible to go on experiencing explosive climaxes in lovemaking indefinitely? She couldn't imagine that anyone would voluntarily give up that side of marriage, not unless one's partner was someone like Arlen Bickford.

They giggled about it secretly, observing the tiny courtesies and courtly speeches directed at Winnie by the only male in the household. They waited for the

242

return of their own men, and for the pace of their lives to quicken its tempo once more.

Rebel was deeply touched when Winnie approached her one evening when she was sitting alone in her room, embroidering initials on a pillowcase. The desultory conversation in the parlor intruded upon her private thoughts, so she had chosen to stay upstairs.

"Rebel, dear, I want you to have this," Winnie said, unexpectedly thrusting a small purse at her.

Rebel looked up in astonishment. "What is it? Oh, Aunt Winnie, I can't take your money! Where did you get this? I thought we were all nearly broke when we got here, and you can't have earned . . ."

"Please. Please, Rebel dear, just take it," Winnie said earnestly. "I'm earning a wage here, and my room and board as well, and Evelyn is in no particular need of money at the moment. I'm sure that Mr. Cotton Stirling is going to propose to her any day now, and he's wealthy enough to provide her every comfort and convenience."

She gave the impression of wringing her hands without actually doing it. "I've carried a burden of guilt for so long. Let me ease it now, by providing you with a wee bit of a trousseau."

Rebel forgot her stitching. "Aunt Winnie, what are you talking about? What guilt?"

Winnie sank onto the adjoining chair as if her legs could no longer hold her. "Oh, Rebel, don't you think I've known for years what a coward I've been? I allowed my papa to force me into a marriage for which I had little taste. There was someone else, but he was poor, and I hadn't the courage to give up everything I knew, all the luxuries, the security, and run away with a young man who might have given me something more important than those things."

Winnie's face twisted into a parody of a smile. "Beryl had more courage than I. She defied Papa to marry Ned Moran, and they were happy together, weren't they?"

"Yes," Rebel said softly. "They were very happy."

"In spite of not having much of the material things my family convinced me were necessary. It was a shock to have my own marriage end the way it did, but I'm sure it comes as no surprise to you to hear that it was a wretched one. I knew on my wedding night that I had made a dreadful mistake." Color blossomed in her face. "Mr. Bickford . . . had no consideration for a young and innocent girl. I hesitate to say this to you, dear, for you are young and innocent, too, but it's important to me to make you understand. I was . . . raped, on my wedding night. There was no tenderness, no love, no decency, even, hard though that may be for you to imagine."

Actually, it was not at all difficult for Rebel to imagine. All she had to do was picture Arlen Bickford, to put herself into Winnie's circumstances with a man she did not love, who did not love her. Rebel put a hand over Winnie's.

"I knew that if I had to continue in the . . . the way that I did for that first six months of our marriage, until my doctor persuaded Mr. Bickford that I was too unwell to . . ." Again the ugly color rose up Winnie's throat and flooded her face. That this was mortifying to relate was clear, yet Rebel guessed that it was something Winnie really needed to do, and kept silent.

Winnie gave up trying to express that particular thought and moved on. "After Evelyn was born, I escaped from my marital duties the only way I could; I became a semi-invalid. A cowardly way out, no doubt, yet I hadn't the spirit to handle matters any differently. In every other way, except in the bedroom, I was as good a wife as I knew how to be. I saw to it that Mr.

Bickford's house was well-kept, that meals were served as he liked them, that he had a hostess when he entertained, though Evelyn, bless her, took on that chore when she was no more than fourteen."

Winnie paused for breath, then plunged onward. "Mr. Bickford had nothing but contempt for your father, my dear, as I'm sure you were aware. He thought your mother a . . . an idiot to have married beneath herself. I didn't agree with him. I'd met Ned Moran, and a handsomer young devil I never saw, but I kept my mouth shut on that score, as on all others that raised Mr. Bickford's ire. I allowed my husband to cut me off from my own family, so that all I had was Evelyn, and she an infant. My own mama died shortly after our wedding, you know, and I had too much pride to confess to Papa how miserable a life I led. What was to be done about it at that point? No one in our family had ever even considered a divorce, let alone obtained one, and Mr. Bickford would have fought such a move with all his resources, while I had none to use at all."

Her smile was watery as she dabbed at her eyes with a lace-edged hanky. "I tried, for a few years when you and Evelyn were babies, to stay in touch with your mama. Beryl and I had been close when we were younger. But I could not bear Mr. Bickford's scorn and mockery; the letters that came from Beryl were but one more weapon he used against me, until at last I stopped replying to them regularly. Oh, there were still messages at Christmas, and on the occasions of Beryl's birthday, or yours, when you were smaller. My need was such that I dared that much, though the consequences were sufficiently unpleasant that I hadn't the resolution to cross my husband often."

Rebel squeezed the hand beneath her own. "Mama understood. She never held it against you, Aunt Winnie."

"Is that true, or are you only being kind? At any rate, I knew I was a coward. Do you know, I even imagined picking up the pistol he kept in his desk drawer and shooting my husband with it on one occasion. I would never have dared to do it, of course, but I thought of it, after Mr. Bickford had . . . well, no matter what provoked me so. What matters is that I never had the courage of my convictions, and I never had the opportunity to set things right with Beryl."

"I promise you," Rebel insisted, immeasurably touched by this unexpected recital, "that Mama never thought badly of you. She knew you were caught in a trap from which there was no escape. She never blamed you for it."

"That eases my heart to hear," Winnie sighed, crumpling the handkerchief into a damp wad. "But I want to make amends now, the best I can, to Beryl's daughter. I want you to take this money—it isn't all that much, really, but it's my own, and I'm free to give it in a way I was never free to offer anything in Mr. Bickford's house—for the things a girl needs when she approaches her wedding day."

Rebel's own eyes grew moist. "Aunt Winnie, that isn't necessary. I have everything I need, and after we're married Luke will see to the rest. I have all those lovely clothes Evelyn passed along to me, most of them like new. I don't need to take your money."

"But I want you to! It's true you look lovely in those gowns, but she didn't have undergarments to pass along to you, not many, anyway. A bride needs pretty petticoats and camisoles and nightgowns dripping with ruffles and lace—" She laughed a little. "You see, all those years with Mr. Bickford did not entirely deprive me of my romantic notions! So take the money and buy yourself some pretty things for the bedroom, the kind of things every bride should have."

She rose decisively, resting a hand for a moment on Rebel's shoulder. "God bless you, my dear, and grant you a long and happy marriage. Take it from me, I know a good man when I see one, and your Luke fills the bill."

She left Rebel staring after her with mixed feelings. Winnie's parting remark made Rebel hope that her perceptivity about Luke was more acute than it had been years earlier about Arlen Bickford.

She put the purse aside after inspecting its contents with gratitude. It was true that she would like a special garment to wear on her wedding night, though she already surmised that she wouldn't wear it long enough to matter much.

It bothered her own conscience a little that Winnie thought her so pure and innocent. If she had it to do over again, Rebel told herself, she would have found some way to resist temptation. Yet she could not really regret what she and Luke had shared.

She couldn't wait until he returned from Little Rock, until he drew her once more into his arms.

Rebel was smiling as she resumed her embroidery on the pillowcases. But on the following morning the nightmare began.

# Chapter Twenty-four

EVELYN WAS IN HIGH SPIRITS AS THEY STARTED OFF FOR
school that morning. She expected Cotton back either
that day or the next, which was reason enough for
happiness, and the day was glorious: a few puffy white
clouds drifted harmlessly in a blue sky and the warm
wind teased the budding trees into a dance of spring.
While Rebel had no reason to expect Luke until the
middle of the following week, if he kept to his planned
schedule, she, too, was elated over the weather and the
prospects of going over onto Garrison Avenue after
school to shop for lingerie: the first time in her life she'd
ever had the money to buy something frivolous and
luxurious.

As they neared the school, however, Evelyn commented on the knot of boys clustered outside, deep in
conversation instead of engaged in their usual rough-
housing.

"Now what? I hope there hasn't been another bank robbery, or an escape attempt from the jail," she commented. "It stirs them up so much they can't pay attention to a mere teacher."

As they approached the edge of the group, one of Rebel's favorite students saw them and detached himself from the others. His name was Eben Hawker, and he was twelve years old. He lived on a farm and he rode seven miles every morning and afternoon in order to attend school; he loved to read, and he soaked up the stories Rebel read to the class like a sponge, always eager for more. She had already begun to plan a competition for Eben's benefit: she knew he would win an essay assignment, and she'd buy out of her own funds a prize for the winner. There had never been a book in the Hawker household except for a family Bible, and she was determined that Eben should have a book of his own.

She smiled at him now. "Good morning, Eben."

His freckled face lighted up with excitement. "Morning, Miss Moran! Have you heard the news? The Eureka Springs stage was held up yesterday afternoon and they got away with the cash box! Shot the driver and two passengers as well, and one of 'em died. They were only a mile from our place. We all heard the shots, and Pa went over to see what was going on and found the wounded. Mr. Tisdale, he was hurt the worst. He's still at our house and my ma's taking care of him. He was shot in the thigh and he sure bled a lot. Pa wouldn't let me go look at the feller that was killed."

Evelyn had gone white, and Rebel extended a hand to touch her cousin's arm. "Cotton wasn't on that stage," she said quickly.

"No, ma'am," Eben confirmed. "Mr. Stirling was on the stage day before yesterday. I saw him getting off when I was riding home. I could tell it was him because of that big hat he wears, only one just like it in Fort Smith, I reckon. Besides, I recognized his horse."

Rebel felt a wave of uneasiness sweep through her. Cotton wasn't supposed to be back yet, and if he'd returned to Fort Smith day before yesterday, why hadn't he communicated with Evelyn?

Evelyn spoke as if her lips had gone numb. "You saw him from a distance? Then it's possible you're mistaken about who it was, Eben."

The boy shook his head, oblivious to the cause of her distress, eager to alleviate her anxiety by assuring her that Cotton Stirling was safe and well. It was, of course, no secret to the children that Cotton often met Miss Bickford and drove her home.

"No, ma'am. It was him, all right. There's no mistaking that gelding of his, marked with a white blaze and white feet the way it is. Ain't—" he glanced quickly at Rebel and amended, "There isn't another horse like that in the whole territory, I don't reckon."

"And you say this was near your home, north of town?" Rebel asked quietly, not wanting to draw the attention of the boys who were by now beginning to act out the stage robbery in dramatic fashion.

"That's right. The stage don't—doesn't—usually stop out our way, but I see it go by sometimes. It stopped and let Mr. Stirling off, and he got on his horse and rode away to the east."

"His horse was just . . . tied there, waiting?" Rebel was unaware that lines of bewilderment etched themselves into her brow. "For . . ." she calculated rapidly, "for the three days Cotton was gone?"

"Oh, no, ma'am." Eben gave her a pitying look, but he was willing to make allowances for a city schoolmarm. "Wouldn't nobody—*any*body—stake a horse out for that long. No, Mr. Kittering met him with the horse, ma'am, and they rode away. So they're both

250

safe. They wasn't—weren't on the stage when it got robbed."

Vertigo assailed her. Rebel stared into the earnest, lively face. The boy wasn't making this up. It was true—or he believed it was true. Her throat worked for a few seconds before she could produce the words.

"Mr. Kittering?"

"Luke Kittering, yes, ma'am. I know him and his horse, too. That big black stallion. There's more blacks like that, but they all belong to the Kitterings. Mr. Luke was there, waiting, behind the trees, and when the stage stopped and Mr. Stirling got off, they galloped away like there was a fire or something."

"You must be mistaken," Evelyn said, still having trouble with numbed lips. "Luke Kittering went to Little Rock and he hasn't come back yet."

"Oh, yes, he's back!" It was clear the boy had no idea of the distress he was causing in his eagerness to assure them of the safety of both men. "Too bad he wasn't on the stage. Luke Kittering's a dead shot with a six-gun. I seen him—saw him—shooting against some braggart once that thought he could outshoot any of the locals. Everybody that bet on Luke Kittering won."

From the top of the schoolhouse the bell tolled, and the children began to move toward the front door. Eben beamed up at the teachers. "You don't have to worry. The man got killed was a stranger from up at Eureka Springs, nobody we know." He turned and trotted off after his friends.

Evelyn and Rebel didn't move. Evelyn had a white line around her mouth, and Rebel felt as if she'd been kicked in the stomach by a mule.

"I don't understand," Evelyn said, almost in a whisper.

"No doubt they'll explain, when they come back," Rebel said unsteadily. "Though I can't imagine how—

they don't even *like* each other, so why would Luke meet Cotton with his horse, and stop the stage seven miles out of town?"

"And why would Cotton say he wouldn't be back from Eureka Springs until today or tomorrow, when he must have arranged ahead of time for Luke to meet him day before yesterday?"

"Unless," Rebel's speculation was feeble, "Cotton telegraphed Luke in Little Rock and asked him to come back early for some reason."

"Did you know where Luke was staying in Little Rock?"

Rebel shook her head. "No. But . . . his family probably did."

"And how would Cotton know? He couldn't ask the family, not from Eureka Springs. Rebel, I don't like this. It upsets me no end."

Rebel bit her lower lip until she tasted blood. Evelyn didn't know the half of it; there were all kinds of things she had not confided in her cousin. Things like that wound in Luke's shoulder, sustained at about the same time the fracas had taken place at the Ox Bow Saloon.

"They used to be very good friends, when they were boys," she said softly, trying to think. "And they've never acted like *enemies* when they met."

The bell had stopped ringing, and they realized all the children had vanished into the building. They moved after them, but Rebel, at least, still felt stricken and sick.

Something peculiar was going on, and she couldn't guess what it was. Dread suffused her body with a chilling lethargy, and it was all she could do to call her class to attention and concentrate on the lessons she had outlined for the day.

* * *

Evelyn was organizing a choir and holding try-outs after school, so Rebel went alone downtown to do her shopping.

She had considered canceling the excursion; today's disturbing news had her wondering if she ought to be buying a pretty nightgown for Luke Kittering's benefit at all. Yet since she had told everyone at the boardinghouse she was going shopping, she wouldn't be able to go home without making explanations.

Her enthusiasm for the project was considerably diminished; she kept coming back to Eben's story, and it remained baffling and unsettling.

She revived a little when she began to look at the gowns. Fort Smith might not offer the merchandise found in places like Little Rock or New York, but the selection was far greater than she'd ever seen in Lyons Falls, and for once she had cash money to spend. The soft fabrics, the ribbons and laces and tiny pleats, were enticing.

The shopkeepers, even those she had no recollection of having met, knew who she was. They knew she was being courted attentively by Luke Kittering even if they didn't realize the couple was already engaged to be married, and they put themselves out to be helpful to her. After all, Mrs. Luke Kittering would presumably be a good spender in the years to come. Establishing a good relationship with her now was only good business sense.

She bought a soft cambric gown in white with blue ribbons, a simple, virginal-looking gown, not too elaborately decorated to be practical. And then, on impulse, Rebel added a rather daringly seductive gown as well, that would reveal more than it would conceal. If she hadn't so many misgivings because of Eben's story, she would have thoroughly enjoyed this almost wicked purchase, though she shrank from showing it to anyone else, even Evelyn. She knew instinctively that Luke would find it both provocative and amusing.

The thing she didn't know was whether she would be amused by Luke's explanations of his present conduct. If he and Cotton were engaged in something innocent, something legitimate, why had both men deliberately misled her and Evelyn about what they would be doing while away from Fort Smith?

They couldn't have had anything to do with the stage robbery.

The thought hit her mind with the impact of a sledgehammer—shocking, yet not totally unexpected. It must have been there, suppressed in the back of her mind, all day.

Why hadn't she asked Eben about the holdup men? If the driver and most of the travelers had survived, they must have had some description of their attackers. And since Cotton, and probably Luke as well, were known to the stage driver and the local passengers, they would have to have been insane to consider any such thing. If a schoolboy could recognize both men and their mounts, so could anyone else, and Luke and Cotton would have known that.

Only why was there this ongoing correlation of timing between Luke and the terrible things that had happened? He'd been in New York, and outside the Bickford home, the night of the jewel robbery. He'd been injured then, inexplicably, and again at about the time the shootings had taken place at the Ox Bow. He had not been with her the night of the escape attempt from the Fort Smith jail. And now there was a stage robbery, which would never have seemed to implicate Luke in any way if he hadn't deceived her as to where he was when it took place, and if he hadn't met Cotton

254

with a horse seven miles out of town at a time when both of them were supposed to be hundreds of miles away.

The whole thing was making her head ache.

Rebel emerged onto the sidewalk and was crossing the bricked surface of Garrison Avenue when a familiar figure stepped off the curb on the other side of the street, heading away from her.

This time she had a good long look at the man in profile, and in spite of the addition of the beard the likeness was unmistakable.

It *was* Jubal Hake.

Damn him, Rebel thought with a viciousness that astonished her in its intensity. The man was responsible for Arlen Bickford's death, for the loss of reputation and social standing of the entire family, and if he were somehow tied in with Luke Kittering, it was time she knew about it. She had played ostrich, with her head stuck in the sand so that she could not see what went on, long enough. When Luke returned from Little Rock, or wherever the devil he had gone, they were to finalize their plans for the upcoming wedding. An engagement party was scheduled at the Kitterings, and the formal announcement would appear in the newspaper the following day. How could she go on with the doubts that continued to plague her?

Since Eben's story this morning, she supposed she had known, deep inside, that she could not marry Luke without being sure she could trust him.

Jubal Hake had long legs and his strides were rapidly carrying him away from her on the opposite side of the street.

Rebel clutched her forgotten packages against her bosom and set out after him.

She dodged a wagon and a pair of cowboys heading

for the nearest saloon, changing her angle to cross the street when she saw how rapidly Hake was moving away from her. He must not disappear this time, she thought desperately, he must not! She must learn where he went, and where he could be found by the authorities.

Cotton, when pressed, had shrugged off their queries. No one by the name of Jubal Hake around that he could find, he said. Perhaps it had only been someone who looked like the man who had led to the downfall of the Bickfords in New York. Or maybe it was the same man and, unlikely though it seemed, he'd changed his name when he'd inadvertently followed them to Fort Smith.

Or, Rebel thought grimly now, gaining the far curb and hurrying after the tall figure ahead, maybe Cotton *knew* Jubal Hake and simply wasn't admitting it.

Cotton had told them to stay away from the man if they did spot him again. If it was Hake, he pointed out, he could be dangerous if he recognized them.

Rebel was well aware of the truth of that, whether there was a connection between Hake and Luke or not. Yet she had to take the risk of finding out. She simply could not go on with her life until she knew what was going on.

The sun caught her hair as she passed a shop window, reflecting back at her in a glorious coppery nimbus that Hake could hardly fail to recognize if he looked back. She prayed that he would not and juggled her parcels, trying to draw the hood of her light cloak up over her head to conceal her curls.

Hake was, she realized a moment later, heading for the same corner where he'd vanished before. She had to get there before he entered one of the buildings and escaped from her again.

The sun dropped behind a cloud and Rebel glanced

up, startled, to see that it was later than she'd thought. In another half hour it would be dusk.

There was no one between her and Jubal Hake, now, and Rebel broke into a run. It would be easier without the packages and the purse that slapped against her thigh as she ran. They were slowing her down. On impulse, she slowed enough to thrust them all onto the stoop of a closed shop, then sped after her quarry.

Once more he rounded the corner before she reached it, but he had been only moments ahead of her. Rebel stopped, breathing heavily, heart pounding. Where? Which door? It had to be one of those very close to Garrison Avenue; he hadn't had time to get much beyond the first few buildings, nor even, she thought, time to wait for someone to reply to his knock at a private house.

There were spaces between the buildings, now deep in shadow. Could he have gone through one of those places, perhaps to reach a rear door?

Cautiously, Rebel took a few steps, peering into first one and then another of those narrow walkways between the buildings. No one. She clenched her teeth. Damn, damn, *damn!* Where had he gone?

She saw and heard nothing, no step behind her, no breathing. There was only the rough hand closing painfully over her mouth, a powerful arm pulling her nearly off her feet, against a lean, hard masculine body.

And the voice, remembered after all this time. Jubal Hake's voice.

"Stop fighting, Miss Moran, or I'll have to hurt you."

# Chapter Twenty-five

THE BIG HAND COVERED HER NOSE AS WELL AS HER mouth, and Rebel fought desperately for air. She tried to kick backward, but her captor was easily able to avoid that contact, and she cursed her confining skirts.

My God, he was suffocating her! She had to breathe or die, Rebel thought wildly, and now there was no coherent thought, there was only a savage battle for air.

He had drawn her into a shadowed area between two brick buildings, and the shadows grew rapidly deeper, first in dark spots before her eyes, then spreading, spreading into complete darkness as she lost consciousness.

The voice she heard was unfamiliar, coarse, and angry.

"What in the hell are we supposed to do with a girl?"

Rebel drifted upward through layers of gray gauze,

at first unable to attach meaning to the words, aware only of discomfort. Her teeth and lower jaw ached, and she was lying on a hard floor, a dusty floor, which made her feel like sneezing. She tried to put up a hand to her itching nose and found that she could not; her hands were secured behind her, adding to her discomfort.

"I don't know yet, but I told you—she followed me. She recognized me and she followed me. What was I supposed to do, let her run for a posse of U.S. marshals?"

She knew *that* voice. Rebel was still too stunned to sort it out at first, and then her senses rapidly returned. Jubal Hake. He had cut off her breath and dragged her . . . where? Where was she? How much time had elapsed?

She felt as if she'd been thrown down a flight of stairs. Involuntarily, she moaned.

"She's coming around," Jubal said, and a moment later she was grasped by the hair and her head lifted off the floor so that he could look into her face.

The gray gauze dropped abruptly away, and Rebel was not reassured by what she saw. There was a grim sort of humor in the man's bared teeth.

"Recognized me in spite of the beard, did you, Miss Moran?"

Her vision had cleared, but her mind was still fuzzy. To what lengths would this man go to silence her?

"You're hurting me," Rebel said. She sounded thick and slow.

He let go of her hair and her head thudded against the floor so that she yelped a protest. Jubal Hake squatted beside her, looking like one of those cowboys or ranchers who roamed the streets of Fort Smith, not like the diamond merchant he had purported to be in New York. His face was only a couple of feet from her own, so that she could see the separate hairs in the dark

259

beard and smell the sour odor of something alcoholic on his breath. Instinctively Rebel tried to pull away from him.

"You should have minded your own business, Miss Moran," he said. "How did you follow me here?"

Her chest still ached from the struggle to breathe. "I saw you crossing the street."

"I don't mean to this house, I mean to Fort Smith. How did you know where I was?"

"I didn't know. How could I?"

"Then what are you doing here?"

Unexpectedly, the other male voice replied. "She's one of them new schoolteachers. What are we going to do with her? Somebody'll be looking for her before long, when she doesn't get home for supper."

"Schoolteacher? That right? Who else is here with you? Your aunt and uncle, and that cousin?"

"My uncle killed himself because of what you did," Rebel told him. "There's only Aunt Winnie and Evelyn and me left."

"That right? Well, old Bickford was no great loss, was he? Not even to his family, I should think." He turned away from Rebel to his companion. "We'll have to get her out of here as soon as it gets dark."

The other speaker moved into Rebel's line of view. He was a man of medium size, in his mid-twenties, and would have been moderately attractive had it not been for a jagged scar that disfigured one side of his face. It had healed poorly, leaving a raised ridge from cheekbone to jaw. He had a mustache, but it didn't grow across the scar, giving him a lopsided, villainous look.

"Where you going to take her, for God's sake?"

Rebel's head was rapidly clearing, and it was a question in which she had a vital interest. Was it a good sign that Hake hadn't throttled her when he first dragged her off the street?

Instead of answering his cohort, Jubal leaned toward Rebel. "Who's going to come looking for you when you don't show up at home, girl?"

Not Luke, she thought, feeling the flutter of the pulse at the base of her throat. Luke was in Little Rock—no, unless Eben was mistaken Luke was somewhere closer at hand, but who knew where?—and Cotton, he, too, was beyond Evelyn's ability to reach, which left only her cousin and her aunt. What could either of them do against someone like Jubal Hake?

"Who else knows I'm in Fort Smith?" the man asked when she didn't reply. "Answer me, damn you."

"Nobody," Rebel said. "I saw you . . . crossing the street. I didn't have a chance to tell anyone else."

He gave a grunt that might have been satisfaction. "You'd better be telling the truth, or your friends could get hurt. Another day and this would all have been over. You'd have saved us both a lot of trouble if you'd pretended you didn't see me, Miss Moran. Now you're just going to have to live with the consequences of your foolishness."

"Like what?" the younger man demanded impatiently. "If they come looking for her they'd better find her dead body."

Rebel's heart felt as if it turned over in her chest, and the blood drained from her face.

Jubal stood up, towering far above her; he was more than a head taller than his cohort. "Shut up, Norse. I'll decide what we're going to do, and when we're going to do it. Right now we're going to fix this little lady so she can't yell and create a fuss until we get back."

The handkerchief he stuffed in her mouth was clean, but the one he tied over it, to hold it in place, smelled of horse. The cloth bit into her flesh and for a few seconds, until Jubal adjusted the binding, she thought she was going to be suffocated again.

Rebel had never been more terrified in her life. Luke, Luke, she thought, where are you? Do you love me? Can't you feel what's happening to me? Dear God, wherever you are, help me!

There was no indication that God was listening, and no reason to think that Luke would be aware of her plight, either. Whatever he and Cotton were doing, it was absorbing and important to them. Nothing less would have induced them to mislead—she avoided the term *lie to*—the women they loved.

Cotton was expected back in Fort Smith by tomorrow night. Evelyn would inform him of Rebel's disappearance, provided he actually showed up then. As for Luke, she hadn't expected him for another five or six days, and now she didn't know what to think.

In five or six days, in even twenty-four hours, what would happen to her?

The two men had moved away from her and Rebel looked around. She was in a room with dirty white-washed brick walls; there were cobwebs and spiders in the corners. The wooden floor looked like it hadn't been swept in years. There was no furniture, only some shelves, mostly empty except for a few dimly discerned items that might have been tools.

A storeroom, Rebel decided. An unoccupied shop, maybe. Not a place where anyone was likely to come looking for a missing schoolteacher.

Evelyn knew about Jubal Hake, of course. Would she put two and two together when Rebel didn't return home? If she did, without Cotton or Luke to turn to, would she go to the authorities? To Judge Parker, or the U.S. marshals under his direction? And even if Evelyn acted promptly, how would they find her, particularly if she were moved from here?

She couldn't be sure, but Rebel thought she was in

one of the buildings on Fifth Street, just off Garrison Avenue, very close to where she had been when Jubal Hake took her by surprise. Evelyn knew that this was where Rebel had lost Hake before. Would this area be where searchers would begin to look for her?

She forced herself to be still, to try to breathe normally, to think. To plan. Her best bet was to pretend to be immobilized by fear, she decided, which was not so far off the actual mark as to make it a momentous job of acting. Perhaps, if they moved her from this place, there would be an opportunity to attract attention, to get away.

It was a forlorn hope at best. They wouldn't take her outside unless the coast was clear, would they? And she'd presumably still be gagged, unable to call out for help.

The light allowed in by the single window, high on the opposite wall, was perceptibly dimming. It was nearly dark. How long would it be before those at the boardinghouse realized there was something wrong? And without masculine escort, how could Evelyn even instigate a search?

The men left the room, closing the door behind them, leaving her alone. In a way it was a relief to be alone, though her fear did not diminish.

She would not think about the gag that made her mouth dry, which caused her to wonder if she'd choke to death if she became nauseated. She would not dwell on the discomfort of lying in an impossible position on a dirty floor, nor the tug against her shoulder muscles caused by having her hands drawn behind her back, nor the tightness of the bonds around her wrists.

She would think about Luke. She would remember how lovely it had been to lie in his arms, to feel his lips on hers and the ripple of muscles under her hands as she stroked his shoulders and locked her arms around his neck to draw him closer, to experience that bitter-sweet final exultation . . .

It was no use. She couldn't summon the images, the emotions. She couldn't even clearly picture Luke's face.

Tears oozed from beneath her eyelids and Rebel succumbed, for a time, to despair.

The hours passed with incredible slowness. The light faded, and no one came with a lamp. She must be alone in the building, whatever it was, Rebel thought.

With the darkness came sounds, soft scurrying in far corners of the room. Mice? Please, let it be mice and not rats, she thought, and fought the revulsion that rose in her throat. She must not allow herself to be sick. To give in to nausea might be to die.

The silence, except for the rodents and her own ragged breathing, was intense. She strained to hear anything beyond this room, a horse in the street, a voice, anything. There was nothing.

She tried to guess what time it was. Suppertime, certainly. Her grumbling stomach told her that. Would they sit down to Aunt Winnie's boiled dinner (Rebel had carefully written out the directions for it before she'd left home) without her? Or would they become alarmed, knowing that the shops were closed by this time? If anyone came hunting for her—who, though? She couldn't expect Evelyn to wander the streets alone after dark—would they find the parcels she had left on Garrison Street? Would they realize they belonged to Rebel? And even if they did, where would they look for her?

She grew cramped and cold as well as hungry. The bonds on her wrists were painful, and the gag in her mouth made her feel as if her breathing might be cut off completely at any moment. She had shed a few tears, but that was dangerous; if her nose got stopped up, she really wouldn't be able to breathe.

It seemed to Rebel that many hours had passed before she heard returning footsteps.

Her body was instantly bathed in cold perspiration. What would they do now?

The man called Norse carried a lantern, leading the way. He put the light down and stared at their captive; his scarred face was thrown into exaggerated relief, giving him the menacing appearance of a pirate.

Jubal Hake entered the room behind his confederate, crossing directly to Rebel. "Still here, are you? Well, come on, we're going for a ride."

He hauled her effortlessly to her feet, but it was all she could do to stand after hours in cramped repose, and he had to hold her upright. He did it as if he were handling a bag of feed.

"This way, Miss Moran. Wait a minute." He paused to pull her hood up over her head, so far forward that it interfered with her vision. "Can't have that red hair showing; anybody who's ever seen it will recognize it. There, now walk along like a good girl. Don't try anything funny and you won't get hurt."

What could she try? Her hands were still bound, her feet were prickling from having gone to sleep, the gag was still in her mouth, and she was propelled forward with a firm grip on her arm.

The temperature had dropped while she'd been inside and the chill passed through her light cloak. She wished she had the fur-lined one.

There were lights in a house across the street, and at the intersection with Garrison Avenue there was a streetlamp. Here, though, as they came out through the front door of the building, it was dark enough so that she stumbled, unable to see where to put her feet. If

Jubal Hake hadn't had a secure hold on her she would have fallen.

A horse whinnied close at hand. Rebel sensed rather than saw the movement as Norse led a pair of horses out of the alleyway.

"Up you go, missy," Hake said, and lifted her onto a beast that shied, nearly spilling her. She had never felt more helpless.

"How's she going to stay on that way?" Norse wanted to know. "Look, why don't we just leave her here, tied up? Nobody's going to find her."

"They might," Hake contradicted. "And I've been working on this deal too long to have it ruined now by a talkative female."

"It's kidnapping to take her," Norse pointed out.

Hake laughed. "What difference does that make? They can't hang you more than once, not even the great Judge Parker can do that, can he? Here, girl, I'm going to free your hands, so you can hang onto me as we ride, but remember what I told you. It's going to hurt real bad if you try anything, because I guarantee you, you won't get away."

The steel of his knife was icy against her benumbed hands, and then the rope dropped apart. As the blood surged into her fingers Rebel rubbed them, hoping no permanent damage had been done by cutting off the circulation for so long.

A moment later Hake vaulted into the saddle in front of her, speaking over his shoulder. "Better hang on, or they'll find your trampled remains in the morning," he said, and swung the horse around so abruptly that she nearly fell.

The street was empty. There was no one to call to, no one to see.

They rode out of Fort Smith, not fast enough to attract undue attention, not close enough to any of the few stragglers still on the streets for anyone to tell that Rebel was a prisoner.

She lost her sense of direction. She had to cling to Hake or risk falling under the horse's hooves. The sensation returned to her hands, bringing pain with it, but that was the least of her worries.

The big horse broke into a gallop at last, and they left the town behind them.

Luke, where was Luke? If only she could let him know where she was, what was happening to her!

But there was no one to save her. There was only the darkness, the cold wind, the powerful body of the horse beneath her, and the dreaded man in front of her in the saddle.

Rebel hung on and wondered if she would see Luke, or anyone else she knew, ever again.

# Chapter Twenty-six

REBEL WAS SO WEARY, COLD, AND HUNGRY THAT THE END of the ride came as a relief, even though her apprehensions had mounted about what would happen at the end of it.

The lights of Fort Smith had long since vanished, and for the past half hour not even an isolated farmhouse had offered the comfort of a lighted window.

When the flicker of firelight ahead of them broke the darkness Rebel tried to draw herself together, emotionally and physically.

There had been no conversation during their ride. Jubal Hake took the lead, with the scar-faced Norse behind him, the horses thundering along the road and then taking to the low hills.

Now, as they came over a slight rise, there was the fire, and three dark figures standing around it.

Rebel did not admit even to herself, until she'd been

allowed to slide off the horse and approach the fire, that she had been terrified one of the men would be Luke or Cotton. The relief of seeing only unfamiliar faces left her weak in the knees.

Dear God, had she really thought Luke would be tied in with a gang of desperados?

Hake shoved her forward toward the fire, which gave off a welcome warmth. There was no indication that there was anything to eat, however; Rebel's stomach growled audibly and the men turned toward her and the other newcomers.

There was a muttering of disapproval among the men already there. "What's going on? Who's the girl?"

"Someone who recognized me from another job," Hake said smoothly. "She's just going to stay out here for a day or so, until it's safe to let her go. By the time she's found, we'll be well away from Arkansas, and she can tell the marshals anything she likes."

The ripple of uneasiness increased. Rebel held out her hands to the flames, almost afraid to look directly at any of the men for fear that might be signing her own death warrant. Were they all going to flee the state, or would there be those who intended to remain in Arkansas who would not want anyone around who could identify them?

"Why bring her here?" one of the men demanded. He was a burly fellow in a wide-brimmed hat that concealed most of his bearded face, and his voice held a note of authority. "What if somebody followed you? There's more at risk here than just your own hide, Salters."

Salters? Rebel sneaked a quick glance at her abductor, who had released her and was warming his own hands, but she wasn't quick enough. Hake, or whatever his name was, grinned at her, intercepting her look.

"A man in my line of work changes his name from

269

time to time," he told her. "Got a batch of cousins who loan me a name when I need it."

The challenger stepped closer to Hake. "Nobody gives a damn what you call yourself. But to bring a female out here the night before a job we been planning for months don't show good judgment."

Hake's grin vanished, and there was a wolfish twist to the mouth, nearly covered in the heavy dark beard. "Who made you head of this outfit, Grimes?"

The bulky man thrust his face closer to the fire so that Rebel saw the flames reflected in his eyes. "I may not be the boss, but my tail's in the crack same as everybody else's if you foul up. And I sure as hell didn't sign on to knuckle under to you, breezin' in with your crazy ideas after we already had things lined up."

Hake straightened to his full height. "Tracker and I talked about this job nearly a year ago, before you ever did anything more exciting than steal a steer from a farmer. He waited until I came back so we could work it together, and the reason he was willing to wait is that I can *think*. I can plan. And I add the class to this operation that none of the rest of you can do. You're hired guns, nothing more, Grimes. Without me, all you're doing is robbing a train and taking a chance on getting your heads shot off."

Robbing a train. The words were implanted in Rebel's mind as if burned there by a branding iron. A hanging offense, and one that would send Judge Parker's marshals after them all no matter where they fled. Her heart sank. How could they afford to let her describe them or risk allowing her to testify against them in court?

Grimes was obviously having similar ideas. "You ain't so damn smart if you brought that girl here. She's seen us. She's heard some of our names. You gotta get rid of her."

Hake was cold and he emanated an air of authority unmatched by anyone else in the circle. "I'll decide about that. I did some thinking on the way out here, and I've got plans for Miss Moran. She's going to contribute an air of legitimacy to this operation. That's the trouble with you, Grimes, you have no imagination, no class. That's what Miss Moran is going to help us with, so I don't want her marked up anyplace it'll show, and I don't want her clothes mussed up, either. She's going to look like a schoolteacher when she gets on that train with me, and nobody's going to suspect a thing."

For long moments the two men glared at each other across the campfire. Then Grimes swore and turned away, unconvinced but unwilling to put the other man's determination to the test.

Rebel's legs felt like rubber. What did Hake mean? What was he going to make her do?

She was torn between horror at the idea of being forced to participate in a train robbery and the hope that, in the presence of other people, she might be able to sound a warning to the potential victims and to effect her own escape.

"Everything's ready?" Hake asked sharply, and there were reluctant nods among the men. "All right. We're going on ahead as planned. Tell Tracker, when he gets here, that everything's set on my part. I need another horse for the girl. We'll make better time if mine's not carrying double."

There ensued a brief and bitter discussion of which mount could best be spared. Rebel wondered if there were any chance that the thieves would have a falling out before they achieved their objective; certainly they were at odds over any number of things, and Hake was more feared than respected or liked.

A horse was brought forward, and Rebel was assisted to mount. There was no sidesaddle, of course, and she had to ride with her skirts drawn up immodestly high. It was the least of her worries, though it made her uncomfortable to have the ruffians around the fire gazing at her exposed ankles ·and undergarments. To guess by the bold, lewd glances, she was lucky indeed that Hake wasn't leaving her here with these men.

Hake himself was not a reassuring companion, of course. And he was taking no chances with her. He retied Rebel's wrists, in front of her this time so that she could cling to the saddlehorn, and then secured her mount to his own. He was leaving her no option but to follow after him.

Rebel could see nothing as they left the campfire behind them and rode out across the prairie. The ride seemed endless, hour after hour in the night so dark she did not know how Hake could tell where he was going.

It seemed that he did, however, for after so long a time that Rebel feared she would doze off in exhaustion and fall from the horse, she heard Hake's muffled exclamation of satisfaction.

She straightened a little, peering beyond him, and saw the flicker of light through a grove of trees.

Not a campfire this time, but a house, surely. She came out of her lethargy, willing her mind to clear, her body to be ready to respond should there be any opportunity to escape.

There was no such opportunity. Hake approached the small building that was barely discernible through the copse, dismounted, and dragged Rebel off her horse, leaving her hands bound.

She realized, as Hake threw open the door, that the place was a railroad depot, one of the small ones scattered along the tracks between Fort Smith and Little Rock.

He shoved her ahead of him into the lamplight, laughing when a man with a rifle rose quickly from his seat beside the cast iron stove. Before anything else registered, Rebel smelled the stew that simmered there, making her mouth water.

"Put the gun away, you fool, it's only me. Everything under control?"

The man with the rifle was close to sixty, a grizzled fellow in garments so stiff with grease and grime that they surely must have been capable of standing alone. He lowered the weapon and glowered at Rebel.

"Who's that?"

"A young lady who is going to add respectability to my performance tomorrow. Or should I say, later on today?" He pushed Rebel toward the bench the old man had vacated, and she fell onto it. "Give us a plate of whatever's cooking. Where's the stationmaster?"

Rebel already knew the answer. She was staring into the terrified eyes of an old man in the corner, trussed like a turkey for the oven, with a gag similar to her own.

"He ain't gonna get to the telegraph, or warn nobody," the man with the rifle said. "Nobody told me there was goin' to be no female involved in this. You can't trust no female."

"I don't intend to trust her," Hake asserted. He took off his hat and dropped it on the bench, then bent to untie the kerchief that held the gag in her mouth. "Nobody around to hear you make any ruckus, Miss Moran, but if you do this'll go back in without you getting anything to eat."

The relief was incalculable. She felt bruised, dehydrated, ready to collapse. And the hunger gnawed at her stomach so that she shook when the old man brought her a bowl of the stew and a chunk of bread to go with it.

The trussed-up stationmaster made sounds deep in his throat and Hake paused in his chewing to look at him. "He been fed?"

"No. I wasn't about to let him loose to eat, not with just me here to watch him. He already tried for a gun, and I had to break his hand to get it away from him."

Hake resumed eating. "Untie him long enough to eat. There's plenty for all of us. Then we'll tie him up again and Miss Moran and I will get some sleep, so we'll look rested up like regular travelers when we get on the train tomorrow."

Rebel's stomach almost rejected the longed-for stew. She hoped he did mean *sleep,* not anything else. The thought of having Jubal Hake touch her in an intimate way was so revolting she forgot, momentarily, how close she was to being starved.

The stationmaster, freed from his bonds, accepted his plate of stew and ate hungrily before he spoke. Then he looked at Hake.

"You're never gonna get away with this, mister. You might get on that train, but you're never gonna get that cashbox that's goin' to the bank. They got guards on it will shoot you dead."

Hake bit off a chunk of the bread and chewed. "Maybe. Maybe not, old man. At any rate, you're not going to telegraph for the marshals. Eat up, it may be your last meal for a while."

"Even if you get away with the money," the stationmaster persisted, "they'll hunt you down. Hang you on the gallows in Fort Smith, the whole lot of you. I seen 'em hang six men at one time, all of 'em kicking and jerking 'til it was over. Think on it, mister."

Hake scraped at his plate, then ladled out another helping of the stew. "If they catch up with me they'll hang me now, so one more job isn't going to matter."

Rebel found her voice, now that she had something

in her stomach and her knees were no longer shaking. "Why are you doing this? You have all those diamonds and the other jewels you stole in New York."

"Ah, but jewelry is no good until you convert it into cash. And you have to be careful where you do that kind of business." He gave her a sardonic smile. "This will be cash money that can be spent anywhere, and will get me far enough away so nobody will ask where I got the diamonds. Nobody will care."

Rebel watched him, baffled. "You speak as an educated man, yet you're a common thief. I don't understand."

"Oh, not a *common* thief, surely." He laughed. "I thought that business in New York was fairly clever. Yes, I had a reasonable education, my uncle brought me up the same as his own sons. But the schooling wasn't worth anything. It didn't earn me any money. It didn't give me any real family, any prestige or position or power. When the chance came along to improve my lot, why, I took it. And when this job is over, I'll be able to live like a gentleman, whether your cousin thinks I qualify or not."

So he had noticed that Evelyn observed his table manners and his conduct with some amusement. She had not been unkind about it, though.

Rebel could not quite summon the courage to ask the question uppermost in her mind: were Luke and Cotton in any way involved in what was going on? Or was there a perfectly rational and legitimate reason for the two of them to have misled people as to their whereabouts and their friendship, and to have met at the Eureka Springs stage stop yesterday?

She did, however, give voice to her most immediate concern. "What are you going to do with me?"

She saw by the malicious glint in his eyes that he understood that concern only too well. He sighed and stretched out long legs toward the stove, setting aside his plate.

"Well, I'm sorry to disappoint you, Miss Moran. I'm too tired, and too absorbed in working out details for procedures tomorrow, to feel amorous. And I probably won't have time afterward, either, unless you'd like to accompany me when I leave this part of the country forever."

Rebel swallowed her fear. "Thank you. I think not."

Hake laughed. "Very well. Let's get some rest, so that in the morning you may play the part of my wife when we board the train. No one will suspect a man who travels with a wife who is unwell, do you think? A wife who leans heavily on his arm and clings to him with weakness as well as affection?"

He stood up and crossed the small room to a door, throwing it open. "One bed. We'll have to share, then. You won't mind? I assure you I'm going to fall asleep very quickly, with my boots on. There's only the matter of making sure you don't get up to mischief while I'm snoring."

She was not entirely reassured by this declaration, for she was assuredly helpless with her wrists tied at the head of the bed, her ankles at the foot. Hake meant what he said, however, for within moments after he joined her on the straw-filled mattress, he was asleep.

Rebel, though exhausted, did not as readily succumb to slumber. She was not comfortable, though in truth this was much better than being hog-tied on horseback, and certainly better than a dirty floor. The blanket Hake had thrown over them smelled as if it could do with a good washing, but it was warm.

Gradually Rebel's fear sank into temporary abeyance, and she, too, slept.

# Chapter Twenty-seven

THE NIGHT SPENT SHACKLED TO AN UNFAMILIAR BED HAD not been particularly restful, yet when they stood on the platform waiting for the train the following morning, Rebel felt curiously alive and strong.

Her stomach was fortified with bitter coffee and lumpy oatmeal, so that it would be hours before hunger became a problem again.

This was not to say she felt at ease. Rather, she imagined herself as a chained tiger, sleek and powerful, ready to make a break for freedom the moment the keeper's attention was distracted elsewhere.

It was warm enough in the sun so that the cloak was an unwelcome addition to her rather crumpled garments, but Hake had insisted that she wear it, with the hood pulled securely over her coppery curls.

"I don't want anybody looking at you, and that hair's like a torch," he told her after a critical inspection.

"Don't talk to anybody, and don't let go of my arm. You're sick, remember. Don't overdo the acting, it's better if nobody pays any attention to you at all. And don't try to interfere with what I'm going to be doing, because your life depends on it."

Rebel didn't doubt that he meant what he said. He wore a six-gun under his coat, and the way he'd loaded it while she watched had assured her he was at ease with it. She knew he would shoot her if it was to his benefit.

The train puffed to a steaming stop, and Hake took her firmly by the arm and helped her climb the steps. Rebel gave a quick backward glance toward the station-master, who had been freed to appear in the doorway and wave at the engineer and the conductor. If the rifle held against his back by the unseen conspirator made him fear for his life once his usefulness was past, the old man concealed it fairly well.

Rebel didn't know his name or that of Hake's cohort, but the stationmaster had managed to convey, while he dished out the oatmeal with trembling fingers, that he had worked for the railroad for many years, and that even this involuntary cooperation with its enemies shamed him. She hoped that he would not be shot when the train left, nor lose his job if he survived.

There was no time to worry about the old man, however. In the next hour, somewhere between here and Fort Smith, her own fate would be decided, and she must be alert and ready to seize any chance to save herself.

Hake guided her along the aisle looking like a solicitous husband but his fingers dug painfully into her arm and she was conscious of the bulge of the gun under his coat.

The car was no more than half-filled. Rebel had blurred impressions of cigar-smoking men in western garb like that she was used to on the streets of Fort Smith, a traveling drummer in his cheap suit and a derby, so different from the wide-brimmed Stetsons, an elderly couple sharing a picnic basket, and a young woman with a sleeping infant.

She probably would have been oblivious to all of them except that her eyes scanned the other passengers in a forlorn hope that somehow Luke would be returning home early, that Eben was mistaken about having seen him north of town with Cotton. There was no one who looked like Luke. Or Cotton. Or any of the men they had met around the fire in the hills last night. Only strangers, unsuspecting, vulnerable.

Was there anything she could do to save either them or herself?

If he's going to kill me anyway, when he's accomplished his purpose, she thought grimly, I might as well try, when the time comes.

The trouble would be in knowing when that time arrived, and in acting quickly enough.

In the meantime, she would be submissive, meek . . . and watchful.

Hake shoved her ahead of him into a seat at the far .end of the coach. When they were seated, they had a clear view of the entire car.

Rebel had to fight the tendency of her mind to go blank, to withdraw from reality. Unless she stayed aware of what went on around her, perhaps found someone among the other passengers who might be an ally during the crisis that was rapidly approaching, she had no chance at all of coming out of this to meet Luke when he returned home.

For a moment she clung to the memory of Luke. She was able to recall his face in every detail: the shape of his mouth, the way the dark brows grew over the hazel eyes, the bold nose and firm jaw. Would she see him again? If she did, Rebel determined, she would ask him point-blank for explanations about everything that troubled her, and she wouldn't settle for evasive answers. And then they would make love without reservations, because Luke would come up with all the right answers, even though she couldn't imagine now what they would be.

Hake settled himself beside her on the dusty-green plush, lifting his feet to rest them on the facing seat. Rebel stared at his boots, scuffed from the stirrups, knowing that if the man had looked into her face at that moment he would have read the hatred, and the bitter intent, there. She swallowed. She must make him think she was docile, cowed, not dangerous in the slightest.

Hake took out a two-day-old newspaper and began to read, or pretend to read. Rebel willed her breathing to level off and her mind to work. Who among the passengers might possibly help if she tried to get away from her captor, or to interfere with the robbery that was scheduled to take place? She didn't want anyone to be hurt, but it seemed a foregone conclusion that guns would be brought into play when the plan was set in motion.

She saw no one who looked like any of the men from the campfire last night, which didn't necessarily mean none of them was on board in another car. Or perhaps they would be getting on at a station nearer to Fort Smith.

She examined two men halfway down the car who sat facing each other, clouds of smoke drifting between them. In their forties, perhaps, and they looked capable and intelligent. She was pretty sure she'd noticed at least one of them wearing a six-gun too.

Yet they would be taken by surprise, and an attempt to draw a gun might only mean the man would be shot and killed before he could get the weapon free of its holster.

Rebel let her gaze drift from one passenger to another, evaluating them. The mother with the baby would be of no use; the woman opposite her looked the type to start screaming the moment one of the robbers made himself known. No help there.

There was one armed man at the far end of the car from where she sat. He might be an ally, though it was hard to judge since she couldn't see his face. He appeared to be sleeping, his hat tipped forward to cover everything but his jaw-line, which showed a stubble of dark beard. He wore a faded plaid shirt and leather vest, and the toe of one booted foot, visible where he rested it on a seat across the aisle from her side of the train, suggested that he spent most of his time in the saddle.

He was broad through the shoulders, trim through the waist and hips, and even in slumber exuded a lithe masculine grace. If he weren't one of Hake's confeder- ates, who had gotten on the train ahead of them, he might prove of some value.

On the whole, though, it appeared there was no one she could count on. What, then, could she do to stop a train robbery and whatever was planned for her when it was over?

Since she knew nothing except that what was to happen must take place within an hour, Rebel could only bide her time.

The conductor, a genial man with a shock of white hair that reminded her of Judge Parker, came along and punched their tickets. "Have a nice trip," he said, handing the pasteboard stubs back to Hake.

Hake nodded, not speaking. When the man had gone on along the aisle, there was no one within hearing distance of them. Rebel wondered what her companion would have done if this very last seat had already been occupied when they got on the train, as it was obvious Hake had chosen it with an eye toward keeping track of everything that took place.

Rebel shifted uneasily, and Hake gave her a sharp look.

"I'm too warm with this cloak on," she told him defensively, and it was true, though part of her perspiration might have been the result of nervous tension as well.

"You uncover that hair and you'll be sorry," he told her coldly.

"I'm sorry already. Sorry we were civil to you, even kind to you, when Uncle Arlen brought you home with him," Rebel said with asperity, though not in a voice that could possibly carry to anyone else. "You repaid our hospitality very poorly, Mr. Hake."

"Arlen Bickford was a fool," he told her.

"Perhaps so, but he didn't deserve to die for it. Did you give any thought to what it would do to him, to be blamed for something that was not his fault, when you took all those jewels?"

He shrugged. "Not much, no. It's a dog eat dog world, Miss Moran. Nobody ever gave me anything. I figured out by the time I was fourteen that if I was ever going to have anything I was going to have to take it. The easiest way has been with a gun, and if you think I'm going to be apologetic about helping myself, you're doomed to disappointment."

She considered that, loathing him. "You have enough education to have made a living doing something acceptable, not going against the law."

He gave a low bark of laughter. "Doing what? Being a clerk in a dry goods store? Working in a bank?"

That reminded her of Luke and his aversion for the

family business. Hake gave her no time to dwell on that.

"I did work in a bank once, as a matter of fact, and I hated every minute of handling other people's money while working for a salary that enabled me to subsist in a hovel with none of the finer things of life. That's why, one day, when the bank manager was out of town on business, I filled up a satchel with money, hung the closed sign in the window, and never looked back. Luckily I'd had the foresight to take the job under the name of another of my cousins, so they have the wrong name on the wanted posters, and the likeness of me isn't particularly accurate or flattering, either."

Rebel was surprised that, under the present circumstances, he would talk this much. Perhaps that was his weakness, and she might be able to exploit it. If she kept him talking she might put him off guard as well as learn something useful. She realized, uneasily, that this could be dangerous. If he was frank about his past misdeeds, it could mean only one of two things: he was confident that his escape could be managed without leaving a trail for the marshals to follow, or he didn't intend that Rebel should live long enough to provide the law with any information that could result in Hake's arrest. Yet she could not stop now.

"You had forged credentials, and real diamonds to sell to my uncle."

He lowered the newspaper and gave up the pretense of reading it. "He was a fool, but he wasn't stupid enough to have been taken in by a perfect stranger or to have bought stones that weren't genuine. I took that for granted when I found his name listed in the little book the diamond dealer carried."

Rebel's mouth was dry. The "possible" young man had shifted position in his sleep, flinging out a hand with a heavy ring on it, set with a dark stone. She couldn't see his face any better, though, for if anything, the hat covered it even further.

"And you . . . killed that diamond dealer?"

"Not at all. I only knocked him over the head when he was foolish enough to walk out into the dark after he'd let it be known he was carrying valuable 'samples.' I'm sure he recovered after a week or two. Not that I'm against violence when it's necessary, so don't get your hopes up in that direction. I may have killed a man who made the mistake of following me when I was too busy to be bothered with him, at least I hit him hard enough to crack his skull. So don't think I won't crack yours, too, if it suits me."

She told herself to ignore that. Succumbing to fear wouldn't help her. "How . . . how did you do it, getting the addresses and the keys to all the houses of my uncle's guests?"

His lips drew back in a feral manner that made her fight to keep from cringing away from him. "Ah, that was a bonus. The high and mighty Bickford was so eager to sell a diamond necklace to some society matron that he didn't even notice I'd been into his safe at the back of the shop, and you and Miss Evelyn were most cooperative: inviting me to the party, leaving a guest list where I could find it, showing me where everyone left their wraps so I could get at their keys. Actually, I had a master key that worked on most of the locks. You'd be amazed how easy it was to get one."

The train was up to full speed, racing across the countryside. It won't be long now, Rebel thought, her nails digging into her palms. He would have to act soon. The robbery would take place before they reached Fort Smith, and the minutes were ticking away like a time bomb.

"You worked alone that time, didn't you? I'm surprised you'd be involved now with all those other men.

**284**

Men who don't seem your type at all," she said, not to flatter him but because it was true.

"I work best alone, or with a single partner," Hake admitted. He folded the newspaper and tossed it onto the seat beside his feet. "But this job was set up a long time ago. Do you have any idea how much money they ship between banks in this part of the country? I didn't know there were going to be so many other men involved—it splits up the profits too much. I'll never work again with a gang. But this is a special shipment, and it's big enough to go around."

He sat up suddenly, leaning toward her to look out the window. This brought his shoulder against hers, and Rebel steeled herself not to flinch. Her gaze followed his, but there was nothing to see except barren prairie.

No. Wait. The train was slowing. Wasn't it? Were they approaching another station, perhaps the last one on the route before they reached the depot in Fort Smith?

And then she saw them coming over the rise: half a dozen horsemen. A few seconds later Rebel noticed they all wore bandanas tied over their faces and identical dark hats. Her shock was no less profound because she'd anticipated something like this, for she still had no plan, no weapon. The train began to swing on its tracks, heading for the horsemen, who then vanished from sight.

No one else among the passengers seemed to notice anything amiss. Some dozed, the young mother was discreetly nursing her baby behind a blue blanket, the smokers were still talking above the clack of the wheels on the rails. Rebel's chest began to ache, and she forced herself to inhale and exhale.

Beside her, Jubal Hake rested a hand on the butt of his six-shooter.

Rebel wildly considered making a grab for the gun herself, but what would that accomplish except that he'd probably shoot her? She looked at her only hope, the sleeping cowboy—and froze. She felt, quite literally, as if the blood stopped moving in her veins, having turned to ice.

The man was no longer sleeping. As Hake eased his weapon free of its holster, the man with the heavy ring reached down to the kerchief knotted around his neck and drew it up over the lower part of his face as he raised his head.

The train suddenly shuddered, brakes screaming, and the passengers were jolted from their lethargy. Before they had come to a full stop, Jubal Hake was on his feet, speaking in a voice loud enough to carry over the exclamations of the others.

"Just stay in your seats, folks, don't anybody reach for a gun, and everything will be all right." In his arrogance, he hadn't even covered his own face, although of course if he shaved off the beard that would alter his appearance considerably.

Hake stepped into the aisle, ignoring the gasps and a profane protest from the man ahead of them who was wearing a gun. Hake had observed that, also. "Take off the belt and throw it on the floor," he commanded, and with Hake's weapon aimed at his head, the man reluctantly complied.

Hake's hand reached down for Rebel's arm. He propelled her to her feet and ahead of him, kicking the discarded gun ahead of him. His grip was like steel, there was no twisting away from him, even if he hadn't been armed.

The bandit at the far end of the car had risen and moved into the aisle, too, glancing over his shoulder. Rebel couldn't tell what he saw through the window toward the front of the train, but apparently it was reassuring, for he gestured with his own weapon.

"Go on through," he told Hake, and Rebel nearly fainted.

For she recognized the voice, and even if it had been disguised, she would have known the hazel eyes that stared into hers from above the concealing bandana.

Nausea washed over her in a scalding wave that made her, for a moment, wish that Jubal Hake *had* shot her. Anything would have been better than this.

# Chapter Twenty-eight

SHOCK MADE HER SENSELESS. REBEL STUMBLED AND SHE would have fallen had not Jubal Hake, with an angry oath, held her up.

"None of that, Miss Moran, or I won't bother with you any longer! Walk, damn it!"

Rebel walked, her mind reeling. It wasn't possible, was it? She knew Luke, she loved him, and he would never be involved in anything like a train robbery.

Yet he was back there in the car she had just left, with a kerchief concealing his face and a six-gun in his hand, holding the frightened passengers in their seats.

If it hadn't been for that flashy ring, Rebel thought, she might have recognized him, even though he'd kept his face covered by the brim of his hat.

Had he been informed she would be there as Hake's prisoner? Or had he been as stunned as she was, to come face to face that way?

Hake shoved her ahead of him into the next car where another gunman had the situation under control. The passengers who had been wearing guns had been adroitly deprived of them almost before the train came to a stop, the men who had carried them registered anger and frustration. Everybody else looked scared. One woman was sobbing openly, which struck Rebel as a dangerous thing to do.

"All right here?" Hake demanded.

At the grunted affirmative, Hake steered Rebel back onto the platform between the cars, and then to the ground. She felt as if she were moving through a kaleidoscope, with jumbled impressions of her surroundings that shifted and twisted just before she managed to retain them. Terrified eyes, masked faces, gun barrels that looked large enough to blow anyone's head off, hard voices barking orders, swift-moving feet.

Once off the train, Rebel saw why it had stopped. Some sort of barricade had been erected across the tracks ahead, formidable enough to derail an engine if the engineer had been brave enough to risk hitting it. She was spun around involuntarily when Hake headed toward the caboose. He was so rough that even if she hadn't felt shattered and sick she would have had trouble keeping her footing.

It wasn't the caboose that drew Hake, however. The doors to the baggage car were open, and its contents were spewing onto the ground beside the tracks, thrown or pushed by unseen hands. She heard a muffled cry, then Hake's grunt of satisfaction.

"Here it is!"

The box was plainly marked as the property of a bank, and though it wasn't overly large, it could certainly contain a sizable quantity of cash. It fell and rolled, and Hake put a foot on it to stop it going on down the embankment.

Rebel wasn't expecting the shot, and for a moment she was deafened when the gun went off so close to her. Hake put the six-shooter back into its holster and tossed aside the padlock he'd shot off, throwing open the lid of the box with the pointed toe of one boot without loosening his hold on her arm.

"This is it," he said, and Rebel stared down at the bundles of bills and the bags of coins. "Anything else worthwhile in there?"

There were sacks of mail, and through a haze Rebel listened to them debate whether or not there was likely to be anything worthwhile in those. In the end, the pouches were emptied out, and two of the bandits pawed through them looking for select envelopes or packages.

A shout brought all heads around toward the head of the train. A man Rebel guessed to be a brakeman had grabbed a gun from somewhere, but he wouldn't get the chance to use it.

Hake swung Rebel in front of him, facing the railroad crewman, and reached up to jerk off her hood. She knew what her hair was like in the sunlight—a coppery halo of curls.

"Put it down, or I'll shoot your schoolmarm right here," Hake said, and the crewman wavered.

A moment later, the gun was shot out of his hand by the masked youth holding the horses. The brakeman swore and clutched at his bloodied hand; the horses reared and whinnied, so that they had to be calmed.

Through it all, Rebel allowed herself to be manipulated as if she were a mindless puppet. If it hadn't been for the staggering realization that the man she loved was among those robbing the train, she might have found some way to resist. As it was, she was reduced to jelly, both in mind and body.

Gradually, after Hake shoved her aside and personally emptied the strongbox into canvas bags which were then secured on the back of a packhorse, Rebel's mind began to function again. It was very painful and she would almost rather have remained insensible.

She didn't see Luke, he was still inside the train making sure none of the passengers interfered with the robbery of the baggage car, and there was no one among the men she could see who resembled Cotton.

She began to edge away from where Hake had left her, though as yet she had no idea where she could go. Surely when they had what they had come for, the gang would gallop away as fast as they could and there would be no reason to hurt any of the passengers or the crew members. Would Hake think it worthwhile to search her out, if she disappeared from his sight?

She was afraid he might, for she knew who he was, or at least the name he was currently using and the one he'd used in New York. She also knew what he looked like, both with a beard and without one.

Yet it wasn't likely that he'd drag her along with him indefinitely. No, there was a strong possibility that when her usefulness was ended—which it probably had—Hake would simply shoot her.

She had backed up against the side of the passenger car. Would it make any sense to get back on the train? There was no one on it who could protect her against armed men, but there was no hiding place here on the plains.

Hesitantly, Rebel turned toward the steps, then, seeing that Hake was still occupied with the saddlebags full of loot, she swung up the steps onto the platform between two passenger cars.

There was no hiding place here, either. She had the choice of entering the forward car or the rear one, each of them guarded by an armed man. Getting off on the far side would be of no help; they would see her skirts under the train, and beyond would be only miles of open country in which she'd present herself to a pursuer like a mouse to a hungry hawk.

She chose the one to her left, the one where Luke Kittering stood easily covering the passengers with that deadly six-gun.

He heard her enter and turned his head. Their eyes locked, and Rebel supposed her anguish and fear were clearly written in her own. She read nothing in his.

Luke stepped to one side and waved her past him in the narrow aisle. "Sit down," he said crisply. And then, to one of the cigar smokers who made an abortive movement to rise, "You, too! I don't want to put a bullet through your hat, because I might not be a good enough shot to miss your head."

The man subsided, flushed, sweating. Rebel sank into the indicated seat, facing the rest of the car. Surely Luke would not let Hake kill her, would he? He'd professed to love her, he'd asked her to marry him, yet would he be able to do anything to save her without destroying himself?

A shout went up outside. "Come on, let's get out of here!"

Luke took a step backward, onto the platform. "Don't anybody move for at least ten minutes. You, with the gold chain, pull out your watch and time it. Anybody sticks his head outside sooner than that will lose it." Only then did he glance down at Rebel. "Stay right there. Don't move."

It was said in the same tone he'd used for the rest of the passengers, and was not in the least reassuring. Because, as she'd dreaded, Jubal Hake shouted, "Is she in there? The schoolteacher?"

Did Luke hesitate? Did he draw a deeper breath before the demand was repeated, before he yelled a response?

"I want the schoolteacher out here!"

"She's here," Luke replied. "Leave her here, she'll just slow us down."

"Bring her! If we need a hostage, we couldn't find a better one," Hake shouted back. "Now! Move! Get her out here!"

Surely this time Rebel didn't imagine the perceptible hesitation. But then Luke jerked his head toward her, indicating that she was to precede him off the car.

For a matter of seconds their eyes met again. Was there, this time, a message for her? If so, she couldn't read it. She was damp with perspiration, her hands were icy, and her mouth was so dry as to be painful when Rebel stepped off the train one more time.

Her captors were exuberant, exhilarated. They rode hard, heedless of their mounts. As they all thundered away Rebel glanced backward and saw flaming debris in front of the train, set afire to delay the train's removal.

The engineer had been underestimated, however. Before the gang was out of sight, he put the train in motion, going backward. If the telegraph lines at the previous station had not been cut, he would be able to get a message through when he reached it. Rebel would have felt a pang of concern for the stationmaster there if she hadn't been so terrified about what was going to happen to her.

She was not a rider. While Rebel was not normally afraid of horses, this was a different situation. Her mount was unused to female riders and excited by the other horses and the whooping and hollering of the triumphant outlaws. Rebel clung desperately and prayed that she would be able to keep her seat, because falling would probably prove fatal.

She didn't know where Luke was. Somewhere behind her, she guessed—turning around to look was too precarious. She blanked everything out of her mind except surviving.

They had not ridden far when the leader turned his horse in a wide, sweeping turn. They reached a river—the Arkansas?—and slowed their horses somewhat to follow its bed without leaving a trail. Though it was still rough going, Rebel now had time to think, and her thoughts were the most painful she'd ever had in her life.

She would not cry. She *would not,* she told herself grimly. She would not give Luke the satisfaction of seeing her weep.

All of her doubts flooded back, everything she had rationalized away, and now she could view Luke only as a deceiver and worse. There were so many things, and they all pointed to a bleak and dreary future for herself, even if she managed to live through this. And she found little reason to think this likely.

As on the night before, they rode for hours. The hot sun was high in the western sky before they stopped to rest. They ate cold food, not bothering with a fire, though Rebel thought they were so far from any civilization that smoke wouldn't have given them away to any possible pursuers, not even if a posse had been formed by now and had failed to be thrown off by their maneuvers in the river.

Luke was there, all right. They had all removed their bandanas, which increased Rebel's apprehension. Why would they let her go when she could describe them all? Yet even without believing she'd ever have that opportunity, she began consciously to try to do this. She was careful about it, not obvious.

She tried not to look at Luke. When she did her throat ached so badly that she had trouble breathing, and the tears she'd sworn not to shed stung her eyes.

Luke didn't come anywhere near her, nor did she feel his gaze upon her. She sat on the ground, apart from the men, and chewed on the bread and jerky, fighting the rebellion of her stomach to the food. Whatever was to come, she would need all her resources, including the strength that would come from eating.

The sun was hot, tempered by the breeze, and it made her remember the day in the shelter of the new house beside the Poteau. The dappled sunlight through the budding cottonwoods, the touch of the cool spring air, the warmth of Luke's mouth and his hands, the lean length of his body resting lightly on her own, her fingertips tracing the healing wound on his shoulder—

Rebel blinked hard against the forbidden tears. Fool! Fool that she was to have allowed Luke to convince her that it was an innocent injury instead of the bullet wound it had obviously been. Fool, to have allowed him to seduce her so easily.

No. Rebel was more honest than that. Luke hadn't seduced her, at least not against her own will. She'd wanted him to make love to her. She had been hesitant only because it was all new to her and she hadn't known what to do or to expect, but she'd been willing enough to be taught.

And oh, dear God, what a teacher Luke had been!

She was glad when the man called Norse stood up and said, "Let's get going. The sooner we get to Indian territory the better."

She would not be able to think and ride at the same

time, not if they kept up the pace they'd set previously. And she'd rather concentrate on her fear for her life if she fell off than remember what it had been like having Luke make love to her.

She'd be better off dead, Rebel reflected, than never knowing that ecstasy again.

The sun was dropping enough to make it clear that they traveled westward, into territory that even Judge Parker's marshals had not been able to tame completely, and for a time Rebel was too sunk in apathy to care what was going to happen next.

# Chapter Twenty-nine

FATIGUE TOOK THE EDGE OFF HER FEAR. WHEN SHE WAS finally allowed to dismount at dark, Rebel was reeling with limbs numbed by unaccustomed hours in the saddle, aching muscles, and hunger. Her stomach growled, but more than anything she longed for a hot bath and a soft bed.

After holding up the train, the gunmen had ridden east to throw off eventual pursuers, then crossed the Arkansas and worked their way back to the west, well out around Fort Smith. From what Rebel gathered from the conversation around her, they all expected to disappear into the vast Indian territory beyond the Arkansas border, some perhaps even going as far as California.

Hake didn't mention his destination. In fact, he talked to the others very little, and then only when it was essential. It was clear that he considered himself a cut above the others, and equally apparent that they both disliked and resented him.

The only one in the group who spoke less than Hake was Luke. He might almost have been a deaf mute. He helped gather wood for the fire and he drank his share of the coffee in a tin cup from his saddlebag, which also supplied another cold meal of bread and meat.

The other men were in high spirits. No doubt a posse was on their misleading trail by now, headed in the wrong direction. They thought it amusing that they were camping for the night so close to the city and the intimidating judge. There were coarse jokes about hangings if they were caught, but Rebel saw that they had no expectation of such a thing. They were too clever, too fast, and had planned too well.

Nightfall brought a chill, and Rebel huddled against the trunk of a big cottonwood, unable to fight the misery she felt. She knew without hearing it put into words that by tomorrow, when they were well past Fort Smith, her usefulness would be at an end. There would be no need for a hostage. When the money was divided between them, the men would split up and go their own ways, riding hard and fast. At that point her fate would become known.

After hours of feeling that it didn't matter what they did with her, Luke's betrayal having killed all feeling, she began to revive. She began to care again. Her mind, perhaps sharpened by hunger and discomfort, showed the stirrings of hope, of searching for a plan to survive this nightmarish ordeal.

She was too far from the fire to derive any benefit from it, yet under no circumstances would she have called attention to herself by approaching its warmth. Bottles had been brought out of saddlebags, and a celebration was underway. The only prudent thing for a female to do was to become invisible, insofar as this was possible. Rebel drew her cloak more closely around her and hoped the men would forget she was there.

Suddenly a tin cup was thrust at her silently. Startled, Rebel looked up and saw Luke standing over her.

For a moment she hesitated. Then common sense and the need for the steaming coffee won out over what she felt about him. She reached out and took the cup.

The coffee was not his only offering. He had unobtrusively taken a blanket from his bedroll and dropped it now beside her, speaking in a low voice that was nearly drowned out by a burst of profane hilarity from the fireside.

"Wrap up in this, as far back in the shadows as you can get. Don't take your shoes off. If anything happens, run like hell, in that direction." He gestured with his head.

Astonished, she forgot to drink from the cup. Before she could think of a response, Hake shouted from beyond the fire.

"Get the hell away from her!"

Luke turned, casual, relaxed. "Just giving her a cup of coffee." He walked back to his horse, evincing disinterest in either Rebel or his comrades. Hake, however, continued to stare after him.

"Where'd he come from? He wasn't in the original plan, was he?"

"Wasn't nobody in the original plan 'cept you and me. But it worked better with all of us, didn't it? Kittering pulled his own weight, kept people under control while Norse and Hughes emptied that baggage car." The speaker was, Rebel had figured out, the nominal leader, though they were such an independent lot that they tended to question any authority. "We run across him a few months ago, invited him in."

Hake had his hat pushed back on his head, his face

clearly visible in the firelight, creased by a scowl. "Kittering? Isn't there a Kittering family owns a bank in Fort Smith, and another one in Muskogee?"

"Same family," Luke said easily. "Only I prefer outdoor work."

Somebody guffawed, and after a moment the others followed suit, except for Hake. He took another swig from the bottle he was not sharing. "Just stay away from the schoolteacher."

"Sure," Luke agreed, and sat down with his back to one of the cottonwoods, several yards away from Rebel, to sip at a bottle of his own.

Rebel's heart was thunderous. The tin cup was hot against her fingers, and she made herself drink of it, cautiously. What was going on? The exchange between the two men seemed to rule out any prior collusion between Luke and Jubal Hake. Yet here they were, having both taken part in a robbery that would send them to the gallows together if they were caught.

The coffee was an infusion of courage. Of hope. Why should Luke, after studiously ignoring her all this time, have suddenly taken pity on her? Was it possible that, even though he had criminal proclivities, he *did* have some feeling for her? That the words whispered to her in moments of love had been genuine?

A few minutes ago she had thought she hated him. Now Rebel drank the coffee, wrapped herself in the blanket, and studied Luke covertly, being careful not to do so in a way that Hake would notice.

Her breath caught in her throat. His face was so dear, so beloved—how could he *not* be the man she had believed him to be?

He made a slight gesture, and Rebel, uncomprehending, saw him motion with his hand, close to the ground, unnoticed by the other men. She put down the cup, but she made no other movement until he increased the urgency of the signal. It *was* a signal, she decided at last. He wanted her to move farther from the fire, out of the light.

She gave no nod of understanding, in case Hake was watching. But she began to inch away from the tree, and then around it, and then . . . long minutes later . . . eased into the deeper darkness behind it. Her pulse was so rapid that it seemed to be leaping, making the blood pound in her ears.

Luke wanted her to get away. He didn't want her used as a hostage if the posse caught up to them, nor for Hake to eliminate her once he no longer had a use for her. And Luke put himself at risk to accomplish this, for she knew that Hake would not hesitate to shoot them both if he realized what was afoot.

Perhaps, she thought, if she were to lie down—if Hake glanced over and saw her apparently going to sleep—it would then be less obtrusive when she crawled away.

Luke had told her to go that way, directly behind the tree she'd been leaning against, but it had not been quite dark when they'd halted here and she had seen that there was nothing out there but low hills. Where would she go, unable to see anything, with no destination in mind? Or would it be enough simply to escape the notice of the men, to worry about being rescued, or finding her way to a house or a trail, later on, after Hake had given up and gone on without her?

A burst of raucous laughter covered the sounds of the twigs cracking beneath her. The party was livening up. "Let's split the money now," someone suggested, and there was a sound of approval, with one dissenting voice.

"We agreed to do it in the morning, when everybody's sober and we can see what we're doing."

"We got a fire to see by, and who knows what'll

happen during the night?" The voice belonged to Norse. Rebel didn't look at him. She wriggled awkwardly a few inches farther, dragging the blanket with her. "What if we're wrong about misleading the posse? They're sure to have one out by now, even if it's just because the train didn't show up in Fort Smith with that strongbox. Bloody Parker's got every marshal in the district out looking for us, you can bet on that. So what if they show up here? If we each got our own money, we can run with it. If we all go in different directions, a marshal or two can't follow us all at the same time."

Good, Rebel thought, and dared to get to her hands and knees to crawl a bit farther. She must be almost invisible now to those around the fire, and if they either divided their loot, or argued about it, they wouldn't have time to notice her.

A backward glance showed her that Luke remained seated, beyond the circle of men lighted by the flames or silhouetted against them. Rebel crawled several feet before stopping. Suddenly she gasped in shock as a whisper issued out of the surrounding darkness.

"Rebel! Lie flat, be absolutely still!"

Shock dissolved in incredulous delight as she recognized the voice. "Evelyn?" Rebel whispered back.

"Shhh! Give the marshals time to surround them!" Her cousin's hand descended on her outstretched wrist, pressing her downward, and Rebel thought her heartbeat must be audible even over the voices of the men behind her.

She risked a question, for Evelyn's ear was no more than inches away. "How did you find me?"

"I found the packages you'd put down, and I knew they had to be yours. And I remembered where you'd followed that wretch of a jewel thief before, and assumed you'd done it again. I figured this time he'd caught you at it, so I went for help."

Rebel raised up enough to look over her shoulder. She was surely beyond the reach of the firelight here, and the men—except for Luke, still lounging against his tree, visible only as a shadow with a wide-brimmed Stetson—were engrossed in the contents of the strongbox.

"Who? Cotton? Did Cotton come back?"

"No, and I went to Mr. Kittering, but he didn't know where Luke was, said he hadn't sent him to Little Rock on any business, and he didn't know anything about building supplies coming from there, when they were all available right here in Fort Smith." Evelyn paused to check out the situation, too, and Rebel bit her lip. So even that had been a lie.

"I did the only thing I could think of," Evelyn said. "I went to Judge Parker—"

At that moment a shot rang out, bringing the men around the fire to immediate attention, reaching for their six-guns. Before any of them could fire a commanding voice rang out of the darkness.

"U.S. marshals! We have you surrounded and outnumbered! Throw down your guns or we'll shoot you where you stand!"

Several of the outlaws obeyed, reluctantly allowing their weapons to thud onto the ground. Two others didn't, and the ensuing gunfire drove both girls to press their faces into the earth and cover their ears against the onslaught.

Luke, Luke! Rebel thought frantically. He wouldn't have drawn a gun, would he? Eben had said he was a crack shot, but against such odds as these, with the outnumbering marshals impossible targets in the darkness, he'd have no chance at all if he resisted.

Rebel jerked herself up onto her hands and knees, and Evelyn violently tried to pull her back down.

"Don't be crazy, you'll get caught in the crossfire!"

She wasn't thinking about her own safety. She broke free of Evelyn's restraining hands and sat up, then wished she hadn't. It was a scene of carnage, or so it seemed for a moment or two until the shooting stopped.

It had been no bluff. There were a dozen marshals who walked in from every direction, and one of them called out, "Miss Moran? Are you all right?"

"Over here!" She sounded shaky, and her legs trembled when she rose to her feet, Evelyn behind her as they emerged into the light.

"You all right? And Miss Bickford?"

"We're fine," Evelyn cried, and then ran toward one tall figure who, though not wearing a badge, was holstering a gun. "Cotton, are you all right?"

Bewildered, Rebel watched her cousin fling herself into Cotton's arms, saw the way his arms came around her in a tight embrace that sent vibrations through Rebel. She bit hard on her lip and glanced around for Luke.

Jubal Hake had been one of those attempting to shoot it out. He had been shot and was now groaning and swearing, holding a hand to a bloody shoulder. Norse had had even worse luck. He lay in a crumpled heap, gun just beyond his dead fingers.

Rebel tried to slow her breathing, tried to think. Now that the worst was over, *she* was safe, but the men who were being rounded up and put into shackles would eventually face the hangman. No matter what Luke had done, she could not allow him to go to the gallows.

No one was paying any attention to her. She inhaled deeply and moved, not too quickly, to avoid drawing attention to herself, toward the fallen Norse. She was unused to guns, and this one was undoubtedly ready to fire, but she forced herself to pick it up, very carefully, and held it pointing earthward beneath the cover of her cloak.

Luke stood apart from the others and she moved toward him, cautiously, careful to attract no attention. In a minute or so they'd have him shackled with the others, and that might be too late.

She reached his side, saw the light spark in his eyes as he realized she was there, and turning so that no one could see she pressed the gun into his hand.

"Here," she said unsteadily. "Nobody's watching the horses. Take this and run."

# Chapter Thirty

IT WOULD BE A LONG TIME BEFORE REBEL FULLY FORGAVE Luke for laughing. He took the gun from her hand and put it carefully aside before he swept her into his arms and kissed her. Thoroughly, thrillingly, and infuriatingly.

Relief that he was still alive and fear for his eventual safety allowed her to melt momentarily against him. But as the kiss deepened, indignation and bewilderment drove her to free her lips and draw back, to look up into the face she had alternately loved and despised, oblivious of the activity around them.

"If I'd seen you pick up that gun I'd have thought you were going to shoot me with it." There was a teasing note in the words. "Thank you, darling Rebel. I wouldn't have blamed you if you'd been annoyed with me, just a trifle."

"A trifle! I could kill you myself—" her voice broke,

then steadied, "but I couldn't bear to have anyone else do it—" She could not hold back the tears.

Immediately his amusement died, to be replaced with infinite tenderness. "I'm sorry, I didn't choose to do it this way, but I had no choice."

"They'll h-hang you—"

"No." He lifted his hands to cup her face, holding her firmly when she would have torn herself away from him. "Judge Parker has a reputation for being a harsh man, but he's never yet hanged one of his own marshals."

For a moment, too stunned to move while her mind tried to sort this out, Rebel simply stood there. "M-marshal?"

"I work for Judge Parker. Not as a marshal with a badge, but under his authority anyway. I had a chance to infiltrate the gang when I got wind of what they were planning—keeping bad companions sometimes has its advantages—and I talked to the judge. He persuaded me to pretend to be one of them, and we set them up for this capture tonight. We even got a bonus, capturing Jubal Hake, or Jim Skilly, which is his real name, we think—he's used so many it's hard to know for sure."

The tip of her tongue moistened her lips and she put her hands over his and made him let go of her face. "Then you weren't . . . a confederate of Hake's, in New York?"

"You thought I was? And you still fell in love with me?" His hands rested on her shoulders now, a touch as gentle and loving and intimate as the caresses they had shared in the framework of their new house.

"I . . . didn't want to think so. But you were there when he robbed my uncle and all those people . . ."

"I followed him there." He spoke quietly, so that she could hardly hear him over the cursing and orders being issued around them. "He robbed a bank over in

Muskogee, one Pa's a partner in. It was a big loss, one that my father took personally because he made up most of it himself. I thought I could find out where the man you call Hake had stashed it, and then I realized he was setting up something else with a jewelry merchant. I followed him the night he left that party, not knowing what he was doing but hoping for a lead to Pa's money, or what's left of it, but he must have realized I was following, and he stepped aside to let me get ahead of him on a dark street. Then he clobbered me hard enough to put me in a hospital for weeks."

Gradually the truth was filtering through all the misconceptions she had carried through the past twenty-four hours. "I thought I'd lost him for good when I came home to Fort Smith," Luke went on. "And when I found out he was going to be part of the gang I'd joined up with for this train robbery, I was afraid he might recognize me from New York. I almost pulled out. But he didn't know me, he'd only seen me in the dark before, and he was in a hurry to get away from me that time."

"You could have told me," Rebel began, and he stopped her with a kiss.

"No. No, I couldn't tell anyone. I was sworn to secrecy. And you'd have wanted me to get out, which I couldn't do. Not until it was finished. I had to manipulate the gang to the extent of getting them here tonight, all still together and with the strongbox intact, so the marshals could surround them. I never guessed you had suspicions about what I was doing. And I never dreamed you'd show up with Hake on that damned train, and then I was afraid you'd give me away and blow up the whole business."

She didn't know whether to be angry, relieved, or thrilled. Her emotions were in a turmoil. She glanced around and saw Evelyn and Cotton still locked in an embrace—or perhaps it was a different one—and asked, "Is Cotton a marshal, too?"

"No. Well, maybe they deputized him for this one operation, since he was here with a gun. No, Cotton's just a good friend. I couldn't be seen anywhere near Judge Parker or any of the men who work for him, so we got messages back and forth through Cotton. He has business in the courthouse often enough so that nobody would think anything of it if he spoke to Parker occasionally. Rebel, I love you. And even though you were furious with me, you weren't angry enough to want to see me die, whether I was guilty or not. I'll never forget that."

"And I'll never forget the hell you put me through, thinking you were a killer—"

"I thought so too, at first," Evelyn said, materializing at Rebel's elbow with a grinning Cotton behind her. "When you didn't come home for supper last night I got Mr. Sylvester to go with me looking for you. When I figured out what must have happened, I didn't know what to do except go to Judge Parker. I told him about Jubal Hake, and when that didn't seem to galvanize him into action I added everything else I could think of. I told him how suspicious we were about Cotton getting off the Eureka Springs stage and being met by Luke, who was supposed to be in Little Rock on business his father said he didn't have there. I even," and she smiled wryly, "resorted to a slight case of hysterics. I've found it works wonders in an emergency to get a gentleman's attention. I think the judge was afraid the neighbors would think he was murdering someone, so he just told me to shut me up, that Luke was working for him and that Cotton was their go-between."

"And then," Cotton added, grinning widely, "she convinced him that she needed to come with us. I wouldn't have believed that was possible. He's a man who makes his own decisions about things, and be damned to what anybody else thinks—even the Congress of the United States has felt the back of his hand a few times and pulled away."

"It was perfectly safe," Evelyn interjected. "You had the robbers outnumbered and took them by surprise. I would have died waiting back there in Mrs. Tolman's parlor with a group of people who didn't know anything about it, wondering whether you'd all been killed."

It didn't seem to occur to her that there was some illogic in her reasoning, and when both men laughed she only hugged her cousin. "You are all safe, so I was right to come, wasn't I?"

Rebel's stomach made a protesting growl, and she began to come down to earth a little. "I'm starving. Did anyone bring anything to eat?"

"I have some biscuits left," Luke offered. "And a strip or two of jerky. Come on, you can eat on the way. Everybody's ready to leave, and it's going to be an hour's ride back to Fort Smith."

"I don't know if I can ride and eat," Rebel said. "I had a terrible time just staying on that horse. Oh, and where is that blanket? I left it somewhere over there under the trees."

"I'll get it." Luke took a few steps away from her and then stopped. "Maybe we should stay here while you eat, and we'll catch up with the others later. They won't be riding fast going in, not the way they did coming out."

For long moments Rebel stared into his face. How could she have believed for a moment that this man was a liar and a villain? Her instincts had been right, and she thanked God she had given in to them rather than taking the situation at face value.

"Yes," she said, "that would be easier. You . . . you go on with the others, Evelyn."

She didn't hear her cousin's answer. She was barely aware of the sounds of the horses' hooves as the posse and the gang left them alone by the dying fire.

What she was aware of was Luke: tall, broad in the shoulders and deep in the chest, lean of waist and flanks. Luke, waiting for her with open arms.

She drew in a deep breath and stepped into them, letting her arms encircle his neck to draw him close. His mouth closed on hers, hungrily, eagerly, yet holding something back.

Rebel slid her hands down his neck and then around his waist, allowing her lips to part beneath his. And then, as passion built within and between them, there was no holding back on either side.

She closed her eyes and let the sweet sensations fill her. Never again would she doubt anything about this man. He was hers, as she was his, and that was all that mattered.

# Tapestry

## HISTORICAL ROMANCES

POCKET BOOKS

# TAPESTRY
# ROMANCES